SCORED

THE VIRGIN PLAYBOOK
BOOK 1

LILI VALENTE

SCORED

By Lili Valente

ABOUT THE BOOK

Begging my brother's best friend—aka NHL superstar, Ian Fox—to help me ditch my V Card wasn't part of my "make it big in NYC" plans.

But after years of being "cute little Evie," I'm tired of waiting for Mr. Right. I'm ready for Mr. Right Now and Ian is everything I've ever wanted in a first time. He's kind, funny, confident, and has a legendary...stick.

Seriously, his stick has its own page of search results, complete with gray sweat-pants shots hot enough to make even a clue-less virgin drool.

And yes, my brother will murder us if he finds out, but we're both grownups.

We can keep a secret. We have to since I just landed an art therapy job working with his troubled team.

All we're doing is a little practice. (Or...*ehem*...**big** practice.)

Too bad my heart didn't get the memo.

PROLOGUE

DEAR DIARY
Evie

Dear Diary,

Three months! Just three months until I'm a twenty-four-year-old virgin. As if being a twenty-three-year-old virgin isn't bad enough. At this point, I only have sixteen years until I'm old enough to be the star of a HYSTERICAL romantic comedy about having the oldest V-Card on the planet.

And sure, sixteen years is a long time, but look how fast the past sixteen years have zipped by. It seems like just YESTERDAY I was turning eight years old. Maybe the day before yesterday, but you get it.

I can still remember the smell of the scented markers I got for my birthday and how Dad freaked out when I gave myself "tattoos" all over my face with them.

Ugh, I wish I had a pack of scented markers right now. Cam is experimenting with collard greens in the kitchen. The entire apartment smells like death, covered in lemon juice and the bitter zest of dying dreams.

I know, I'm being dramatic.

I'm just so tired of being overlooked, ignored, or passed by for someone with a better sex vibe. Or...any sex vibe.

Maybe Vince was right. Maybe I'm about as sexy as a lump of cold mashed potatoes, covered in collard green slime.

If so, I'm not sure what to do about it. How does one develop a sex vibe, Diary, and do high heels have to be involved? Like so many things that are supposed to make you beautiful and attractive to the opposite sex, heels just...hurt.

Am I crazy to think that beauty and sex-vibing shouldn't have to hurt?

Yes?

No?

Heavy sigh...

I continue to be disappointed with your lack of answers, Diary.

Please remember to hurl yourself into a fire if I meet an untimely end, okay? I don't want my legacy to be a journal filled with whining about my hymen. Ha! We should write a song—"Whinin' 'Bout my Hymen." Or YOU should write it. I'm a visual artist, not a musical one.

So, get on that, okay? If you're not going to answer questions, you can at least spend your free time wisely.

Virginally Yours,
    Evie

CHAPTER ONE

Evie Eleanor Olsen

A (nearly) twenty-four-year-old virgin
about to be disemboweled by a colored pencil

*T*his is it, I guess.
This is how I die.

I always hoped I'd die in bed, surrounded by loving children and grandchildren—or at the very least that there wouldn't be large amounts of blood involved—but you don't always get what you want.

I learned that a long time ago.

Around age eight, in fact, when my mother left.

Dad had no idea what to do with a girl (and made zero effort to learn). My much-older brother,

Derrick, attempted to make up for our father's lack of interest by becoming the kind of hyper-protective big bro my girlfriends thought was the swooniest thing ever, but that secretly drove me insane. Derrick was *always* in my business, from bullying me into eating healthy foods instead of Pop-Tarts, to cleaning my room, to questioning my love of bug-themed school projects and my preference for spending time with art supplies over most people.

But if I had to guess, I'd bet my brother's constant hovering is part of the reason I became an artist in the first place.

When I was lost in my art, I forgot that my brother cared too much, and my father cared too little. With a paintbrush in my hand, layering washes of watercolor to create the perfect fall maple leaf, I didn't feel anxious or worried or not good enough.

I felt like I was where I belonged, doing exactly what I was supposed to do, and that I had everything I needed to make my dreams come true tucked away inside my own creation-loving soul.

I was hoping to cultivate some of that same calm, steady confidence within the twenty-seven professional hockey players glaring at me from the card tables set up in the old equipment room the New York City Ice Possums' management appro-priated for my two weeks of art therapy class. I thought the guys would be excited for a break from murdering each other on the ice, brutalizing their bodies in the weight room, and talking about feelings with the group therapist brought in to help defuse the Possums' pervasive attitude problems before the preseason.

After all, I'm not asking anyone to *talk* about their feelings. I'm asking them to draw them, using shiny new pastel crayons and high-quality colored pencils.

Colored pencils like the pink one currently aimed at the center of my chest, held by the agitated goalie towering over me in my slip-on Vans, making me wish I'd worn my tennis shoes with the platform soles.

At five foot two, I'm never the tallest person in the room, but I'm feeling especially wee today, surrounded by enormous men with bruises all over their arms from scrapping on the ice and a collective bad attitude so intense it felt like I was wading through a swamp of icky vibes as I handed out their "anger iceberg" drawing templates at the beginning of the session.

The extra height wouldn't offer any real protection, but I'd feel less vulnerable than I do right now, as I squeak, "Excuse me? What's the problem exactly?" to the scowling man glaring down at me like I killed his kitten and stole his comic book collection.

"They keep breaking," he grunts, his hint of a Slavic accent helping jog my memory as to his name.

This is Slavic Sven, one of two Svens on the team, not to be confused with Sassy Sven, who told me I reminded him of a sheep as I handed out his worksheet.

"The hair," he said, smirking at my tight blonde curls, which I've always worn in a pixie cut. "Do you curl it like that on purpose?"

"No, it's natural," I'd said, forcing a smile and refusing to let him shake my confidence on my first day.

This gig is part of my community involvement hours for my master's in art therapy and a job my brother went out of his way to secure for me.

Derrick is still as overbearing as ever, but these days he mostly uses his bullying powers for good, like pushing me to apply to NYU in the first place and then helping me land this gig working with the Possums during their team-building camp. He's been a junior manager for the franchise for years and has major street cred with his bosses. He didn't really have to stick his neck out for me, but I still don't want to let him—or myself—down.

Besides, sheep are adorable.

I could remind Sassy Sven of far worse things.

Like a pin cushion. Or a pencil sharpener, or whatever Slavic Sven is thinking as he jabs the tip of his pencil closer to my heart again, making me so nervous I take a few steps back, bumping into my own desk and sending pencils rolling onto the floor.

I flinch, jumping a few inches into the air and then jumping again as a deep voice rumbles from my left, "What's the problem, man?"

I glance over to see Ian standing a few feet

away, and my shoulders relax away from my ears. Ian is one of Derrick's best friends from our old neighborhood growing up, a star defender for the Ice Possums, and one of the nicest people I've ever met.

He won't let Sven gut me with a colored pencil.

And maybe, now that he's here to join in the fun, the other guys will loosen up and play along, too. He's their team captain, after all, and one of the few Possums who isn't constantly in the penalty box for lashing out on the ice. But he still has to attend group therapy, art therapy, and all the other team-building activities planned throughout the next two weeks.

If he can have a good attitude about it, the rest of them would be big babies not to follow suit.

"These fucking pencils keep breaking," Sven practically shouts. "And I can't draw. All my people look like cats."

"Retarded cats," a voice calls from one of the tables, eliciting a round of muffled laughter from the rest of the less-than-thrilled artists in the room.

"You can't say that word," Sven shouts over his shoulder. "It's fucking insensitive. And my cousin has Down's syndrome, and that kid is ten times smarter than all of you meatpie heads put together."

"And probably ten times better looking than you," a defenseman I believe is named Pete shoots back, summoning another round of guffaws.

"Yeah, maybe, but your mother wasn't

complaining last night," Sven says, prompting Pete to shout for him to "shut the fuck up," and a blond guy to dissolve into snorts of laughter so intense he blows his drawing-in-progress off the table onto the floor.

"Okay, everybody calm down," Ian says as he shifts closer, making me feel even safer.

Should Slavic Sven experience a mental break and lunge at me with that pencil, I have no doubt Ian will have him on the ground begging for mercy in five seconds flat. I've seen Ian's protective reflexes in action. One time, a couple of years ago over holiday break, Derrick and I were out for drinks with Ian, his girlfriend, Whitney, and a bunch of their friends and some drunk asshole grabbed Whitney's ass while she was playing darts.

Before she had time to do more than cry out in shock, the creep was under Ian's knee, begging for mercy.

I'm not usually the type who gets weak in the knees over displays of aggression, but Ian was just so calm and efficient about the whole thing. He didn't yell or freak out, he simply put the man out of commission and gave him a stern talking-to while the guy whimpered that he was sorry and swore he'd never touch a woman without permission again.

By the time Ian lifted the groper into the air and carried him to the door by the back of his shirt, he'd transformed the ovaries of every woman in that bar into puddles of quivering goo.

He's just so chivalrous and gorgeous and

protective in a way that's sexy instead of smothering. Derrick barges into other people's business, certain he's the only one who can solve their problems. Ian is happy to stand back, respect his friends' boundaries, and let people make their own decisions, only stepping in when it's clear his help is needed as an ally and decent human being.

He's just...the best, a fact he proves as he puts a hand on Sven's shoulder and says, "I don't think it matters what the drawing looks like, man. Just that you get your feelings out while you're working." He glances back to me. "Isn't that right, Evie?"

"Yes. Absolutely." I shoot Sven what I hope is an encouraging smile. "And if the pencil tips are breaking, I can set you up with something sturdier. I have some thick crayons or—"

"Sven's getting downgraded to crayons," Pete says, guffawing again. "Does he have to use the blunt scissors, too?"

Sven spins toward him, his eyes burning. "I swear to fucking God, I—"

"That's enough," Ian says, moving between Sven and the chortling Pete. "This is part of our team-building work for the next two weeks. And yeah, we may think it's a waste of time to sit around coloring our feelings like we're five years old, but this is what happens when you lead the league in penalties three seasons in a row. A bunch of you decided it would be fun to lash out like children on the ice, so now we're being treated like children behind the scenes. And throwing another fit about the punishment isn't going to make management happier with any of us."

"This isn't a punishment," I pipe up in a thin voice, shocked that Ian, a guy I've never seen put anyone down is being so dismissive of my work. "Art therapy has been proven to reduce stress, improve communication skills, and promote feelings of well-being."

"See there." Ian motions toward me, but he doesn't sound convinced and his next words make it clear he still isn't on board with art therapy as a valuable tool for solving the Ice Possums' problems. "So, buckle down, draw a pretty picture for Evie, who's way too sweet to be forced to deal with your bullshit, and we can be out of here in twenty minutes. That's plenty of time to hit happy hour across the street. I'm buying the first round for everyone who gets a thumbs-up from the teacher."

Spirits buoyed by the promise of an adult beverage waiting at the end of their assignment, one by one, each set of massive shoulders hunches as they focus on their paper. Even Sven takes the package of easy-grip crayons I pass over and returns to his seat looking less upset about the state of his cat people.

Ian turns to me with a dazzling grin that would normally make me beam right back at him.

Instead, I whisper, "Thanks, but next time, I have to keep them the entire ninety minutes. It's in my contract."

"Of course," he says, squeezing my shoulder

before he bends to collect my pencils from the floor. He sets all of them back on my desk, save one, which he holds up between us with a conspiratorial wink. "Okay if I use this for my masterpiece?"

"Sure," I say, forcing a smile as I hand him an anger iceberg worksheet. "Just write down a memory you have of being angry or out of control during a game or practice on the top of the iceberg. Then, under the water, draw pictures of things that contributed to you feeling out of control or frustrated in that situation."

"Got it," he says, but I can tell he isn't taking this seriously, even before he lengthens his six-foot-two frame into a chair at the end of one table and proceeds to whip out the fastest stick figure drawing I've ever seen.

My nose wrinkles and I'm filled with a heavy, sinking feeling.

Who is this Ian?

And what has he done with the man I've always idolized?

CHAPTER 2

Evie

*H*ow long have I been Ian's biggest fan?

Since I was in second grade, and he started giving Derrick a ride to and from hockey practice. I'd hang out with them while they gorged on after-practice snacks and go watch them play with my best friend, Harlow. And sometimes, Ian and Derrick would take us out for ice cream after the games as a special treat for being their most loyal fans.

Ian is the oldest of eight kids and has the patience of a saint. He never made me feel silly or babyish for wanting two scoops of bubblegum or for going on and on about whatever boy band Harlow and I were obsessed with at the time.

Though usually Harlow was the one who was truly obsessed. I went along with whatever my friend liked because she fit in with our peers so much better than I did. Even as a kid, Harlow knew how to dress and was on the cutting edge of cool.

I, on the other hand, don't have a cool bone in my body and still dress like I'm in elementary school.

Or, according to my ex-boyfriend, like a reject from a clown college.

Vince was always begging me to put on something tight and slinky, or at least something other than paint-splattered overalls. But I spend all day working on my own art or helping my students with their projects. By the time I'm done with work and school, I'm usually too tired to get dressed up in skintight Lycra, even if I wanted to... which I don't.

I'm perfectly happy the way I am. And if Vince had been the right man for me, he would have been happy with me, too.

But he wasn't. So, I'm single again.

And that's fine. Better than fine.

I don't mind being single. Or I wouldn't mind it as much, if Vince hadn't delivered a killer parting shot on his way out of my life...

"It's not just the clothes, Evie," he'd said as he did a shitty job of "letting me down easy" over funnel cakes at a festival in the East Village last summer. "It's your whole...vibe." His dark eyes filled with pity as he added in a softer voice, "You have zero sex appeal, baby. I'm sorry, but it's true. I thought I should be honest with you about that before we go our separate ways. You know, in case you want to try to get therapy or something."

He turned to leave, then swung back around, leaning in to add in a stage whisper I'm sure half the people watching me fall apart on a park bench heard loud and clear, "And you really should try to get someone to have sex with you before you're any older. You're at an age where it's getting a little weird that you're still a virgin, you know?"

Yes, I *do* know. And it *is* getting weird, but only because other people are making it that way!

I'm twenty-three, not thirty-three, and I was a late bloomer. My sophomore year, I was still the size of a flat-chested twelve-year-old. I didn't develop until my final semester of high school and by then the few guys I thought were interesting were too busy prepping to leave our tiny New Jersey town to notice my modest blossoming. (I'm still only a B cup and can wear most of my overalls from middle school.)

In college I was too excited to finally be spending all day every day studying and making art to stress about boys. Growing up, I'd learned to hide my obsession with drawing and painting as best I could. My mother was an artist—that was allegedly why she left us, because she wanted to study in Europe like painters did in the 1920s.

Anytime Dad saw me working at my easel in the backyard or mixing papier-mâché materials in the kitchen, it would put him in a bad mood for hours. I'd usually end up getting in trouble for something I couldn't even remember doing not long after.

So, art became my secret love, one I was only free to openly adore once I left home.

That newfound freedom was so all-consuming I didn't notice I'd forgotten to date until all my girlfriends in the freshman dorm started spending Saturday nights with their boyfriends. Seeing them snuggled up on the couches in our rec room, watching scary movies and making out in between bites of popcorn made me feel left out all over again, the way I had back when Harlow and my high school friends giggled over prom dress choices and whether or not to get on birth control before the big night.

I made finding a guy of my own more of a priority, but every time I found a cutie to take to art openings or dance parties on the town square in our little Virginia college town, I would eventually end up in the friend zone. Without fail, within two to three months, the man in question would tell me what a wonderful person he thought I was, beg for the chance to stay friends, and then express his desire to date someone he was more attracted to.

They didn't say the last part most of the time, but despite what people think about art majors, I'm *not* stupid.

I was more than capable of reading between the lines.

But then Vince, an art history major, and I started dating the end of my senior year. He was the first boyfriend to last a full six months and the first who seemed to enjoy kissing me as much as I enjoyed kissing him. And he was moving to the city after graduation, too, so we wouldn't have to deal with the stress of a long-distance relationship!

Everything seemed to be going pretty well until that steamy August night when he dumped me like a hot potato.

No, like something less exciting than a hot potato. He dumped me like a cold lump of oatmeal someone had sloshed into his palm—unflavored oatmeal without so much as a teaspoon of maple syrup to make it more enticing than eating paste.

"Done!" Pete shouts, bolting up from his chair so fast that it tumbles over onto the tile behind him. He doesn't bother righting it before cruising around the table and thrusting his paper into my face.

"Great. Let's see what you discovered." I hold it back far enough to study his work, fighting the urge to frown as I take in the empty top of the iceberg and the wild slashes of red and orange beneath it.

I hate giving my students critical feedback, especially on the first day. Putting yourself out there creatively is hard enough without someone jumping down your throat with criticism your first time out of the artist gate.

So, I force a smile and add, "This is a solid start. What are these slashes symbolizing for you?"

"Fire," he says, grinning. "Because I'm fire on the ice."

It takes all my strength to keep my side-eye

under control. "Okay, but the assignment was to draw things you feel contribute to you losing your temper during a game. Could the flames maybe symbolize something from your past? A memory that makes you feel fiery and irritable, for example?"

He shrugs. "Sure. Can I go now?"

My shoulders slump as I sigh. "Of course. Go ahead. We'll try again on Monday." Maybe, by the end of the weekend, I'll have figured out a way to keep my reluctant students on task.

"Cool, can I be done, too?" the blond guy asks, holding up a paper that seems to be filled with doodles of pizza. "I'm starving. Need to grab a few slices before happy hour or I'll get wasted. I've got a low tolerance on an empty stomach."

"Pussy," a deep voice pipes up from the opposite end of the table.

I turn to see a guy with hands the size of the Incredible Hulk's holding up his paper with a shit-eating grin that makes more sense as he adds, "Speaking of pussies. That's what I drew. It symbolizes how much I hate refs who bitch about things getting a little rough on the ice and how much it sucked to grow up with three little sisters and one bathroom. There was never any room in the cabinets for my shit. They were always full of pads and tampons."

"That must have been frustrating." I step up to collect his drawing, cheeks going hot as I take in the highly detailed sketches of female genitalia, each one more intricate and original than the last.

I clear my throat, but my voice still emerges as a squeak as I say, "These are actually really good."

"Yeah?" the guy asks, laughing as he adds, "Then why do you look like you're about to toss your cookies, teach?"

"Aw, teacher's blushing," Sassy Sven pipes up. "Look what you did, Laser. You've got our sweet little sheep all flustered."

"I'm n-not flustered," I stammer unconvincingly as the rest of the players push back their chairs, either abandoning their work unfinished or tossing it playfully on the card table in front of me on their way by. "Please come with a good attitude on Monday." I raise my voice to be heard over the sound of men grabbing their things and chatting as they head for the door. "We'll be working with clay. If you like what you make, I can take it to the studio and fire it for you. That way you can keep it as a souvenir of our time together."

My last sentence is shouted into the sudden silence as the last player disappears through the open door.

No, not the last player.

Ian is still here, I realize, as he appears on the other side of the card table and adds his paper to the top of the pile.

He shoots me a sympathetic smile and shrugs. "Seriously, don't worry about them, Evie. They're idiots. You're never going to get through to them, but that's their fault, not yours."

"Oh, I'll get through to them," I say with more confidence than I feel. Forcing a smile, I add, "And

I'll see you at happy hour. I'm meeting my roomies there at six."

"Cool," he says, adding with a laugh, "It's still so weird that you're old enough to drink."

"Have been for almost three years now," I say, surprised to find irritation tickling at the back of my neck as I add, "I'll be twenty-four in December." The irritated feeling gets worse as I glance down at Ian's paper to see two stick people with hockey pucks and nothing at the top of the iceberg. Glancing back up at him, I tap two fingers onto the paper. "What is this?"

"My drawing," he says, chuckling again. "I can't draw, either."

"First of all, everyone can draw," I insist. "Secondly, this wasn't about honing your artistic skills, it was about expressing yourself. I don't see any of you in this drawing, Ian. And you didn't follow the directions for the assignment."

His gray-blue eyes widening, he says, "Okay. Sorry, Evie, I'll try harder next time."

"Please do," I say, adding in a tight voice, "The others look up to you. If you take this seriously, there's a better chance they will, too. And honestly, this could be good for you, Ian. I know you aren't one of the team members with anger issues, but we all have suppressed emotions. Especially men who play professional sports. Our society puts a lot of pressure on you guys to ignore your feelings and be tough all the time, and that isn't healthy."

He nods, a new respect in his gaze. "You're

right. I'll bring my A game on Monday, and you and your friends' first round is on me. How's that?"

"That sounds like my generous boyfriend," a female voice purrs from the doorway. "Hey, Evie, how are you, doll?"

Whitney, Ian's gorgeous girlfriend of three years, sashays into the room wearing a slinky red dress far too fancy for happy hour at the beer garden/sports bar across the street from the Possums' midtown arena. But that's never stopped her before. Whitney is an assistant designer at a major fashion house. She has a wardrobe any New York City fashionista would kill for and zero concerns about standing out in a crowd.

"I'm good. You?" I ask, ignoring the sinking feeling in my gut as she wraps her arms around Ian and leans in.

Whitney and I are about as opposite as two people can get, but when our paths cross, she's always polite. I don't know why seeing her with Ian makes my stomach snarl into a stress knot.

Maybe it's just that I wish Ian were with someone...friendlier, a woman who appreciated his sense of humor and kindness as much as his studliness and fame. Whitney sighs at his jokes and shushes him when he laughs too loud, and it's always bothered me.

The world can be such a hard place. It just makes sense to enjoy the good times and embrace laughter and happiness whenever possible.

Whitney should be amplifying Ian's joy, not warning him to take it down a notch.

That's probably why I want to pry her fingers off Ian's abs with an extra-sharp colored pencil.

Or maybe it's something else, something I've never admitted to anyone—even myself.

Sometimes I suspect that my feelings for Ian aren't purely of the surrogate-little-sister variety and that what I'm feeling when I watch him hug Whitney isn't concern for a friend who's dating the wrong woman, but plain old jealousy, rearing its ugly head. But if it *is* jealousy, it's completely stupid—Ian will never see me as anything but a kid-sister type—so I do my best to ignore the ugly little prickle across my skin whenever it arises.

"You look so cute, Evie," Whitney says, rubbing a possessive hand over Ian's pecs through his long-sleeved Ice Possums t-shirt. "Like a little farmer doll about to go feed the goats."

"Or the sheep," Ian adds with a wink and a laugh. "I'll talk to Sven before Monday's class, too, get him to ease up on the sheep stuff."

I roll my eyes. "Don't worry about it. It's fine. There are worse nicknames, and if it gets out of hand, I'll shut it down myself. I don't want the guys thinking I can't fight my own battles. If they're going to open up to me in their work, they have to respect me first."

"Aw, she's so cute," Whitney says, doing that thing where she talks about me like I'm not standing right in front of her, which also drives me crazy. "Little Evie, all grown up, with a real job."

Her gaze shifts from Ian's face to mine, her voice cooling a degree or two as she adds, "It doesn't matter that your brother had to pull strings to get you this gig. I'm sure you're going to do a fabulous job."

"Thanks," I grit out, accepting the backhanded compliment with as much grace as possible as Whitney takes Ian's hand and starts for the door.

"Come on, honey, we're going to be late," she says. "I want to get a table on the roof before they're all gone."

"See you there, Evie?" Ian asks, smiling back at me as he follows her.

"Yeah, see you there." I force a grin until they're out of the room and then let it fall away as I exhale an audible breath.

That could have gone better.

But it could have been much worse, too.

As I collect the drawings, I see a few that are actually right in line with what I was hoping for, proving this team isn't a lost cause. I'm already getting through to a few of these men. On Monday, I'll reach a few more. With a little luck, by the time I write my final evaluations, I'll have helped the players connect with their feelings and process them on the page instead of out there on the ice.

By the time I've cleaned up the space and repacked all my art supplies, I'm feeling cautiously optimistic and eager to start the weekend with my roommates and very best friends.

Harlow and I have been tight since second

grade, Jess joined our crew when she moved to town in sixth grade, and Cameron was welcomed in as our boy bestie not long after, when he helped us pass our elementary school's mandatory cooking class. He was already a foodie and amazing in the kitchen, while the three of us couldn't boil water without burning ourselves.

For the most part, we still can't. When we moved in together at the start of last summer—thrilled to finally be making our dream of living together come true after attending different undergraduate programs—we quickly realized Cameron was still the only one who could be counted on not to poison people with his culinary offerings. Jess, Harlow, and I agreed to pay for groceries and keep the common areas clean in exchange for homemade meals.

It's been working out great so far, but even with healthy, delicious food waiting for us at the end of each day, the past three weeks have been grueling. Harlow is in one of the most competitive forensic accounting programs in the country, Jess is working for a video game company doing coding so complex I'm pretty sure I saw her brain leaking out of her ears a few days ago, and Cameron is a sous chef at one of the swankiest, and most demanding, restaurants in the city.

And me...

Well, I'm getting mistaken for one of the homeschooled high school kids who take art classes at NYU, even in the watercolor technique class where I'm the teaching assistant. I'm also getting overlooked in my studio classes, just like I did when I was in undergrad, proving my new professors are just as disdainful of art involving adorable baby animals as my old ones.

Which just...sucks.

Why does the art world have to be so pretentious? Why can't they see that sweet, happy art is just as valid as the edgy, violent stuff?

Sure, I could paint my next panda bear with part of its skeleton exposed, sitting in a puddle of blood or something to please my critics, but...*ew*. I want to paint a happy panda hugging its baby in a misty bamboo forest. Why can't pandas be allowed to live in peace?

At least in paintings...

I cross the street to the bar to find Harlow waiting for me under the awning of the coffee shop next door, looking elegant as always in a pair of vintage wide-leg trousers and a white button-up with a brown bow tied at the neck that perfectly matches her long, glossy brown hair.

I lean in for the hug she offers and ask, "Why can't the pandas live in peace, Harlow?"

"Because the world is a fucking shit show," she says without hesitation, proving why she's still my best friend after nearly sixteen years. No question is ever too random or weird. "And people are garbage who don't deserve good things like pandas. How was your first day with the sweaty grunt monsters?"

I grin. "Okay. They kept the sweating and grunting to a minimum. They also kept the art making to a minimum, but I think our next session will be better. Ian is going to help me get through to them."

Harlow's nostrils flare. "Oh, is he? How *nice* of him. The others are waiting up on the roof, by the way. I told them to go ahead and save us a table in the garden, so we don't have to sit at the indoor bar with the men yelling at televisions."

"Great. And yes, Ian *is* nice," I insist as we start toward the entrance to the pub and the elevator that will whisk us up four flights to the beer garden on the roof.

"Compared to your brother, maybe," Harlow says. "But that's like saying Hitler isn't bad compared to Satan."

I laugh as we tuck ourselves into an empty corner of the elevator beside a group of chatty tourists wondering if they'll have time to order dinner before their show starts.

"That's horrible," I say, pointing a chastising finger up at her face. Like most people, Harlow has several inches on me, even in flats. "Derrick isn't Satan. And he's apologized for that bonfire thing in high school at least twice."

Harlow sniffs. "I don't care. I still hate him like wet socks. But I'll be nice to him if we host Thanksgiving this year because I love you."

"I love you, too," I say, tucking my arm through hers and leaning into her shoulder with a sigh. "I'm looking forward to a drink. It's been a week."

"I hear you." She heaves a sigh of her own. "My

study group is driving me insane. They keep mansplaining litigation support procedures, which would be irritating enough if they were in possession of correct information about said procedures. But sadly, they are not."

"Have you talked to your professor?"

"No," she says, with a weary flap of her arm. "Every time I stop by for office hours, he's asleep, but he's like a hundred years old, so I feel bad about waking him."

"Aw, you..." I nudge her shoulder with mine. "You're getting soft in your old age."

She wrinkles her nose. "Or I'm just secretly worried that he's dead, not sleeping, and I don't want to be the one to find the body."

"Always a good goal," I say as the elevator doors slide open. "To be the one who *doesn't* find the body."

"Amen," she agrees as we step out into the cooling air.

It's still unusually warm for early September, but it's going to be a gorgeous night. The breeze from the river has swept away the exhaust stink from the streets below and the setting sun feels good on my face as we weave our way through the tightly packed tables to the high top in the corner where Cameron and Jess are waving their arms.

I wiggle fingers back at them and hurry around Harlow to hurl myself at a nervous-looking Jess, hoping her first review with her new manager didn't go too badly. She's been stressing out about it since she started with the company in July.

"Hey, babes, how did it go?" I ask, hugging her tight.

"So good," she says, her voice trembling. "I think I got promoted."

I pull back from our embrace, my eyes going wide. "What? What do you mean you *think* you got promoted?"

"I don't know." She brushes her straight, black bangs from her forehead with a shaking hand. "I was so nervous that I'm not sure I heard Zip clearly. It was like he was underwater or one of the grown-ups from the Charlie Brown cartoons." She grins, her brown eyes lighting up. "But I did get a key to my very own office, so I think I'm now the head of my very own team."

"Huzzah!" Cameron cheers, lifting his glass of water into the air. "I'll drink to that." He glances over my shoulder across the crowded garden. "Assuming a server ever finds us way over here in the boonies. Want me to go order from the bar?"

"Yes," Harlow says, settling into one of the tall seats and draping her purse over the back. "And be sure to flirt with the cute bartender while you're over there. She totally has the hots for you, and you should ask her out."

Cameron sticks his tongue out good-naturedly. He and his girlfriend just broke up recently, too. He's been too down in the dumps to date but that doesn't stop Harlow from trying to find him a rebound girl. "Yes, Mom," he says. "Pale ale all around?"

"Old-fashioned for me," Harlow says as I slide

into the chair facing her and Jess, with a view of the skyline behind them. "I need something serious to dampen my seething rage."

Jess pushes her glasses up her nose. "Oh no, more mansplaining?"

"So much mansplaining," Harlow says. "And Chas suggested I might want to switch to decaf if caffeine makes me twitchy. But it was Chas making me twitchy because he wouldn't stop drumming on his textbook with his pencil."

"Monster," I say in mock horror. "How dare he make unnecessary noise?"

Harlow has a thing about "unnecessary noise."

"Seriously," she says, her lips pushing into a pout. "It's awful, Evie. You don't understand. It's like tiny, rabid zombie squirrels are being unleashed inside my skull. I need you to empathize with my psychic pain."

"Uh-oh," Jess says, sinking lower in her chair. "Speaking of pain, I think we might want to find another table." She leans in, adding in a whisper, "Don't look now but I'm pretty sure that's Vince behind us."

My shoulders instantly tighten, but I force a smile. "Oh, well...that's okay. I'll just pop over, say hi, and wish him a great night. It won't be weird."

"Except that he's not alone," Jess says, her forehead furrowing with empathy.

Harlow's eyes widen. "Oh, yeah. He's *really* not alone."

"Intensely not alone," Jess agrees.

Harlow's lip curls. "Grossly not alone, as well."

"What are you..." My words trail off as I peek over my shoulder to see Vince sitting at a table for two with a blonde in a clingy black dress welded to his face.

They're making out like they're drowning, and the only source of oxygen is located deep inside each other's throats. Vince is making little moaning sounds I can hear over the music and the dull roar of laughter and after-work conversation filling the air. Meanwhile, the blonde is petting his neatly trimmed beard—the beard I once thought was so cute I drew a cartoon series called "Adventures of the Beard" that I gave to him for our three-month anniversary—like a beloved pet.

And that isn't even the worst part.

Seeing him all over someone just three weeks after he told me I had no sex vibe would be bad enough, but then I see it...

On her left ring finger.

A rock the size of a jumbo crayon tip.

It's an engagement ring. Vince is *engaged*.

And my next diary entry just got a hell of a lot more depressing.

CHAPTER 3

Ian Fox

*A man who's confused about his wonderful life,
and why it isn't making him feel so wonderful anymore...*

She's a grown woman.

Like she said, she's almost twenty-four and absolutely old enough to make her own choices and deal with the consequences.

I know this. But it still takes every ounce of my willpower to keep from crossing the garden and encouraging Evie to slow her roll. She's had at least three old-fashioneds in the past hour and shows no signs of stopping.

"Don't you think, babe?" Whitney asks, squeezing my thigh under the table.

I flinch and pull away, making her full lips turn

down at the edges. "Sorry," I say, dragging a hand through my hair. "Just a little jumpy."

"A little distracted, too," she says. "Did you hear anything I just said?"

"Sure," I lie, scrambling to recall what we were talking about before I zoned out on Evie pounding whiskey. When I can't, I decide it's best to change the subject. "I'm just worried about Evie. I'm not sure she realizes an old-fashioned is pretty much all hard alcohol."

Whitney sighs. "Yeah, well, she'll figure it out. We've all had hangovers in our early twenties. We're still alive."

"Right." I chew my bottom lip for a beat before I add, "But she probably only weighs like...a hundred pounds. And she's not eating any of the flatbread they ordered."

"Oh my God," Whitney mutters. "Stalker much? What's with you and that girl? It's like you're obsessed with her. Should I be worried?"

I rip my gaze from Evie, a frown clawing at my forehead. "What? Of course not. She's my best friend's little sister. I've known her since she was a tiny little kid. I just care about her, that's all. I don't want her to get hurt."

"Must be nice." Whitney crosses her arms and sits back in her chair, clearly winding up for a prolonged pout. "Seems like you're just fine with the rest of us getting hurt."

I fight the urge to roll my eyes.

I'm so tired of having this same argument with

her, over and over again. Honestly, I'm so tired of most of our relationship.

Things haven't been good since last Christmas, when Whitney didn't get the engagement ring she was apparently expecting she'd find under the tree. Ever since, she's acted like there's something wrong with me, with *us*, because we missed some benchmark I'm not sure I ever want to reach.

My parents have an incredible marriage, but they're abnormally sweet, laid-back, optimistic people—which I assume is the only way they were able to stay sane while raising eight children—and they're the exception when it comes to happily ever after, not the rule. Most of my friends' parents are divorced and the ones who aren't don't seem very happy about being together.

As far as I can tell, the institution of marriage isn't in a healthy place right now, and I'm already trapped in one unhealthy institution with a team that refuses to act like one, so I'm in no hurry to join another.

"I'm not fine with you getting hurt," I say with as much patience as I can muster. "Of course, I'm not. I'm not trying to hurt you, Whitney. I'm just not ready to get married. It has nothing to do with you. It's me. I just need time to decide if that's something I want for my future."

"And while you're doing that, what am I supposed to do? Sit around with my fingers crossed hoping you'll finally decide that I'm good enough for you?" Her lips pucker into a cat anus of irritation.

Whitney is a gorgeous woman, but that face is the worst.

But how to ask your significant other to stop making cat-ass shapes with their lips? That's not something I know how to do any more than I know how to stop having this same fight every seven to ten days like clockwork.

"This has nothing to do with you being good enough for me," I say for at least the dozenth time. "If anything, I..." I trail off as a sharp clatter and several sharp gasps sound from Evie's corner of the beer garden.

I look over to see Evie on the ground with her wrought iron chair on top of her and mutter a curse beneath my breath.

"I'm fine, nothing to see here," Evie calls out, flashing a thumbs-up as her friend Cameron lifts the chair. A beat later Jess and Harlow are on either side of her, helping her to her feet, but she winces in pain and quickly lifts her weight off her right foot.

She's hurt.

That's all I need to see to get me out of my chair.

"Where are you going?" Whitney demands sharply.

I tuck my chair under the table. "I'm going to check on her. I'll be right back."

"If you leave, then I'm leaving," Whitney says, her hand balling into a fist on the table. "I'm serious, Ian. I won't let you ditch me for another woman in the middle of a date."

This time I can't control my eye roll. "I'm not ditching you. I'm going to help a friend. And you know it. But do what you need to do, Whitney. I'll catch up with you later. Or...not."

I turn, leaving her making outraged huffing noises behind me as I cross the garden. A part of me is shouting that I can't end a three-year relationship like this, that I have to go back and talk to Whitney, make her understand where I'm coming from and assure her that I'm taking her hopes for our future under serious consideration.

But I'm so tired of fighting and making up, so tired of reassuring her about things she shouldn't need reassuring about.

Like this insanity with Evie. Yes, I love Evie, but not in that way. My chest gets warm and tight when I'm with her because she's my first and most loyal fan, the little girl who stole my heart the day I met her.

I'd swung by her house to pick up Derrick for practice our sophomore year to find Evie curled up in a ball on the sagging couch on their front porch with tears streaking her cheeks. I'd asked her what was wrong, she'd told me her dad had taken her crayons away because she forgot to clean her room, and I'd pulled out a pack of colored pencils I'd bought for art class and handed them over.

I'll never forget the way her face lit up or the reverence in her voice as she said, "Oh thank you so much. I'll be so careful with them, I promise."

"You don't have to be careful with them," I'd assured her. "Just enjoy them. Have fun."

She'd nodded seriously, her green eyes wide and her mouth trembling as it pressed into a tight line. "Okay. I'll try."

By that point I had six little brothers and sisters and another on the way. I had loads of experience with little kids, and I'd never heard one say he or she would "try" to have fun.

Having fun, as far as I knew, was something kids did naturally.

Looking back from an adult's perspective, it's obvious that Derrick and Evie's dad was a neglectful, and occasionally mean-spirited, jerk. But at sixteen I didn't know much about their family or how to tell if an adult was truly bad news or just doing the usual, fun-killing things adults do in the name of keeping their kids safe. I did know, however, that Evie's sad, serious, and oh-so-determined face touched something inside of me that hadn't been touched before.

From that moment on, she was under my protection. If anyone wanted to hurt that little girl, including Derrick when he complained about letting her tag along to all our games, they had to come through me, first.

And that's still true. I hope she knows that, even though we've grown apart since she went to undergrad in Virginia.

I arrive at their table just as Harlow is looping Evie's arm over her shoulder and hissing, "It's fine, just keep your head high and don't cry."

"I'm not going to cry," Evie squeaks in a voice that sounds like she's about five seconds from a breakdown. She glances up, blinking faster as her gaze connects with mine. "Oh, no. Did you see me fall out of my chair? Did all the other players see it?" Her lips turn down hard at the edges. "Now they're never going to respect my authority," she slurs, sniffing as Harlow snaps her fingers in front of her face.

"Yes, they will," she says. "Stay focused. Cameron's paying the bill and Jess is downstairs calling a car. We can be out of here in two minutes if we stay on task." Harlow casts a pointed look my way as she whispers, "Help me, jerk. Her ex is right behind us, watching this entire meltdown."

I dart a quick glance over her shoulder to see a man with dark hair and a cheesy pirate beard watching Evie with a pitying expression. The equally cheesy blonde in garish red lipstick beside him is smirking, clearly of the opinion that she's a finer specimen than Dickhead's former girlfriend.

But she isn't fit to lick Evie's tennis shoes, and a part of me wishes I hadn't been raised to be a nice guy so I could tell her so.

"I shouldn't drink whiskey," Evie says, weaving unsteadily as Harlow reaches back to grab her purse and Evie's art bag. "It tastes like fire and then your brain goes...squishy." She lifts a hand, poking a finger into her temple. "See? Right there. Squishy." Her eyes go comically wide. "Do you think I broke my brain, Ian? Is it going to be squishy forever?"

"No, your brain's fine. I'm more concerned about your ankle," I say, sliding in to wrap my arm around her waist. "What do you think, short stack? Can you hang on for a piggyback ride downstairs?"

"Yes," she says with a heavy sigh. "But let's go quick or I might barf in your hair."

"You're not going to barf in my hair." I turn and squat down low enough for her to climb on my back. Hooking my arms under her knees, I hoist her up and add in a softer voice, "But if you do, it's not a big deal. No worries. That's what showers are for."

"Thank you, you're the best," she says, clinging to my shoulders as I start around the table.

As we pass her ex, I make a point not to look his way.

We're nearly past him, and I'm debating whether I should text Whitney once we're downstairs and tell her I'm going to help get Evie home, when the guy surges to his feet and says, "Holy shit, you're Ian Fox! From the Possums. Aren't you?"

Well...fuck.

CHAPTER 4

Ian

I reluctantly turn his way, summoning a soft groan from Evie. "Yeah," I say, "but I'm kind of—"

"Totally. I won't bother you, man," the guy says, his eyes bright above his dark, evil-villain-shaped beard. He looks like he escaped from a cartoon. Or 1910. "Just wanted to let you know I appreciate everything you do for the team. They'd suck even harder than they do already without you."

I force a tight smile. "Thanks."

"So, how do you know Evie?" he asks, his nearly black eyes darting to my left shoulder, where Evie is still moaning softly beneath her breath, a long—*uhhhhhhh*—sound that isn't comforting.

I wasn't lying when I said I'm okay with getting barfed on if it can't be avoided, but I'd prefer we both make it to her place without baptism by bile.

"She never mentioned you," he pushes on. "Not even when we went to a game last February, though I wondered how a college kid could afford seats like that."

"I'm not a *kid*, asshole," Evie slurs into my ear. A second later, her arm flops limply over my shoulder to point a finger at Beard Guy's face. "I'm a fully grown woman with wants and needs and urges, just like everyone else. Yeah, that's right, I have urges, too! Tons of urges."

Heat creeps up my neck. I have a high-tolerance for embarrassment but apparently a *low* tolerance for hearing my surrogate little sister talk about her "urges."

I squeeze Evie's leg. "Okay, Evie, I think—"

"Dark, sexy urges," she continues, wiggling her finger closer to his face. "Urges so naughty you would swallow your tongue if you knew half of the things I thought about when we were kissing. And you weren't even the best kisser I've ever kissed! So there!"

"Come on, Ian, we need to get her downstairs," Harlow urges, tugging at my sleeve.

"No, I want to stay," Evie says, "I'm not finished yet."

"You should have been finished two old-fashioneds ago, doll," Harlow says, before adding in a voice for my ears only, "She's never had this much alcohol at once. We need to get her home and get water and crackers in her. Stat."

"Gotta go," I mutter to Beard Guy and the

blonde, who is doing a shit job of concealing her amusement at Evie's meltdown.

I turn to follow Harlow, but Evie lets out a wail that has the half of the beer garden not already staring turning to gawk.

"No, I'm not finished," she insists, pointing more emphatically at her ex's face. "Here is what people don't understand, Vince. Women can be more than one thing. I can be cute in the street and a savage in the sheets. I can draw adorable baby animals and still make deep and meaningful art. And I shouldn't have to choose between being a 'good girl' or a 'hot girl.' We, as humans, contain multitudes. Multitudes!"

That last "multitudes" is said with such force, such passion that I'm not really surprised when it's followed by a stream of projectile vomit a television comedy sketch team would be proud of. It emerges as a churning tornado of whiskey-and-cherry-scented sickness that whizzes over her ex's shoulder as he ducks to the right to splatter all over his date.

Now it's Blondie's turn to wail in a thick, Jersey accent—"Oh my God, Vince. Oh my fucking Gawwwwd!"

Evie lets out a soft burp and mutters, "Oops. Sorry," as Harlow tugs more urgently at my sleeve and demands, "Out of here. Now. Before they start naked vomit wrestling or something equally heinous."

She doesn't have to ask me twice. I hustle to the elevator behind her, slipping inside as Vince is stripping off his jacket to help clean Blondie up and she's screeching, "Somebody stop her! She's gonna pay for this damage. My Balenciaga bag is ruined. It's fucking ruined!"

"It's Balen-SEE-aga, not CHEE-aga," Harlow mutters as she jams the "close door" button until the doors glide shut. "It's Spanish, not Italian. If you're going to dump that much money on a bag, you ought to at least be able to pronounce the designer's name correctly."

"You tell 'em, Lo," Evie mutters against my shoulder, where her head is once again resting heavily.

Harlow props her hands on her hips. "I told *you* to stop several drinks ago, Slimer," she says, the reference to the barfing ghost hitting me hard after what we just experienced.

"I'm sorry," Evie says, her voice small. "I was trying to drown the sad knot in my stomach, but it didn't work. I can't believe they're engaged, Harlow! It's only been three weeks! He dumped me, forgot me, found a new partner, fell in love, and proposed in three weeks!"

"I seriously doubt that's what happened, sweetie," Harlow says as the elevator arrives on the first floor. When the doors part, she extends an arm to keep them open as I step through with Evie.

"What do you mean?" Evie asks.

"We'll talk about it later, love," Harlow says, casting me a hard look. "When we're alone."

I clear my throat. "I figured I'd come along in the cab, help you guys get her up to your place."

Harlow waves a breezy hand as we step out onto the sidewalk where their friends, Cameron and Jess—both of whom I remember dimly from when they were all in middle school, hanging out at the ice rink on free skate afternoons—are waiting next to an SUV with an impatient-looking older man behind the wheel. "It's fine. Cameron's big and strong, right, Cameron? You can carry Evie up the stairs to the apartment."

Cameron, who is now a couple inches taller than my six foot two, nods. "Totally. But thanks, man. I appreciate your help."

"I don't need to be carried," Evie says as I set her down beside the car waiting at the curb. "Oh God, not again." She bends over, dry heaving into the gutter.

"No way, not gonna happen," the man behind the wheel says. "No pukers. I don't get paid enough for that shit, and you young people never tip."

"I tip all the time," Harlow shoots back. "And she's not going to be sick. See, she's just...convulsing. Not actively—"

"I'll get her home," I assure them. "I'll get her sobered up and—"

"Nope," Harlow cuts in. "Not going to happen. We don't leave fallen soldiers on the field of battle. Evie's coming with us."

"Not in my vehicle she isn't," the older man says, reaching for the gear shift on the wheel, clearly intending to bail.

"Five hundred bucks. Cash," I say, reaching for my wallet in my back pocket as I help Cameron hold Evie upright with the other. "It's yours to keep, no matter what happens on the ride. And we'll do our best to keep her from being sick in the car. I'll catch it in my hands or something if I have to."

"See, Harlow, he isn't Hitler," Evie says. "He's the nicest and the best." Evie lifts bleary green eyes to mine. "I'm sorry I'm gross right now, Ian. Please don't tell Derrick, okay? You know how he freaks out."

Harlow huffs as she reaches past Evie, snatching the bills from my hand and passing them over to the driver. "Fine, you can come with us, but you have to leave as soon as we get Evie upstairs."

"Okay, fine," I say, but I have no intention of leaving until I know Evie's okay and doesn't need to be taken to the emergency room for alcohol poisoning.

Her friends may not believe in leaving "fallen soldiers" behind but I don't believe in trusting the health and safety of my nearest and dearest to other people. Evie may have been out of my orbit for most of the past four years, but she's back in it now, which means she's back under my protection.

Twenty minutes later, we arrive at a five-story walk-up in the West Village and I learn these lunatics live on the fifth floor. By the time Cameron and I drag a still groggy, but no longer gagging, Evie up the stairs between us, we're both covered in sweat and smell like whatever repulsive meat-and-onion dish their downstairs neighbor is whipping up for supper.

"Okay, I'll take it from here," Harlow says, ushering Evie into the bathroom off the combination living room and kitchen. She casts me a pointed look. "Goodbye, Ian. Don't let the door hit you on the way out."

She slams the bathroom door, leaving Cameron and I standing in the buzzing silence in the living room as Jess hurries into what I assume is Evie's room to fetch her fresh clothes.

"I'm sorry," Cameron says softly, dragging a hand through his shaggy brown hair. "I don't know why she hates you. I know why she hates Derrick. Sort of. We all hate Derrick a little, except Evie, but you...I don't get."

"Really?" My forehead furrows. "Why? I mean, I know Derrick can be a little bossy sometimes, but he's devoted to Evie. Always has been."

Cameron's brows shoot up his forehead. "Um, yeah...that's one way of looking at it."

"What's the other way of looking at it?" I ask, genuinely curious.

"He's a control freak," Cameron says. "Who bosses Evie around like she's still five years old. It's disrespectful. She's a grown woman with a good head on her shoulders." He winces and lifts a hand in the air. "Usually. Tonight was just a bad night. Vince really did a number on her."

"She was into him, huh?" I ask, vaguely disgusted by the thought. That guy was so cheesy. Evie deserves so much better than a douchebag with a cartoon beard.

"No, not really," Cameron says, moving into the kitchen and opening one of the cabinets to fetch a glass. "I mean, yeah, she liked him, but they weren't to the 'I love you' stage or anything. It's more what he said to her on his way out the door, if you know what I mean. It fucked with her head."

I'm about to ask what he said when Harlow calls from the bathroom, "Cam, where's that water? Our drunk pumpkin is coming around in the cold shower and would like a drink, pretty please."

"Just a second," Cam calls out, filling the glass and moving around me to head toward the bathroom.

I'm left alone in their kitchen, staring at pictures of the four friends throughout the years stuck to the fridge with donut-shaped magnets, feeling like an interloper.

I should leave—the rest of them clearly have Evie well in hand—but for some reason I linger, studying each photo, marveling at how little Evie has changed since the shot of her and Harlow on the boardwalk when they were kids. She still has the same halo of blonde curls, the same bright, but slightly anxious light in her eyes, even the same paint-splattered overalls, though the ones in the photo are obviously a much smaller size.

I've always assumed that was just Evie being Evie—she found her signature style at a young age and stuck to it, nothing wrong with that. But what Cameron said, combined with Evie's words at the beer garden, about having to choose between being a "good girl" or a "hot girl," make me question that assumption.

Memories of Derrick giving Evie shit for wearing lip gloss in seventh grade and telling her to go change when she tried to get into the car wearing a short skirt one morning not long after drift through my head, making my stomach tighten.

Maybe Derrick has been overstepping with Evie. And maybe that's been happening for longer than I realized...

I reach for my cell to send Derrick a text asking if we can get together for a talk—I've found it's better to confront problems with friends right away than to let them fester—but when I pull out my phone, I'm confronted with several missed texts from Whitney.

I can't believe you're leaving with a girl who just puked all over the place in public.

That's it, Ian.

I can't do this with you anymore.

If you decide you're ready to grow up, let me know. Maybe I'll still be single by then, but maybe I won't. You aren't the only one who can find someone else to go home with, but my new guy won't be a kid who can't handle his liquor.

Have a nice life!

Fuck. Well, looks like I don't have to worry about making up with my girlfriend. I don't have one anymore.

CHAPTER 5

Evie

For the first thirty minutes after arriving home, I'm too out of it to worry about anything but staying upright in the shower, eating the crackers and water Harlow shoves through the shower curtain for me to munch as I'm standing under the spray, and brushing my teeth for at least five glorious minutes.

But once the crackers are digesting, I'm dressed in a pair of flannel pajama pants and an oversized t-shirt, and feeling more peaceful in my body, the implications of what happened tonight start to hit—hard.

I sink into the couch in the living room, clutching one of our throw pillows as I squeak, "Tell me I didn't shout at Vince about my dark sexy urges. Please. Tell me that was a hallucination."

"Not a hallucination," Jess says from the plush

chair across from me, her expression sober in the soft glow from her laptop. "And already going viral. I ran a search of the top social media applications. #DrunkGirlUrges is already trending on several."

I cover my face with my hands and let out a long groan.

"I guess that means you don't want to see it?" Jess asks, nodding toward her screen. "You look cute for a drunk girl. Until the vomiting starts. The vomit shot is already a meme, by the way."

I put the pillow to my face and wonder how hard I'd have to press to render myself unconscious.

"Don't stress. It'll blow over in a few days," Cameron says from behind me in the kitchen where he's whipping up scrambled eggs and savory pancakes for a late dinner. "The internet has a short attention span."

"But a long memory," I say, dropping the pillow to my lap. "That's going to stay with me for the rest of my life. I'll be seventy and opening a show in Tribeca and the write-up in the *Times* will refer to me as the artist also known as Drunk Girl with Urges."

"But at least you'll have a Tribeca show," Jess says, looking on the bright side. Usually, that's my job, but I'm not feeling very bright right now. I'm feeling like a huge idiot and the worst part hasn't even hit yet.

When it does, I groan again and sink lower into the cushions. "Oh God, my dad and Derrick are going to see it. You know they will. If it's going viral, everyone will see it. Absolutely everyone." I squeeze my eyes shut as a wave of shame washes over me, making my recently settled stomach roil again. "Dad already thinks I'm too naïve to live in the city and warned me not to come crying to him if I get mugged or thrown under a subway car. He's going to be so mortified."

"Fuck your dad," Harlow says. I feel the cushions dip and look up to see her stretching out on the other side of the couch with a sour expression on her face. "He's an asshole. And so is Vince. And that woman deserved to be puked on. Though I wish you'd hit Vince, instead, that slimy little cheater."

My brows pinch together. "What?"

"He had to have been dating that girl the same time he was dating you," Harlow says, making me remember something she said as we were leaving, something about doubting Vince found true love in three weeks. "There's no other way they could have gotten to the engagement stage so quickly."

"Maybe they're just impulsive as a couple," Jess says, her nose wrinkling at something on her screen. I'm tempted to ask what she's found now but think better of it. I'll look myself after dinner and a good night's sleep.

I'll be strong enough to handle it then.

Maybe.

Right now, thinking about Vince cheating and me having no clue about it is enough to handle.

"That's why he wasn't pushing you to have

sex," Harlow continues, still scowling. "It was because he was getting laid elsewhere."

"No, I really don't think so," I say. "There were...other factors."

Harlow arches a brow. "Like what? Erectile dysfunction? Because that's also a sign of cheating. If he can't get it up for a cutie like you, it's probably because his dick was exhausted from fucking someone else." She shrugs. "Or he has a porn addiction or something. Men are weird."

I hug my pillow. "No, he didn't have erectile dysfunction, we just... *I* just..." I pull in a breath, and blurt out, "I'm a virgin. I've never done it and Vince knew that and he didn't want to rush me since I've already waited so long and..." I glance back and forth between Jess's and Harlow's shocked faces.

"You might not want to talk about that right now," Harlow says, but I cut her off with a wave of my hand.

"No, it's time," I say. "I want to be honest with you guys, no matter how embarrassing it is."

"It's not embarrassing," Jess insists. "It's fine. Great even! I just always thought... I mean, you dated so much in college."

"But none of those relationships lasted very long. Not long enough to...you know." I sigh. "And with Vince it never felt totally right. I mean, I wanted to—sometimes I *really* wanted to—but there was always this niggling worry in my head that I wouldn't know how to do it the right way, that I'd be too anxious or weird or something and it would scare him off."

"Then he absolutely wasn't the right guy to be your first," a deep voice rumbles from the kitchen.

A deep voice that *isn't* Cameron's deep voice...

My eyes go saucer wide and Harlow mumbles, "I tried to tell you Hitler was still here, but..."

"Oh God," I whisper, sinking even lower on the couch. After a beat to catch my breath from my sudden case of heart palpitations, I call out, "Ian, I'm sorry I vomited on you and ruined your night."

"You didn't. You missed me entirely and I'm having a great night. I'm learning how to make scallion and miso pancakes. These things are delicious."

"Thanks, man," Cameron says. "I'll give you the recipe if you want. They're super easy and great to make in bulk and warm up later with some fresh eggs or a little cheese. Oh, and I'm a virgin, too, Evie, so don't feel weird about it. You aren't alone."

I pop my head over the couch, a wave of affection for Cam flooding through me. "Really? But you and Mariah dated for almost five years."

"Yeah, but she wanted to wait until marriage. She made a promise to her super religious grandmother before she died, and I respected that," he says, his tone souring as he adds, "Right up until I found her in bed with not one, but two members of the soccer team."

"Oh no," I say, hurting for him. "I guess that's

why you broke up, huh? You could have told us, you know. If you wanted to."

Cam shrugs as he flips another pancake. "I know. I was just embarrassed and worried that..." He sighs. "I don't know...that there was something wrong with me and what I was allowed to do with her in the bedroom. Why else would she hook up with two people she didn't even care about when we were planning to get married after graduation?"

Ian rests a hand on his shoulder. "It wasn't you, man. When people act out like that, it's always about them. Always. And I bet she's going to look back on that decision in a few months or a few years and regret the hell out of it."

Cameron's lips curve in a tight smile. "Thanks. I think she already does. She texts me all the time, but...there are limits. I can't forgive her for that. I just can't."

"And you shouldn't," Harlow says. "The universe gave us hate for a reason. To keep us from getting burned twice by the same loathsome cheater."

Jess lets out a soft laugh. "Geez, Harlow. Are you still mad at Chris? That was senior year of high school."

"Time does not heal all wounds," Harlow says. "Especially cheating wounds."

"Noted," Jess says, pulling in a breath before she adds in a rush, "I wouldn't know because I've never been cheated on. Because I've never had a serious boyfriend and I've also never had sex. So there." She turns back to her keyboard, typing furiously as she adds, "But I'm not worried about it. I figure sex is like skateboarding. It looks fun, but is it worth the steep learning curve and the high likelihood of serious injury? Probably not."

"Well, I think it's great that you guys are waiting until it feels right," Ian says.

"Don't fucking patronize them, Ian," Harlow says. "Or we'll hate you even more than we do already."

"I don't hate you, man," Cameron says.

"Me, either," Jess pipes up. "Anyone Evie cares about as much as you is good people in my book."

Harlow lets out a long, tortured exhalation as she surges to her feet. "Fine, I don't really hate you, either. But you're super dense sometimes and that's annoying." She turns, hands propped on her hips as she adds, "But if you're prepared to step up to the plate around here, then you can join our friend group. On a probationary basis."

"Assuming the super popular and famous pro hockey player is looking for a friend group composed primarily of impoverished virgins," Jess adds dryly, earning a laugh from Cameron and a glare from Harlow.

I'm not surprised when Ian says, "I'd love to be a part of your friend group. Thanks for asking," but I *am* surprised by the enthusiasm in his tone.

He's a sweet guy who does his best not to hurt people's feelings, but he looks sincerely jazzed by the invitation.

"Really?" I meet his gaze over the back of the couch. "No pressure. We know you probably have a ton of friends already, since you've been living in the city so much longer than the rest of us."

"And are super famous and popular," Jess adds again.

"I actually...don't," Ian says with an awkward laugh. "I don't have a lot of close friends on the team, I've lost touch with my high school friends who live in the city, and Whitney just broke up with me, so...looks like I'll have some time on my hands to invest in new relationships." His gaze returns to me as he adds, "And rekindle old ones. Sorry again that I wasn't more help at the art therapy session today. I'll do better next time, I promise."

His words remind me that his teammates were at the beer garden, too, and I drop my face into my hands again. "Oh no, they're never going to listen to me now."

"Sure, they will," Ian says. "You're a meme. That's street cred for most of those cretins, and I'll back you up if you need help. And I..." He shrugs, glancing around the room as he adds, "Well, I might be able to help you guys with the other stuff, too."

"What other stuff?" Harlow asks suspiciously.

"You know, just navigating the dating world with a little more ease," Ian says. "I've done a lot of dating and have experience I'm happy to share. If you're interested in something like that."

"In like...love lessons?" Cameron asks.

Ian laughs. "I guess so."

"Then yeah, man, sign me up. I clearly wasn't doing it right the first time."

"I don't want love lessons," Jess says, still typing away with her gaze fixed on her laptop screen. "But seduction lessons would be great. I'd like to get my first time out of the way before I worry about adding love to the mix. I figure the sex part by itself will be stressful enough."

My jaw drops, but I snap my mouth closed before Jess looks up.

As shocking as it is to hear my proud computer nerd and homebody of a friend ask for seduction lessons, I'm proud of her for having the courage to ask for what she wants.

As far as what *I* want, however...

CHAPTER 6

Evie

"What about you, Evie?" Ian asks as if he's read my mind, a tenderness in his voice that wasn't there before. "I know it might be weird to talk to a big-brother type about dating and sex stuff but I'm here if you need me. And I'm not actually a blood relation, so..."

"I know you're not," I say, suddenly uncomfortable with this conversation.

I *absolutely* know he's not a blood relation. The entire time I was shouting at Vince about my "urges," I was simultaneously experiencing urges related to how good it felt to be on Ian's back, with his strong hands cradling my thighs.

If there was any doubt about it before, there isn't now—Ian makes me tingle in a way no other man ever has.

But Ian wants to help me hook up with another man. He has zero interest in me sexually. Not to mention the fact that Derrick would probably kill me if he thought I had a crush on his best friend and would *definitely* kill Ian if he were in fact interested in me in *that* way.

But he's not. And he won't ever be.

I'm just little Evie from the neighborhood, the kid he used to help wipe ice cream off her face when she was in second grade. That's how he'll always see me, no matter how old I am or how much I grow and change.

You don't know that, doofus, the inner voice pops up, sounding more irritable than usual. Probably because I tried to drown her in cherry-flavored whiskey. Ugh. I'm never drinking whiskey again. Never, ever, ever. *How much have you really changed? You still dress like a little kid, defer to Dad and Derrick like when you were a kid, and sit around with your thumb up your ass waiting for other people to give you permission to do the things you want to do. You also have the tolerance of a ten-year-old. Remember that the next time you try to give me permanent brain damage and stop after one drink.*

I frown. Some of that is true, but not all of it. I don't wait for other people to give me permission to do things, and I certainly don't have my thumb up my ass while I do it.

Oh yeah? Then why not go for this with Ian? Take him up on his "romance lessons," see if you can learn a thing or two. And if you happen to test his methods on the man himself... Well, who could blame you? After all, he did say he and Whitney were over...

My mouth goes dry, and my head starts to pound again.

I can't do that...can I?

Ian would see right through me. And then he'd run away. Or, worse, laugh. Or, even worse, let me down easy with that warm, gentle, "big brotherly" look that's on his face right now.

Just the thought of that is enough to make me want to dissolve into a million microscopic beads and roll between the couch cushions, never to be found again.

Coward.

I wrinkle my nose. I'm not a coward.

Then say yes. At least give it a shot. Even if you don't have the guts to go after the guy you really want, Ian should be able to help you find someone better than Vince.

I chew my bottom lip. The inner voice has a point.

And what do I have to lose? Nights alone in the apartment while Harlow studies late and Cameron and Jess hit the town with Ian, learning how to be Dating All-Stars?

"Okay," I finally say. "I'm game. On one condition—we don't tell Derrick. He's already going to be angry when he finds out what happened tonight. I don't want him all up in my business, hovering and fretting and being weird while I'm trying to learn how to pull tail."

Cameron cocks his head. "I think that slang is gender specific. Like, men pull female tail and women pull...something else."

"Really?" I ask. "Are you sure?"

"Um, no. I'm not." He hands Ian two plates with a laugh. "Are you sure you want to take the three of us on? You're going to have your work cut out for you."

"Yeah, I'm totally in," Ian says, carrying the plates to the long table between the kitchen and the living room area where we eat, study, and play cards on Sunday nights. "I'm excited about it. You guys are great people. Whoever you end up with is going to be hella lucky. And if I get to play a part in helping great people find other great people... then that's awesome."

"I agree." Harlow moves into the kitchen to fetch utensils and cloth napkins from our stash by the sink. "And I believe your intentions are pure, Ian. But that doesn't mean you have the skills to pay the matchmaker bills."

"Well, I won't really be a matchmaker," Ian says. "I'll be more like a coach, training and prepping my team to compete at the highest level." His eyes glitter as he pulls out two chairs and nods toward Jess and me. "The more I think about it, the more psyched I am to get started. You guys are in great shape. You just need a little fine-tuning, and you'll be ready to dominate the New York dating scene."

"But what's in it for you?" Harlow demands. "Don't say the satisfaction of helping other people or I'm going to vomit. And unlike our little whiskey exorcist over there, I never miss my target."

Jess grabs my hand, hauling me up off the couch. "It will keep his mind off his own heartbreak and romantic failure. Right, Ian? You did say Whitney broke up with you, right?"

"Yeah. What happened?" I ask as I settle into my seat amidst the mouthwatering aroma of steamy sausage and pepper scrambles and savory pancakes. "Are you okay? I thought you two were in it for the long haul."

He shrugs before taking the seat across from mine. "Things haven't been great for a while. I wasn't meeting her expectations and didn't know if I'd ever be able to meet them, so..."

"She wanted you to put a ring on it," Harlow says knowingly as she sets silverware beside my plate. "And you want to run free like a wild stallion."

Ian's lips hook up on one side. "No, I didn't want to run free like a wild stallion. I just didn't want to make a promise I wasn't sure I could keep. From what I've seen, marriage isn't easy. It's like... trying to walk a tightrope in an earthquake."

Harlow grunts as she holds out his silverware. "That's a good analogy. And admirable behavior."

Ian's brows shoot up as he accepts the napkin, fork, and knife. "Was that a compliment? From you?"

She rolls her eyes. "Don't get too excited. You're still on probation in the court of my affections. And I will be sitting in on these 'lessons' of yours to make sure you don't lead my best friends astray."

"I won't," he assures her. "Of course, I won't."

"I'm serious, Ian," she insists. "These three

people are my entire world. If you hurt them, I'm going to be very angry with you, and you won't like me when I'm angry."

"You really wouldn't." Jess points her triangle of freshly buttered toast Ian's way. "She's like an Irish banshee—noisy and out to reap souls first and ask questions never. You may think you've seen her angry, but you haven't. And you don't want to."

"So, calling me 'asshole' or 'Hitler' for years was—"

"A symptom of mild irritation," Harlow supplies. "Yes."

"But once she's your friend, she's the best person in the world to have on your side," Jess says, grinning at Harlow as she takes the chair beside hers. "A more loyal, fiercely loving, or funny friend is hard to find."

"Stop it, you're embarrassing me," Harlow says, throwing her napkin at Jess and then instantly leaning in to hug her tight.

"Looks like the only thing left to decide is when class is in session," Cameron says, sitting down with his plate and digging into his scramble.

We all tuck into our delicious breakfast-for-dinner meal as we chat about our schedules. Preseason games don't start for Ian for another two weeks and the rest of us always have Monday and Thursday nights free after work and school. We decide on a bi-weekly schedule to begin in just three days' time.

That gives me three days to build up my courage.

Three days to decide if I have the guts to act on the fizzing, floating feeling that fills me every time Ian shoots a grin my way or if I'm going to let fears about the fallout with Derrick and all the other things that could go wrong scare me into sitting around with my thumb up my ass.

And I swear, that's the exact thought going through my head as a fist pounds on our front door and a deep, outraged voice shouts through the heavy wood, "Evie Eleanor Olsen. Open this door. Right now!"

CHAPTER 7

Ian

*E*vie's eyes go wide and all the color drains from her face. "Oh no."

My stomach clamps down around my eggs and pancakes as I realize I'll have the chance to start making things right with her sooner than I expected.

Surely, it won't be that hard. Derrick is a hothead and a control freak, but he's also been my best friend since we were sixteen years old. And none of us are kids anymore.

Once I give him some constructive feedback about adult sibling relationships, he'll see that I'm right. After all, it's not like I don't know what it's like to be a protective big brother—I have seven younger brothers and sisters, and I'd move heaven and earth to help any one of them—but only if they ask me to.

That's the piece of the puzzle that Derrick's

missing. Evie has to *ask* him for his help and advice, otherwise he's overstepping.

"Evie, open the door," Derrick shouts again. "Or somebody open it. I need to make sure my sister is all right."

"See, he's just worried about you," Jess whispers to Evie as she shoves her chair back. "It'll be fine. But I'm going to wait this out in my room with my noise-cancelling headphones on because conflict is scary, and Derrick is loud."

A beat later, Jess has vanished, and Cameron is quickly gathering up the now empty dishes. "I'll head into my room, too. Give you some privacy."

"Well, I'm *not* going to my room," Harlow says, propping her hands on her hips as she glares at the door. "I'm going to tell Satan to get the hell off our stoop and come back when he learns how to use his inside voice."

"No, I'll talk to him," Evie says, rising unsteadily to her feet. "Putting it off will only make things worse. But I'll take him to a coffee shop or something. You shouldn't have to hide in your rooms all night because I made a dumb mistake and my brother is flipping out about it."

Harlow starts to protest, but Cameron shoots her a hard look and nods toward the other side of the apartment, making me think that staying out of the Olsen family drama is something they've talked about before.

Her fingers clench and unclench at her sides before she finally says in a rush of breath, "Fine,

I'll go to my room, but call me if you need me, Evie, and I'll be there in a hot second, ready to hand Derrick his ass."

Evie's lips twitch but a smile doesn't form. "Okay. Thanks." She lifts crossed fingers into the air. "Wish me luck."

Harlow and Cameron pull their own vanishing act, but I don't have a room to disappear to and I wouldn't go there even if I did. I'm not just an innocent bystander in this family drama; I've been a contributor to the dysfunction by turning a blind eye to it for far too long.

But that stops now.

I'm right behind Evie as she moves past the kitchen into the entryway where the roommates' jackets are hung neatly on hooks with their shoes lined up beneath. She wipes her hands on her pajama pants, pulling in a deep breath as she reaches for the deadbolt.

"Don't worry," I murmur softly. "You've got this."

She jumps several inches in the air and jerks a quick glance over her shoulder. "Oh my God," she says. "You scared me. I had no idea you were there."

"Who's there?" Derrick demands—loudly—from outside. "If you have a guy in there attending to your 'urges,' tell him to get his clothes on right now. Before I kick his ass out onto the street buck naked and covered in boot marks." His fist hits the door again, making it rattle on its hinges. "You hear that, asshole? You think it's okay to take advantage of drunk girls? Well, you're about to learn a lesson about consent, you fucking piece of shit."

"Stop," Evie shouts back, thumping her own fist against the door. "I'm not letting you in until you calm down, Derrick. And I don't have a *man* in here. It's just Ian."

"Thanks," I mutter.

"He helped the others get me home," Evie continues, shooting me a "you know what I mean" look.

And I do know what she means. But for some reason I still don't like it.

"Ian?" Derrick sounds stumped for a second but recovers quickly. "Ian, open the door. We need to start damage control on this. ASAP."

Evie flips the deadbolt, unhooks the chain lock, and turns the knob, whipping the door open to reveal Derrick in a sweat-soaked t-shirt and running shorts, making me think he must have run here all the way from his place in Hell's Kitchen.

He starts to barge in, but Evie holds up a hand, fingers spread wide. "Nope. We're not going to do this. No yelling. No damage control. This is my problem, and I'm going to fix it."

Derrick arches a thick, dark brow. He and Evie share the same pale green eyes, but that's the extent of the family resemblance. He has brown hair instead of blond, olive skin, and towers a full foot over his petite sister. He could easily over-power her and storm inside, but he stops, making me hope my planned intervention won't be necessary, after all.

"And how are you going to do that?" he asks. "Do you have an attorney on retainer I don't know about?"

"No. But I'm prepared to face the consequences of my actions."

"Jesus, Evie, I—"

"But I'm also barely functional right now," she cuts in. "I need to sleep and wake up ready to face all of this tomorrow. On the bright side, I didn't do anything illegal or awful. I just embarrassed myself in front of my ex. I'm sure there are a lot of people out there who can empathize. Who hasn't wanted to give the person who dumped them a piece of their mind?"

"Or barf on their new girlfriend," I add.

Derrick's gaze shifts my way, his eyes narrowing. "So, you were there the entire time? And you just let her get wasted right in front of you, without even trying to stop it?"

"He wasn't sitting with us," Evie says before I can answer. "And Ian doesn't 'let me' do anything and neither do you. I make my own decisions. I'm a grown woman, Derrick."

"You really acted like one tonight," he shoots back.

"Yeah, I did." She slides her shoulders back and lifts her chin. "Sure, I did a dumb thing, but grown-ups make mistakes sometimes. Everyone does. And that's okay. I don't have to be perfect to be a good person or worthy of respect."

Derrick curses beneath his breath before continuing with forced patience, "Sadly, that's not the way the world works, Evie. Especially these days. One mistake, one misstep, one video that makes you look bad and goes viral is all it takes. You can ruin your entire life before it even gets started. Do you honestly think upper management is going to want to keep you on as an art therapist helping the team with their anger issues once they see you can't even control your own temper?"

Evie's shoulders slump. "I didn't think about that."

"Obviously. You didn't think about anything." He drags a hand through his sweat-damp hair. "You got wasted and started running your mouth, just like Dad after Mom left."

Evie flinches. "I'm not like Dad. That was the first time I've ever been that drunk, and I have zero plans to get that way again."

He exhales as he mutters, "Right."

"That *is* right," she insists. "Now, I'm going to get ready for bed. If you want to talk more about this, call me in the morning."

"By tomorrow, the situation will be even worse," Derrick says. "We need to send take-down notices now and get an attorney to start drafting cease and desist letters for—"

"Surely it can wait until morning," I cut in. "She's had a rough night already."

"Your input isn't required, Ian," Derrick snaps. "If you wanted to help, you should have stepped in before she made an ass out of herself."

"Like she said, I wasn't sitting at their table," I say. "And yeah, I did notice that she was hitting the whiskey a little hard, but—"

"And you just let it happen," Derrick cuts in. "Great. Thanks, friend. Way to help a brother out. Now I get to spend my Friday night cleaning up my drunk little sister's mess."

"Also, like she said, she doesn't want you to—"

"Stop! Both of you. That's enough," Evie says, grabbing my arm and pushing me toward the door. "Go. Get out. Go boss each other around because I'm done with both of you."

I step through the doorway to stand beside Derrick, lifting my hands in surrender. "I'm on your side, Evie. I promise."

"You don't even know me anymore," she says, the heat in her tone making us both take a step back. "Neither of you do. But that's not your fault, that's my fault. My inner voice was right, I have been sitting around with my thumb up my ass waiting for other people to give me permission to do the things I want to do. But that stops right here, right now. From now on, I'm going to be my true, authentic self." She exhales a rush of breath. "As soon as I figure out who that is. So you two can either get on board with that or get lost."

She slams the door. The deadbolt turns and the chain rattles back into place and then Evie's soft footsteps pad away, leaving us in stunned silence.

We glance at each other and look away, clearing our throats.

Finally, I say, "Well, I guess that's that."

"She'll come to her senses tomorrow," Derrick mutters.

"I don't think she will. I think she's serious. And I think we owe her—"

"I think you should stop talking," he says. "If you're not going to help, you need to get out of the way." He points a finger at my face. "You're my best friend, but she's my sister, Ian, my only real family. And I'm the same for her. We don't have amazing parents and aunts and uncles and other siblings like you do. We have each other. That's it. And I made a promise to her when we were kids that I would protect her, look out for her, and never let her down. I'm not going to let anyone get in the way of me keeping that promise. Not even her and certainly not you. Just...stay away from her."

He turns and thuds down the stairs, leaving me with the sinking feeling that this isn't over. I have a choice to make—honor my best friend's wishes and make a graceful exit from his sister's life or honor my promise to help Evie and her friends.

I'm still standing in the hallway, debating whether I should knock on the door and tell Evie's crew I'm not going to have time to be their Love Coach, after all, when my cell dings.

I pull it out to find a text from Evie—*If you cancel on my friends because Derrick told you to leave me alone, you're going straight to the top of my shit list, Ian. Cameron is really struggling after his breakup, and I haven't seen Jess this excited in years. I know she prob-*

ably doesn't seem that excited to you, but...that's just Jess. She's shy and has a dry sense of humor, but she deserves love and passion in her life as much as anyone.

Thumbs tapping, I ask—*And what about you? Still up for joining us?*

I'm not just going to join, Evie texts back, *I'm going to be your star pupil.*

Brows sliding up my forehead, I grin. *All right, then. I'll be ready to start Monday night.*

Monday, she confirms, *but come prepared with a solid lesson plan. We may be novices when it comes to love but we're all excellent students.*

"Point taken," I murmur, shooting the apartment one last glance, secretly hoping Evie might decide to let me back in, but the door remains closed.

But that's all right. I'll be back in three days ready to change lives for the better. After slamming my head into the metaphorical wall trying to get my team to pull their shit together, I finally have a group of people who are eager for me to lead them to a better place.

And I intend to do right by them...even if I currently have no idea how to run a love coaching program.

As I jog down the stairs, I search my map app for bookstores and find one just a few blocks away. It's open until nine and looks big enough to have a self-help section. I have my own experience to draw from, of course, but a little assistance from the love professionals seems like a good idea.

An hour later, I'm the proud owner of approximately thirty pounds of relationship books and a collection of raunchy stickers I threw into my pile on impulse at checkout, figuring I can give them out as rewards to my students for making solid progress.

My students...

I'm excited about this, probably way too excited, considering my best friend will disown me if he finds out what I'm up to. I've already lost my girlfriend. If Derrick and I "break up," too, I'll have lost my last long-term relationship outside my family circle.

Well, except for Evie. Until today, I've always thought of her as someone I need to look out for more than a friend, but now...

She's really coming into her own—with a few bumps along the way, but missteps are a part of life. And she's right, people should be allowed to make mistakes and come back from them.

The thought spurs an idea and I whip out my cell again to type myself a quick note to create a lesson on bouncing back from failure and rejection.

Once I'm home, I lay out my books on my dining table and shoot Evie a picture of my haul along with the text—*Preparation in progress.*

She sends back an impressed-looking emoji. *Good job. Maybe you're more than a pretty face, after all.*

Grinning, I type, *So, you think I'm pretty?*

Don't be thirsty, she shoots over, making me laugh. *And don't text me again. I'm ninety percent asleep right now.*

With another chuckle, I type, *Sweet dreams*, and get back to business, determined to blow my students away...and keep my mind off my breakup and the sorry state of my team's morale while I'm at it.

CHAPTER 8

Evie

The next morning, I wake up with a black hole of regret in my stomach and a fiery determination in my chest.

I screwed up last night—royally—but that doesn't mean I can't snap back from this mistake, especially if I'm willing to apologize, take responsibility for my actions, and promise to be a better example for the players moving forward.

As soon as I'm dressed, I place a call to the Ice Possums' administrative offices. No one is there to answer the phones on Saturday morning, but I leave a calm, collected message for Jace, the camp director who hired me for the art therapy gig. I apologize for a rough first day with the team and anything he might have seen online featuring me on a rooftop bar. I promise nothing like that will ever happen again, add that I hope to incorporate my own loss of control into my lesson plan, and encourage him to call me if he'd like to discuss this further before my session with the team on Monday afternoon.

Next, I brew a pot of coffee and sit down with leftover savory pancakes and cream cheese to assess the cyber damage.

I'm braced for the worst but am shocked to find it's...actually not that bad. One of the few benefits of being a tiny human with sheep hair, I'm probably one of the least physically intimidating people on earth.

Even when I'm jabbing my finger at Vince and shouting, I still look sort of cute. And absolutely harmless.

The puking part is, admittedly, super gross, but most of the clips cut out right after. And now that I've seen for myself how Vince's fiancée was smirking at me while I was giving him a piece of my mind, I don't feel so bad about baptizing her in my drunk girl shame.

She was clearly enjoying my meltdown and her perceived sense of superiority.

"What a wretched little beastie," Harlow says, watching the video over my shoulder.

"Which one?" I ask, taking another sip of my coffee.

"Both," she replies, settling into the chair beside me in her black silk robe, looking elegant even first thing in the morning. "So how freaked out are you this morning? On a scale of one to ten? One is completely chill, ten is considering plastic surgery to change your face and moving to Mexico."

I ponder that for a moment. "About a four, I think. Maybe a five if I end up losing my job with the team."

"You won't. Derrick will go to bat for you. You know he will, even if he's pissed off."

I shut my laptop with a sigh. "Yeah. Maybe. But I did tell him to butt out of my life last night, so..."

"I heard that. And that you're going to be your true, authentic self. Sounds pretty awesome."

I glance over to see a soft, vulnerable smile on her face, the one that only comes out when we're alone and my guarded best friend feels safe lowering her defenses.

"Thanks," I say, returning the grin. "Now I just have to figure out who that is."

"You know," she says with way more confidence than I feel. "You've got this, girl. No doubt in my mind. And it's high time Derrick got his own life and stayed the hell out of yours."

"He has a life," I say, instinctively coming to his defense, the way I always do, even though I'm still angry about the way he barged over here last night. "He's busy all the time with the team and he drives down to New Jersey every Thursday to take Dad to his physical therapy appointment because he won't go if he doesn't."

My dad had a stroke eighteen months ago, most likely brought on by the heavy drinking he did when Derrick and I were kids. He's been sober for almost ten years, but the damage was already done.

He did a decent job of going to physical therapy at first, but once he recovered enough to get around the house and handle basic day-to-day activities, he started skipping his sessions. So, he's still on disability, still unable to return to work at the marina repairing boats and being on the water he loves, and still deeply depressed—and pissed—about all the above.

As much as I hoped things might be different, Dad isn't one of those people who had a brush with death and came out the other side a kinder, gentler person. If anything, he's even crankier now than he used to be.

Harlow grunts and takes another sip of her coffee. "Okay. Whatever you say. I'm just glad you finally put your foot down." She reaches over, stealing a piece of my pancake off my plate and popping it into her mouth before she asks in an uncharacteristically anxious voice, "So this thing with Ian... Are we really going to let him be our love guru? In the cold light of morning, does that still seem like a good idea?"

I nibble my bottom lip, debating whether to tell Harlow that I think I might have a crush on Ian. And that I might have flirted with him a little via text last night...

In the end, I decide letting anyone, even my best friend, in on my feelings will only add to my stress. But that doesn't mean I can't enlist her help. My master plan is only half formed, but a makeover—an *authentic* makeover, with no Lycra involved—is absolutely in order and who better to help with that than the most fashionable woman I know?

"I do," I say, "but I think we should also plan on helping ourselves. You up for taking Jess and me shopping later today for a few date-ready outfits?"

Harlow's eyes light up with a feverish joy only her fellow shopaholic fashion hunters can understand. "I'll wake her now. We ride at dawn! Or close to dawn since the sun is already up." She stuffs the last of my pancake in her mouth and claps her hands like a kid who just found a princess chest full of dresses under the tree on Christmas morning. "This is going to be the best day ever! I've been waiting to get my hands on your delicious bodies for years. I'm going to make you both look so fucking incredible the men of New York will hurl themselves at your feet."

"The way you put that was a little creepy," I say with a laugh as she bounces out of her chair. "But I'm down, as long as we can find things that are comfortable, too. You know I can't deal with anything that's too tight or stiff or buttons around my neck. My neck must be free at all times."

"Yes, yes, my pet, never fear, I'll fairy godmother you with a mind to your comfort and button phobia." She waves a hand over her shoulder as she hurries toward her room, stopping on the way to knock on Jess's door and call out, "Come out, come out, it's time to go shopping!"

A beat later Jess's mumbled voice drifts from within. "Not a chance in hell."

"Come on. You can't rock seduction lessons without a seductive outfit," Harlow says, before adding in a wheedling tone, "And if you're a good little shopper, I'll take you to that vintage arcade you like after lunch."

A moment later, Jess's door opens a crack, and she squints out at Harlow. "Really? And we'll stay more than ten minutes?"

"Twenty minutes," Harlow promises. "And I won't make fun of any of the games while we're there."

"Thirty minutes and you have to play, too," Jess counters. "And whatever you make me buy, it has to be something I can wear without a bra. I'm not doing a bra, not for all the sex in Manhattan."

"I can work with that," Harlow says, a devious grin on her face that would make me nervous if I were Jess.

But Jess doesn't have her glasses on, so she probably can't see the way Harlow's eyes are shooting "wicked scheme" sparks. "Okay, cool. I'll be ready in ten minutes. Please put a large amount of coffee in my to-go mug. I barely slept last night. I was too busy having stress dreams about my new promotion."

"Don't have stress dreams!" I say, rising from my chair. "You're going to be great. And I'll get that coffee warmed up for you as soon as I'm dressed."

* * *

Fifteen minutes later, we're out the door, leaving Cameron, who Harlow has dubbed "decently fashionable for a guy" alone to work on a recipe for a new appetizer he's pitching to the executive chef at the restaurant tonight.

Harlow drags us past all the chain stores near the Canal Street subway station, heading uptown, then turning left, toward the upscale designer stores that line Christopher Street and the other trendy areas of the West Village.

"I have a budget of three hundred dollars total," I warn her. "And that's if I make my lunch every day next week instead of hitting the taco truck."

"Tacos," Jess murmurs. "Oh my God, that sounds so good right now."

"It's ten a.m.," Harlow says.

"Shopping makes me anxious, and anxiety makes me hungry," Jess says. "For tacos. Or maybe a burrito, a really fat one with extra guacamole."

"No need to be anxious, sweet squirrel," Harlow says. "And no need to worry about the budget, either. I have a secret, super affordable shopping honey hole I'm going to share with the two of you. But only because you're my best friends and I trust you not to share this secret with others." She sniffs. "And because you aren't my size, so if you get addicted to fashion, you won't buy up anything I want before I can get there."

"I think I'm more likely to get addicted to crack than shopping," Jess says, casting a longing look at a brunch place advertising "the best huevos rancheros in the city!" as we pass by, murmuring, "I bet *they* have tacos. Good ones, too."

"But they don't have vintage Yves Saint Laurent or Coco Chanel," Harlow says, stopping beside a nondescript brick stairway leading up into one of the more dilapidated buildings on this block. "We're here, ladies. Brace yourself. After this morning, you'll never be quite the same."

Jess gulps but I'm buzzing with excitement and not just because I downed another cup of coffee before we left the apartment.

I'm ready for this. Yes, I love my overalls and feeling comfortable while I create. But I'm in a rut. I need to shake things up and expand my comfort zone.

But I'm not going to buy a micro-mini because that's what Vince always wanted me to wear or let my boobs hang out because cleavage is supposed to be sexy. I want to find something that makes me feel beautiful and confident, but on my terms, not anyone else's.

I say as much to Harlow on our trudge up the four flights of stairs, but she just shoots me an indulgent smile over her shoulder.

"I'm serious," I say. "If I can't find something that feels right, I'll go to our first lesson in overalls."

"I hear you," Harlow says, reaching for a steel door with a cheap cardboard sign taped to the front that reads "Maxine's." "And I support this decision. But I want you to promise to try on everything I pick out for you. You don't have to buy it, just try it on. Okay? You trust me?"

Letting out a breath, I nod. "I do."

"I do, too," Jess adds. "But I'm also scared. The last time I went shopping in an actual store was when my mom came to visit last December. She made me spend five hours at Macy's without a pee break or snacks. I thought we were going to starve to death and our corpses be found under the forty-percent-off rack come the spring thaw." She swallows hard and pushes her glasses up her nose. "Are you sure we can't get tacos first?"

"Have courage," Harlow says as she opens the door, revealing a surprisingly bright and cheery loft space absolutely packed with clothes. "We're going to have so much fun. I promise."

And we do.

Not only do we have a blast trying on all the clothes Harlow and a tiny, gray-haired woman in a snazzy, disco jumpsuit bring to the dressing rooms for us, we each find several incredible outfits.

Honestly, they are perhaps the most adorable, sexy, spot-on, true-to-ourselves clothes the world has ever known.

"Wow, this is so comfortable," Jess says, her eyes almost comically wide behind her glasses as she surveys herself in the mirror. The simple black jumpsuit with the wide-leg pants is tasteful, stretchy and soft, but classy, with a deep V front that skims the sides of her full—bra-less—breasts and makes her look—

"Sexy," she says, blinking fast. "I actually look sexy. I look like a person who might have sex. Who like, probably has sex all the time. Loads of sex."

"Oodles of sex," Harlow says, beaming proudly from the tufted couch by the dressing room mirror.

Jess presses a fist to her lips, letting out a soft giggle before she hurls herself at Harlow for a big hug.

Harlow laughs, patting her on the back. "All right, all right. Be careful there, sexpot. We don't want your boobs falling out."

"They won't," Jess says, standing back up and casting her still-contained breasts a pleased look. "This thing fits like a glove."

"I purchased that piece at an auction," the owner says, swinging into the dressing room with another armful of clothes. "She was a petite woman with curves just like you and had all her clothes tailored by the most gifted seamstress on the Upper East Side. I brought you the rest of her things. If you like them, I'll cut you a deal on the whole lot." She winks at Jess. "You're going to knock 'em dead, kiddo. And take it from an old lady, you should all be having oodles of sex. Pickings get slimmer as you age, sweethearts, and you can't take that pussy with you."

Harlow's jaw drops, Jess snorts, and I find myself nodding along like I'm listening to a breakthrough self-help book.

She's right. So right!

You *can't* take your pussy with you. Or anything else.

We're given this body, this spirit, this existence for a finite amount of time and the seasons of life pass so quickly. It seems like just yesterday I was a little girl racing Harlow up the hill behind the school to get the first turn on the tire swing at the back of the playground. Now suddenly I'm nearly twenty-four, with a bachelor's degree and starting on my master's, with students and therapy clients who turn to me for help.

And while I wouldn't have wanted to rush growing up or push myself to have sex before I was ready, I've been ready for a while now. I just haven't been putting that energy out into the world.

It's like Harlow always says—if you want to manifest something in your life, you have to let the universe know what you want. Otherwise, it's like swinging through the drive-thru at a fast-food restaurant and saying "eh...whatever," and then being mad when you get fish with gross, plastic-y cheese on it instead of that burger you were craving.

But not anymore.

From now on, when I want a burger, I'm going to ask for it.

Starting right now.

CHAPTER 9

Ian

I used to love my job.

Back when I was a rookie, busting my ass to prove myself to management and the more experienced members on the team, I couldn't wait to get on the ice for practice or a game. Even if I was bruised and sore from the day before, I'd charge out of the locker room ready to rumble.

Was I occasionally a touch too aggressive?

Maybe.

There were absolutely times when the older guys shouted for me to slow down and keep a cool head, but I only got benched for fighting twice in my first two years and never with my own fucking team members. I idolized the older players and wanted all my fellow rookies to succeed. After all, this is a *team* sport, for God's sake. No matter how talented our forwards or fierce our goalie, we rise or fall *together*.

As I watch Pete tackle Sven the Dick after he pops off with some smartass comment on the other side of the rink, a part of me wants to toss my stick and walk. I love this game and pushing myself to get better as an athlete, but this is fucking ridiculous.

I think back to the last conversation I had with my agent, the one in which Fred assured me he could get me traded to the Portland Badgers without breaking a sweat. They're on my approved trade list, I have friends out there, and that team knows how to work together *as a team*.

But fuck...my entire family is here in the New York and New Jersey area. I see my parents and sisters and brothers at least once a month for a big family dinner. I get to chase my nieces and nephews around my parents' big backyard and am even teaching three-year-old Owen how to play hockey. If I move clear across the country, I might only see them once or twice a year. I won't be there to hold the babies after they're born or to help my dad hang the Christmas lights without breaking his neck.

And I won't be in the city I love best.

I've travelled the world and explored dozens of big cities other people seem to love, but for me none of them can hold a candle to New York. This city feels like it's full of crazy people sometimes, but it's also so...alive. New York has a pulsing, aching, determined, fiercely beating heart at the center of it. This city celebrates together and grieves together. It's a place that's always changing but still somehow always the same. And I love that.

In my more optimistic moments, I imagine taking my own son or daughter to the places my parents took us when we were kids. To the playgrounds in Central Park in the summer, where we ran wild through the water features and played King of the Hill on the giant rocks. To the Zoo and the museums and to ride the ferry around the Statue of Liberty and bikes on Governor's Island.

In my less optimistic moments, I realize I might never be a dad. Most women want marriage *before* kids and considering what a shit job I'm doing of "parenting" this team...

Well, maybe I wouldn't be such a great father after all.

"Is it too early for a drink?" Braxton asks as he skates up beside me, watching our assistant coach pull Sven and Pete apart.

"It's Monday," I say with a sigh.

"Well, fuck," he curses dryly.

The entire team signed a "sobriety pledge" for the duration of our team-building camp. Management made it clear they don't care if we have a drink or two on the weekends, but they expect us to be sharp, sober, and well-rested Monday through Friday.

"Do you think this team is cursed?" he asks. "I thought the new guys were supposed to 'change the chemistry' and make everything all better. But so far... I think they're only making things worse."

"I don't know," I say, hating the heavy, doomed

feeling dragging at my stomach, making it feel like the wrap I had for lunch weighs a thousand pounds. "But something's gotta give."

"Yeah." He shrugs. "Maybe we'll have a break-through during group therapy." He snorts. "Or I'll color a really pretty picture this afternoon and everything will magically be okay."

I shoot him a hard look. "We're taking that seriously from now on. I promised Evie we would. It's disrespectful not to try as hard in those sessions as we try out here. If we really want this team to change, we need to give it everything we've got."

Braxton grunts. "All right, man. But half the team saw her drunk and disorderly at the bar last Friday." He exhales a soft huff of laughter. "You know they're going to give her shit about it. That's what they do. She'll have to prove she can take the heat or..."

He trails off with a shrug, but that's fine. I don't need him to fill in the blank.

As team captain I know these guys better than anyone and even the good-natured among them live to fuck with each other. It's the way they show affection, the way they bond. I'm guessing most of them won't mean to embarrass Evie, or make her feel bad with their teasing, but that's likely to be the result.

Evie's just so...Evie. So sweet and innocent and earnest.

But if they make her run from the art room in tears, I may have to pound a few faces myself.

Hell, maybe I *should* open a can of whoop ass on the lot of them. Maybe seeing their usually calm, cool, and level-headed captain foaming at the mouth and throwing punches will deliver a message—everyone has a limit to the amount of bullshit they'll tolerate and half the men on this team are pushing mine.

Once Coach Vera finally has Pete under control in one penalty box and Sven parked in the one on the opposite side of the rink, we return to our scrimmage, but none of our hearts are in it. Practice this morning was plagued by low energy from the guys who didn't take the "well-rested" mandate seriously, anxiety from our two injured players trying to get back on the ice, and bad attitudes from the rest.

Group therapy before lunch only exacerbated the problem, leading to Russian Sven throwing his sandwich across the room in response to a joke about his twin sister, Anya, who is nearly Sven's size, and which one of them would win in a fight.

And now the afternoon scrimmage is proving to be just as much of a wash.

To say my expectations are low as I shower and change into street clothes for art therapy, is an understatement.

I'm dreading the next ninety minutes and not sure how much support I'll be able to give Evie. Sure, I'm the captain, and most of these men like me as much as they like anyone, but the bad energy is thick in the air today. The team is tired, pissed off, frustrated, and looking to take it out on a vulnerable target.

And I can't imagine a more vulnerable target than Evie.

I toss my things into my bag and hustle to the new "art room" as fast as I can, but by the time I arrive, several of the other players are already there.

Already there and settled peacefully into their seats, drawing with a focus that is frankly...shocking.

Before I can shoot a raised eyebrow Evie's way to silently enquire as to what magic she's worked on these cranky bastards, she pipes up from the corner of the room behind me, "Hey there, Ian, Pete, your materials are waiting on the tables, under the postcard with your name on it. I decided against the clay project. I think this exercise will be more beneficial for where you are as a team."

I spin toward her voice and suddenly lose the ability to hear.

I know she's still speaking—I can see her glossy pink lips moving—but I can't make sense of anything she's saying.

I'm too thrown by her sex siren of a transformation.

CHAPTER 10

Ian

*W*hoa. And...wow.

Evie hardly looks like the same person.

Gone are the grungy overalls and oversized t-shirts she usually wears underneath. Instead, she's wearing a pair of tight black jeans that cling to her curvy thighs, leather boots with a small heel, and a fluttery green sleeveless blouse that emphasizes the bright green of her eyes.

Or maybe that's the eyeliner doing that...

Evie's wearing makeup—not a lot—but the effect is knock-your-socks-off stunning. She looks like...

Like...

"Spit spot, boys," she says, shooing me and Pete—who is also standing stock-still beside me with his jaw dropped—toward the tables. "The faster you finish your first assignment, the faster you get donuts."

She motions toward her desk at the front of the room, where three large boxes from "Dough You Didn't" sit stacked one on top of the other.

"I'm almost done," Braxton calls out from the end of our table on the far side of the room, catching my gaze as he adds in a meaningful tone, "I'm finding today's assignment highly motivating, captain. I think you will, too."

"I'm so motivated," Kyle mutters beneath his breath as I pass behind his chair. "I'm going to break the spell this shithead has over me if it's the last thing I do."

Frowning, I glance over his shoulder to see a drawing of a man with a full beard and tiny, squinted eyes that would look more at home on a mean-spirited pig.

I'm about to ask Evie who we're supposed to be drawing, but when I glance her way, she's already turned back to the corner, where she's taping plain squares of cardboard paper in Ice Possum royal blue to the wall. This also treats me to my first glance of her from behind and the curve of her bottom in those black jeans is nearly enough to cause a cardiac event.

Who knew Evie had an ass like *that*?

I stumble to my chair, tripping over my feet twice because I can't seem to rip my eyes away from Evie, and collapse beside Braxton, who chuckles and pushes a blank sheet of drawing paper my way. "We're drawing a person who has power over our emotions," he says, "someone who gets to us no matter how hard we try to keep our cool."

"Oh, okay," I say, dragging a hand down my face, surprised to feel sweat breaking out on my upper lip.

What the hell is Evie doing to me? And how can I make it stop? This sudden longing to worship my best friend's little sister's ass is bad.

Very, very bad.

Not only would Derrick cut off my dick if he knew—slowly, with a butter knife, so it would hurt more—it goes against every friendly, protective instinct I've ever felt toward this girl.

But she's not a girl anymore. And it doesn't look like she needs protection.

It's true. I expected to step into this room today to find chaos, frustration, and possibly a crying Evie hiding out under her desk while the savages ran wild, scribbling on the walls like toddlers.

Instead, my teammates seem rapt. Focused. For the first time all day, no one is talking smack or giving each other shit.

"Who are you drawing?" I ask Braxton, as I choose a pencil with a freshly sharpened tip and bring it to hover over my paper.

"My uncle Chris," he says. "He used to call me 'fat ass' when I was a kid. He'd buy all the other cousins ice cream from the truck when we played at his house, then toss me a water bottle and tell me to give him twenty push-ups. Then he'd stand there making fun of how sweaty I got. Real grade A shithead."

"Sounds like it. I'm sorry about that, man."

Braxton shrugs and turns his attention back to his drawing. "Thanks. I barely see him anymore, but when I do, I still want to punch him in the face. Makes Thanksgiving and Christmas dinners pretty miserable, so...I'd like to shut that down if I can. I figure it's worth a try."

"And it's fun to draw these fuckers as ugly as possible," Laser pipes up on my other side, holding up a pretty incredible drawing of an old woman with a hideous neck wattle. "My grandma. She kicked me and my mom out of the house when I was five because Mom lost her job at the truck stop. We lived in our car for almost two years before Mom remarried and started having babies with my stepdad like it was going out of style. Meanwhile, Gram went on cruises and gave my mom shit about pulling herself up by her bootstraps."

I wince. "Fuck. With family like that, who needs enemies?"

Laser snorts in amusement. "Right?"

"But that's fantastic work, Laser," Evie says, appearing on the other side of the table. "You have such a strong artistic voice, and your line work around the neck is so striking. That's a powerful piece."

Laser puffs up a little. "Yeah? I used to love to draw. It was the only thing there was to do for fun when I was little. We couldn't afford TV or video games, but Mom always made sure I had crayons and paper."

"She sounds pretty awesome," Evie says. "And so brave. That must have been hard for both of you, living in a car for so long."

Laser's expression sobers. "Yeah, it was. Fucking scary some nights, when the cops would wake us up pounding on the roof or beaming lights through the windows. But you're right, my mom is brave, and she never stopped fighting for a better life for us. She's my hero."

"Maybe you can draw her next." She glances my way as she adds, "We're drawing people or memories that make us feel strong and grounded next. After our donut break."

I nod, willing myself not to gape as her brighter-than-usual green eyes lock on mine. I've always thought her eyes were beautiful but now they're like twin tractor beams sucking me straight out of my comfort zone.

"Could I go straight to that part?" I ask. "I don't have anyone from my past who makes me feel out of control. I had a pretty normal childhood."

Evie crosses her arms. "True, but we all have people who get under our skin. Do a little thinking, I'm sure you'll come up with someone." She nods toward my still-blank paper. "Or just start sketching with that feeling of being out of control and angry held in your thoughts and let your lizard brain do the work for you. You'll be amazed what your creative side can reveal to you when you're willing to listen."

I arch a skeptical brow. Evie responds with a dazzling smile and another nod at my paper. "Just give it a try. In twenty minutes, if all you have are scribbles, you can still have a donut. As long as I can tell that you gave it your best effort."

"I think I'm almost done," Kyle calls from the other table. "Come look, teach. See what you think. I'm pretty psyched about it."

"Be right there," she says, moving his way, taking a moment here and there to offer words of encouragement or praise to the other players as she passes by.

Grateful for the reprieve from her insanely distracting new sex vibe, I turn back to my paper and put my pencil to the upper left-hand corner. I start sketching, letting my pencil scratch where it wants to scratch and linger where it wants to linger. It feels weird at first—to be drawing without knowing what I'm drawing—but I eventually relax into it, amazed that the more I concentrate on that feeling Evie described, the faster the image on the page takes shape.

By the time the alarm goes off on her phone, signaling that our first drawing session is done, I have a face on my paper. It's a weird, ugly face, and doesn't look like anyone I know, but it's clearly a man with dark hair wearing a jean jacket, and it looks like I made an effort.

Hopefully that's enough to earn a donut

because those things are starting to smell really fucking good.

"Okay, pencils down," Evie says, clasping her hands together. "Grab your pictures and follow me. We're going out to the courtyard for the next part of the assignment."

With only a modicum of grumbling and wondering what our pint-sized art guru is up to now, my teammates gather their artwork and head out the door, several making plans to grab coffee in the breakroom on the way back to enjoy with their donut.

I'm having some happy fantasies about a caffeine and sugar infusion myself when I pass Evie and she cranes her neck, asking, "So you did come up with something. Great work!"

I tip the paper her way, feeling a little shy about my still-crappy drawing skills, but happy that she's pleased. "Yeah. I don't know who it is, but I drew him. That trick you gave me really worked."

Her smile stutters as she nods. "Yeah, it sure did."

"Is something wrong?" I ask, glancing between her and the drawing.

"Not at all," she says, pressing her lips together for a beat before she adds, "But I'm pretty sure that's...my dad."

Stunned, I glance down and suddenly I see it.

She's right. That's Xavier Olsen, staring up at me from the page, daring me to say a word about the way he's raising his daughter.

CHAPTER 11

Evie

*Y*ou *can do this. Stay focused.*
Everything is going great, management is giving you another chance, and you're killing it this session. You can't go off the rails now.

I give myself a mental pep talk all the way down the hall and up the two flights of stairs to the courtyard area where players and staff members eat lunch on sunny days, but my confidence is shaken for the first time today.

And right when everything was going so well!

From the moment the players started filtering into the art room, I realized my makeover might do more than potentially help me get laid in the not-so-distant future. These clothes seem to have other valuable powers. Apparently looking like an adult who has her shit together instead of an unkempt toddler goes a long way to convincing other people that it's true.

Right off the bat, I noticed a marked difference in the way the team treated me. Even Sassy Sven kept the sass at a respectful level. I'm sure my threat to withhold donuts from anyone who had a bad attitude helped my case, but even before I laid down the law about making an effort in order to earn their treat, most of the guys were on board right away.

Having them draw someone who holds power over them was a good call, too. I tapped into a source of deep feeling and passion and gave them a clear direction for their work that was much easier to get a lock on than the anger iceberg assignment.

I was already planning my write-up for my advisor and feeling proud of the way I adjusted course with the team when Ian swaggered in fresh from a shower, looking even yummier than usual.

But I blamed the way my belly flipped and my nipples tightened when his gaze locked with mine on my jeans.

My jeans are stretchy and *tight*. They make me aware of my thighs and hips and other intimate parts in a way that I'm usually not. And being aware of those parts makes me think about those parts which in turn leads to thoughts of how much I'd like to rub those parts all over someone else.

Preferably Ian, tonight at our first Hookup 101 meeting.

Sometime in the past two days, my frisky levels have skyrocketed. I don't know if it's the new clothes or the makeup or the way men look at me as I walk down the street—in a way they've never looked at me before—but I have a bad case of Nookie on the Brain. I actually whipped out my vibrator last night for the first time in months in an attempt to take the edge off, but self-administered orgasms felt empty somehow.

I don't just want the release. I want a connection with another person, someone I find sexy, fun, and fascinating, who feels the same way about me.

For a moment there, when Ian was staring at me with shock and appreciation in his eyes, I thought maybe, just maybe, his feelings for me might be starting to change...

But then I saw his drawing.

Oh my God, that drawing...

I can't believe he couldn't see that it was my dad. The jean jacket is just like the one he's worn every fall and spring since I was a kid and the curl on the lip is a dead ringer for my father's. Ian could have drawn anyone in the entire world, but his subconscious brain locked in on my dad as the one person who makes him feel angry and out of control.

If that doesn't prove he still sees me as a little sister, I don't know what does.

And what's worse, we're going to have to *talk* about it. In front of all the other players.

That's part of this project. First, we funnel our feelings into the creation of our portraits. Next, we're going to try to break the hold these people have on us with a simple ritual and a little fire.

"Excellent," Slavic Sven says when we're all

gathered around the firepit in the corner of the courtyard, where in exchange for two donuts, a very nice janitor agreed to keep a fire burning for me this afternoon. "I was hoping we'd burn them."

He starts to toss his picture into the flames, but I lift a hand.

"Wait." I hold up my own drawing, a picture of Vince with a pitying expression that I sketched last night. "Before we burn them, we're going to speak a few words to take our power back. First, I'd like you to briefly state how this person hurt you or why they still upset you so much. For example, I'm angry that Vince blamed me for the failure of our relationship, making me think there was something wrong with me, when in reality he was probably too busy dating two women at once to give our relationship the focus it deserved."

"Oh yeah, he totally was," Sassy Sven says. "No way did he and that blonde meet, fall in love, and get engaged in just three weeks. He was two-timing you, Sheepish. Like a dirty dog."

"Her name isn't—"

"It's fine," I say, cutting Ian off with a smile. I have to stand on my own as much as possible with these men or I'll lose what respect I've earned so far. And this is already going to get weird enough when it's Ian's turn to toss his image into the fire. "Sven is right. And that's a big part of why Vince had the power to make me lose control on Friday. But I don't want to be at the mercy of those kinds of feelings anymore, which brings us to step two. Forgiveness."

"Fuck no," Kyle says. "I'm never talking to my dad again. Not for all the money in the world and two Stanley Cup championship titles."

"And you don't have to," I assure him. "This isn't about repairing these relationships or even making contact with these people. It's about releasing that anger so it doesn't call the shots anymore, so you can finally be free of old baggage that's dragging you down, causing you pain, and affecting your game. It's based on an ancient Hawaiian practice called *Ho'oponopono,* which means to bring things back in balance. It's a simple but powerful tool for increasing self-love and healing old wounds."

Kyle is still frowning, but he nods. "Okay, I'm listening. How do we do that?"

"Just a simple phrase," I say, lifting my paper and locking eyes with Vince. "Vince Victor, I'm sorry. Please forgive me. Thank you, I love you, goodbye." I pull in a deep breath, exhale completely and then open my fingers, dropping the paper into the flames.

Kyle grunts. "But I don't forgive him or love him. I can't."

"Forgiving doesn't mean forgetting," I say. "You don't have to forget but letting go of that anger is vital for your health and well-being. Like Nelson Mandela said, 'resentment is like drinking poison and then hoping it will kill your enemies.' That rage you're holding on to isn't hurting your dad. It's hurting you. And it seems like he's already hurt you enough."

"That actually makes sense," Laser says softly. "Like getting rid of a tumor or something. Get the poison out and then you'll feel free."

I nod. "Exactly. Would you want to go next, Laser? Since this is resonating with you?"

He clears his throat and runs a massive hand through his short-cropped hair. "Sure. Um, this is my grandmother. I'm angry with her for kicking my mom and me out on the streets and for never lifting a finger to help her daughter. I'm pissed that she brags about me to her friends like she had something to do with my success, when I never would have been able to play hockey if my stepdad hadn't paid for it after he and Mom got married." His volume drops and his voice tightens as he adds, "But most of all I'm mad that she taught me how shitty people can be when I was so little. I would have liked the chance to grow up like a normal kid instead of being so fucking jaded straight out of the gate."

Heads nod around the circle, his words clearly hitting home for a lot of us. I feel the same way. I can't remember a time when I wasn't aware of the fact that I was a burden to my dad, an unwanted second girl child when he would have been happier with just Derrick.

"But I don't want to carry that rock around in my gut anymore," he says, standing up straighter. "So, Gram, I'm sorry. Please forgive me and..." He glances up. "I forgot the rest."

"Thank you, I love you, goodbye," I whisper.

"Thank you, I love you, goodbye," he echoes,

dropping his picture into the pit, too. As it catches fire, he lets out a shaky laugh before lifting his gaze to the group with a wide grin. "Wow. That felt good, fam. Like...really good. Seriously, that's some kind of magic."

"And it's something you can repeat, over and over," I add. "If you find those old feelings coming back up and you need a reminder of how good it feels to let go." I scan the faces around the fire. "Who wants to go next?"

Sassy Sven lifts an arm. "Me. I'm so done with my ex."

One by one, the players say their piece and toss their art into the flames until only Kyle and Ian are left.

Kyle is still standing there with his jaw clenched and his arms wrapped tightly around his torso, his body language practically shouting that he's not ready for this, so I'm not surprised when Ian offers to go next.

"This is a guy from my old neighborhood where I grew up," he says, holding up his drawing of my dad. "He was hard on some friends of mine, especially his daughter. She was this sweet, magical little kid. Super smart and talented and just...cool, you know? One of those younger siblings you don't mind hanging out with you and your friends."

He gets murmured responses from Braxton and Laser, but Sassy Sven is watching him with narrowed eyes that he shifts my way after a beat or two.

Say what you want about Sassy, but he's no dummy.

Ian isn't so much as glancing my direction, but Sven is already hot on this trail. I should probably try to redirect in some way but I'm too curious to hear what Ian will say next.

I've always known he liked me well enough, but I never knew he felt this way, that he thought I was "magical." It's a special thing to hear, especially considering I've always found him pretty magical, too. From the day we first met, when he gave me his colored pencils—a gift that felt like the answer to a prayer to a shattered little girl who had no idea why her dad was so mad all the time—I've suspected he might be part guardian angel.

"Anyway, that was my first experience with someone who was just plain mean to his kid sometimes, and it hit me pretty hard. One time, after he locked the little girl out of the house for hours on a cold day because he was pissed about some stupid thing, I asked my mom if we should report him to Child Protective Services. But she said no. That the little girl would probably end up somewhere even worse, and that if she stayed put, at least I could help watch out for her."

He stretches his neck to one side and then the other, his gaze still fixed on the firepit. "But I've always wondered if that was the right call, especially after I got drafted out of the minors a couple years after graduation and moved to the city. She was only twelve and all alone in that house with him. Every time my friend and I stopped by to visit, she seemed quieter than the last time, like she was retreating into herself and..." He shrugs tightly. "That made me feel like shit. And it definitely got in my head. Every time I so much as think of this guy, I get pissed off and frustrated by how little control I have over most things in life."

"But seems like the little girl turned out fine," Sven says, with more compassion than I expected from him. "All's well that ends well."

I sniff discreetly and blink away the tears pressing at the backs of my eyes.

I want to tell Ian that I did turn out fine, that I *am* fine, but hearing someone else's perspective on my dad suddenly puts all the stress of growing up in that house in a different perspective. I've always told myself that it wasn't really that bad—Dad didn't beat me, I never went to bed hungry, and he eventually got his drinking under control—but maybe it was worse than I've wanted to admit.

If I knew a little girl who got shut out of her house on a freezing cold day because she forgot to lock the door on her way to school that morning, would I still think it was just a family squabble?

No, I wouldn't. I would want to save that little girl, to wrap her up in a big snuggly blanket, take her home with me, and make sure she never had to walk on eggshells to stay safe ever again.

That was my childhood—trying to stay safe and fly under the radar. Forget being loved or listened to or understood. That was for other kids, people like Ian and Jess, who both had warm, wonderful parents, and Cameron, whose single mom was devoted to helping her boy grow up strong and happy. Even Harlow's shouty dad and overbearing mother always bossed her around from a place of love.

And maybe *that's* why I've never gotten serious with anyone.

It's not just my body that I've been holding back. It's my heart, too. I've never fallen for one of the guys I've dated. I've never let myself because...

Well, because I guess secretly, I've always assumed that no one would love me back. My own mother and father didn't, so why would a romantic partner?

The realization makes me feel like I'm drowning on dry land.

After years of therapy, I thought I had myself figured out but...guess not.

I fight to pull in a breath, but my lungs are locked, frozen, and my heart feels like it's about to burst.

I'm getting perilously close to losing my shit and my therapist street cred when Ian says, "But this guy doesn't get to live rent-free in my head anymore. I can be there for my friends without wasting another second on his drama. So...I'm sorry that I didn't do what felt right all those years ago. Please forgive me. Thank you, I love you," he says before dropping the drawing into the pit.

I watch the edges catch fire and the flames quickly spread to consume my father's face and I feel...better.

Not only is the worst of this experience finally

over, but I can't help but notice Ian's modifications to the mantra, that his apology seemed intended for me and that he didn't say goodbye.

Ian has never said goodbye. Even when he left for training camp, he always came back to visit. He never deserted me or forgot me. He made me feel cared for, important, special...

How could I have even *thought* about putting that at risk?

Even if he was interested in being more than friends, a few months of hot sex—or however long I managed to hold his much-more-experienced interest—wouldn't be worth the long-term fallout.

I can't lose Ian. I just can't.

Just thinking about it makes me want to run home, wipe off all this makeup, change back into my grungy, oversized clothes and forget I ever pretended to be a grown-up. I'm *not* a grown-up, not like these men are, and I might never be. It's just too damned scary. Better to remain in that murky, not-quite-whole place I've inhabited since I left my father's house and never have to face the demons of my past or the challenges of a fully fleshed-out future.

I'll be the spinster aunt who brings my friends' kids presents and sleeps with her dog every night. And I'll probably end up happier than all those people out there fighting to keep love alive in a world that seems determined to make human connection as hard as possible.

On the outside, I'm still standing in this circle

of men, but on the inside, I'm running back to my safe place as fast as my feet can carry me.

So, when Kyle says in a rough voice, "I don't think I can do this, Evie. I'm sorry. I just can't. Not today," I nod and say, "That's okay, Kyle. I understand."

Because I do.

Boy, do I.

I force a smile, ignoring how fake and stiff it feels on my face as I say, "But I think everyone deserves two donuts. This was some great work, guys. Truly. I'm so proud of all of you."

"But you're proudest of me, right, Sheepish?" Sven grins as he turns up the collar on his track jacket. "Because I'm being such a cuddly team player today and all."

"I wouldn't cuddle you if you paid me ten thousand dollars," Laser says, punching Sven good-naturedly on the arm as he starts back inside. "Last one to the donuts has to eat the peanut butter ones."

"I like the peanut butter ones," Pete says. "Save those for me, dog. I'll eat the shit out of those."

One by one, the team steps away from the fire, until only Ian and I are left.

For the first time since his turn at the pit, his blue-gray eyes settle on my face, a question there I'm not sure how to answer.

But I do my best to fake it, "It's okay," I say, my voice husky. "And *I'm* okay. Like Sven said. But thank you. You've always been a good friend to me."

"I'm not sure about that," he says softly. "But I'd like to be, moving forward. You're a really special person, Evie. One of the best people I know."

I swallow hard. "Thanks. You, too. Want to go eat donuts? I could use one. Or four."

"Yeah. I do." He grins, that smile that makes my skin feel hot all over, opening a whole new can of worms as we follow the others inside.

Deciding that being friends with Ian is my best and only choice is all well and good. But what if my body refuses to get on board with that decision? What if it insists on blushing and tingling and wanting things it can never have?

I don't know.

But I'm pretty sure donuts will make things better.

At least for a little while.

CHAPTER 12

Ian

*a*fter class, Evie bolts out of the art room so fast I don't get a chance to ask her if I should bring anything other than myself when I swing by her place later, so I text Cameron—*I know you're cooking dinner, but I'd love to contribute. Can I bring salad or a vegetable tray or something? Maybe some wine?*

A moment later, Cam texts back—*Yeah, a bottle of white would be great, but I have everything else covered. I'm making shrimp orzo with summer veggies. Tons of it, so bring a hearty appetite.*

Sounds great, thanks—I reply, ignoring the anxiety pricking at the back of my neck as I head home to grab my supplies for our first meeting.

Evie and I talked after the firepit, and she said everything was fine. But I don't feel fine for some reason.

I feel...confused.

When Evie and I were standing there by the

fire, just the two of us, things felt different between us, and not just because she was dressed up and wearing makeup. And not even because I found myself aware of her beauty in a way I've never been before.

It was more than that, but I can't quite put my finger on it, and when I arrive at her place at seven, as planned, Evie answers the door still damp from the shower and wearing her usual overalls over a paint-splattered, long-sleeved white thermal.

She looks like the old Evie, and for a moment I think that's going to be it—the end of the weirdness.

But when she smiles and motions me inside, my stomach does that same clenching, flipping thing it did earlier today. "Come on in," she says. "Food's almost ready and I'm dying for a glass of that." She points to the wine in my hand, and I pass it over, doing my best to ignore the fizzing feeling that shoots up my arm as our fingers touch.

"Yeah?" I clear my throat when the word comes out low and rough. "Hard day at the salt mines?"

"You'd better believe it," she says. "Spent the entire afternoon with a bunch of stinky hockey boys. Had to come straight home and shower the smell off."

"Yeah, about that." I touch her elbow, triggering another squeezing sensation in my chest. "I'm sorry if I overstepped and made you uncomfortable in front of the team. I didn't mean to. I didn't even mean to draw your dad, it just happened."

She glances down at my fingers, still wrapped around her elbow, and pulls in a deep breath before lifting her gaze to mine. "You didn't overstep. But you did make me think. Honestly, I'm still thinking."

I frown. "About?"

"About my dad. About our relationship and what it was like to grow up in his house. About whether I'm as well-adjusted and 'normal' as I've always thought." A tight laugh escapes her lips. "I'm starting to think I'm actually kind of a hot mess."

"Nah, it's just been a rough few days. Starting a new job is always hard and the guys didn't make it easy for you. Though they were better today." I tilt my head, catching her eye before I add, "Seems like you're starting to get through to them."

Her lips twitch but a smile doesn't form. "I hope so. And I hope our sessions help. They're sweet guys, once you get past their outer grouchy and suspicious layers."

I arch a brow. "Sweet isn't the word I'd use, but I hope so, too. Maybe then I won't have to think about transferring at the end of the season."

Her eyes widen. "Wow. Really? You're thinking about leaving the Possums? Where would you go?"

"Portland, Oregon, most likely," I say, with an uncomfortable shrug. "But don't say anything to Derrick or anyone else, okay? I haven't mentioned it to anyone yet. I'm still mulling things over. I just know I can't stay here if things don't change. I'm tired of being the 'bad boys' of the NHL. I just want to play the game without all the in-fighting and drama."

She nods. "That makes sense. But we'd miss you. *I'd* miss you."

"I'd miss you, too," I say, fighting the insane urge to brush her damp curls from her forehead and trail my fingers down her heart-shaped face. To run my thumb over her full bottom lip and see if it's as soft as it looks.

Where is this urge to cross the line with Evie coming from and how can I make it stop?

I have no idea but I'm guessing spending a couple hours teaching her and her friends how to "pull tail," probably isn't going to help the situation.

I'm about to suggest that we head into the kitchen to open the wine—I could absolutely use a glass or ten to take the edge off—when she presses a hand to my chest and whispers, "We can't do this, Ian. I'm sorry. I just...I need you to leave. Now."

"But I promised I would—"

"I know what you promised, and I'm sure you put a lot of time and thought into your lesson because you put time and thought into everything you do, but I can't do this." She shakes her head as she pushes me back toward the door. "I just can't. If you come in here and start talking about flirting and kissing and whatever else you're going to talk about, I'm going to embarrass myself."

Understanding dawns and I bring my hand to cover hers, pressing it closer to my heart. "No, you won't. I promise, Evie. I'm not here to judge. I'm here to help. And I won't breathe a word about this to Derrick, any of the guys on the team, or anyone else. You can trust me."

"I know I can trust you, Ian," she says with an exasperated huff. "It's not about trusting you; it's about trusting *me*. I'm not myself lately. If you don't leave right now, I'm afraid I'm going to do something stupid."

"Like what?" I ask, my forehead furrowing.

"Like this," she says, fisting her hand in my shirt and giving it a tug. I lean forward in response and suddenly Evie's lips are on mine.

For a moment I'm too stunned to respond, but the shock only lasts as long as it takes for Evie to wrap her arms around my neck and press her curvy little body against mine. The moment her breasts flatten against my pecs, it's like a floodgate opens deep inside of me.

A beat later, I have my free arm around her waist, lifting her off the ground as I deepen the kiss. Her lips part, and my tongue sweeps in to stroke against hers, tasting chocolate from the donut she had this afternoon, a hint of coffee, and an earthy sweetness that's Evie's taste.

And it is, insanely good. My new favorite flavor. Bar none.

"We have to stop," she whispers against my mouth, even as she threads her fingers into my hair, the feel of her nails scratching lightly against my scalp driving me fucking crazy. "Harlow and Jess will be home any second and Cam is almost done making dinner. They're going to catch us."

"I'm more concerned about us, Evie," I say, groaning softly as her hip brushes against my erection through my jeans. "Up until about two hours ago I didn't realize I wanted to kiss you, let alone..."

"Let alone what?" she asks, a soft gasp escaping her lips as she apparently realizes that isn't a flashlight in my pants.

"That I want you," I whisper, tightening my grip on her waist, wishing I weren't holding this damned wine bottle so I could squeeze her ass.

"I want you, too." She pulls back to gaze into my eyes with a slightly shell-shocked, but determined expression. "I want you and I trust you and since I've already screwed things up by kissing you..."

"You haven't screwed things up," I say, even as my brain starts spitting out all the reasons getting involved with Evie would be a no-good, very bad idea.

1. She's my insanely protective best friend's little sister and Derrick will cut my dick off if he thinks I'm even *thinking* about getting it close to Evie.
2. She's innocent and inexperienced and chances are I'd end up hurting her

feelings, no matter how hard I would try not to.

3. She's innocent and inexperienced, tiny all over, and a *virgin*, which means I'd probably end up hurting her physically, as well. I'm not a small man in any sense of the word, and even with experienced women, my cock can take some getting used to.

THEY'RE ALL VERY good reasons.

Very, *very* good reasons.

But none of them do a damned thing to soften my dick. If anything, the thought of Evie under me, wrapping her legs around my hips and lifting into me as I push inside her for the first time only makes my cock pulse harder.

I'm still aching when she says, "I'm just saying that we can't go back after this, Ian. And I don't want to. I don't want to be scared anymore. I liked the way I felt today in those new clothes. I liked the way you looked at me when I was wearing them. But instead of acknowledging those feelings or dealing with them, I ran home and showered and hid in my overalls again. But I can't hide forever, and I don't want to. I'm ready to take the next step, to grow up, to try new things and learn new things and..." She swallows, her throat working before she adds, "I want you to teach me, but not like you're teaching the others. I want hands-on experience, and I want you to be my first."

Before I can pull in a deep breath or do anything else to stop the spinning feeling in my head, the door opens behind us, shoving me forward into Evie and sending us both stumbling.

Evie goes down and I trip over her, landing sprawled on a pile of shoes and dusty umbrellas as Harlow steps inside.

She spots us on the ground and huffs in amusement. "Oops. Sorry, guys. I didn't expect you to be lurking in front of the door. Why *were* you lurking in front of the door?" She points a finger my way. "You'd better not be trying to back out, jerk face. We're counting on you. Jess is so excited she made me promise to take her to a bar after the first lesson if she's feeling sassy."

"I'm already feeling sassy," Jess says from outside, poking her head in through the door and frowning as she sees Evie and me still sprawled on the ground. "Are you two okay?"

"They're just clumsy and bad at knowing where to stand," Harlow says, stepping over us before kicking her shoes off beside my head with a sigh. "Mmm, supper smells great, Cameron. Do I have time to take a shower before? Chas patted my back four times while we were studying, and I feel tainted by mansplainer germs."

"Yeah, if you hurry," Cam calls out from the kitchen. "I'm starting the shrimp in five and they only take about two minutes."

"Got it!" Harlow dashes into the apartment,

her purse bouncing against her shoulder as she shouts back to me, "You'd better still be here when I get back, Ian, or I'm going to give you an even worse nickname than Hitler."

"Is there a worse nickname than Hitler?" Jess asks as she steps inside and closes the door behind her.

I rise to my feet as Evie moves past Jess to flip the deadlock. "Probably. I wouldn't put Harlow to the test on that one if I were you, Ian." She turns back to me as she adds, "I think you'd better stay."

"You really were planning to leave?" Jess's tone is so bereft, I promise, "No, of course not. I'm here to share my hard-won dating wisdom. No worries."

"Oh good. I would have been so sad. I'm super jazzed about becoming a sex goddess." Her shoulders relax as she sighs, drawing my attention to the very sexy plunging neckline on the pink blouse she's wearing.

Her jeans look new, too, and tailored to fit her perfectly. For the first time I realize that Jess is stunning, with a curvy figure, glossy black hair that's hanging in a stylish new bob cut, and high cheekbones set off by some glittery stuff I've never seen her wear before.

But Jess's makeover doesn't make me feel anything, aside from aesthetic appreciation for an objectively attractive human and happiness that she seems to have found a look that makes her feel beautiful and confident.

Evie is the one who's working some kind of sex

voodoo on my cock and she's doing it in overalls and no makeup. I'm still sporting a semi even after being knocked to the floor and interrupted —twice.

This is bad news.

But I've already said that I'd stay, and I don't want to let anyone down. And maybe this is a good thing. I'll have at least an hour or two with all the roommates before I'll have to risk being along with Evie again. Hopefully that will be enough time to figure out how to respond to her oh-so-tempting and oh-so-off-limits offer.

CHAPTER 13

Evie

I don't think I've ever seen Ian this nervous, not even before the championship game his senior year of high school, when he knew NHL scouts were up in the stands, ready to break his heart or make his wildest dreams come true.

Ian isn't an anxious person.

He's steady, chill, and confident.

To see sweat beading on his forehead as he moves to stand in front of the darkened television, studying the small stack of notecards in his hand is disarming.

Is he really this stressed about teaching a bunch of virgins how to make a love connection?

Or maybe it's the fact that his best friend's little sister just offered him her V-Card on a platter.

The inner voice has an excellent point.

Maybe I should have left that part out until

after the lesson. I just never expected Ian to be so flustered.

"Okay, so..." He clears his throat and runs a hand over his already smooth hair. "I wanted to start with something that may seem simple... Almost silly, but, um..." He swipes his sleeve across his forehead with a nervous laugh. "Sorry, I actually practiced this last night. Several times. I don't know why I'm fumbling."

"Just relax and imagine us naked," Jess says. "Naked and feeling super self-conscious about it because we've never been naked in front of anyone before." She leans forward and glances to her right, addressing the rest of the hopeless virgins— and Harlow—sitting on the couch. "Have you guys been naked with someone before?"

"Just in the locker room in high school," I say. "Before gym class."

"I've been close," Cam says. "Mariah and I did almost everything but have sex there at the end. But it was always in the dark. She was shy." He grunts. "With me, anyway. When I walked in on her and those two soccer players, every light in her dorm room was on. And she was wearing a strap-on."

Harlow pats his leg. "Don't think about that. She was a garbage person. Your next girlfriend will be wonderful. Right, Ian?"

Ian's throat works as he swallows, but his voice is steadier as he says, "I hope so. And I hope this first lesson will put you all on the road to meeting people who will respect you and your boundaries." He holds up the first card—"Boundaries" is written on it in red—with an adorably shy grin. "Told you it was simple, but all the self-help books I read agreed with me on this one. Before you hit the dating market, you need to have your boundaries and your deal makers and deal breakers fixed in your mind."

Jess raises her hand and asks, "You mean like what kind of partner you're looking for? Height, job, hobbies, things like that? Because that will be hard for me. I'm not super picky. At least not about the physical stuff or whether he prefers to... I don't know, roller-skate or go bowling or whatever."

"Either one of those, there's a good chance he's a weirdo," Harlow says, with a judgmental sniff. "Roller-skating and bowling are both fringe interests in the bad way."

"They are not!" Jess says. "They're fun."

Harlow grunts. "If you like catching fungus from communal shoes and places that smell like feet and despair, sure."

Jess reaches past me to smack Harlow's arm with a laugh. "I love roller-skating. I'm going to put roller-skating on my must-have list just to prove to you that guys who like fun, childlike things are the best."

"Right there," Ian said. "That's the kind of deal maker you want on your list. You want a guy who's relaxed enough to enjoy fun, childlike things. That way you're hitting on a larger attitude, not one trait that might be hard to find. These makers and breakers should be big-picture items. And you don't need a whole bunch of them. Just a couple of each to start. That makes it easy to keep those things in mind as you're vetting potential dates."

"Okay, so for me, a deal breaker would be someone who doesn't value monogamy or keep their promises," Cameron says. "And a deal *maker* would be someone who loves to try new things, so she'll be able to enjoy it when I get experimental in the kitchen."

"Or the bedroom," Jess says, bobbing her eyebrows. "I want that, too. Someone adventurous, who's excited to get out in the world and away from our computers. I mean, I love my computer, but it's becoming a bit of a crutch."

"Or a security blanket," I say, nodding in commiseration. "Same with me and grad school and all my projects. I absolutely want to get good grades and make amazing art but letting work take over because I'm too chicken to go after the other things I want isn't healthy."

Ian clears his throat. "You're both right, and that's a great thing to keep in mind. You want someone who makes you feel safe getting out of your comfort zone. All of this thinking ahead and focusing on the bigger picture can help keep you from getting swept up in a chemical connection that ends up going nowhere. Or worse, damages your self-confidence or self-esteem. You're looking for someone who will be a good fit for the kind of relationship you want right now. So, you need to go in with your endgame top of mind." He nods toward Cameron. "Cam already got started on his, so let's hear from the rest of you guys. Deal breakers and deal makers, spit 'em out as they come to you."

We spend the next fifteen minutes sharing our "wants" and "don't wants," and I'm surprised by how illuminating it is. Deep down, I've always known the type of partner I wanted, but listing the traits for my Dream Guy aloud almost instantly makes meeting him seem more possible.

It also brings home how little any of my past boyfriends resembled this mystery man.

Not a single one of my exes was—

1. So confident in who he is and what he has to offer that he doesn't worry about "being cool" or what other people think about the things he loves.
2. Driven and passionate about his career, but just as supportive of mine.
3. Honest, even when it's hard.
4. Kind but with a killer sense of humor.

AND SEVERAL OF my former beaus exhibited one or more of my dealbreakers. Vince, for example, with his cheating and need to minimize my accomplishments to make his seem more important.

"This helps for sure," Jess says, typing the last item on her list into the notes app on her phone.

"But once we're locked in on our target, how do we attract our dream date's romantic attention? My new clothes are helping already with pulling focus, but a makeover can only take a girl so far. I'm still a nerd with odd hobbies and a weird sense of humor."

"I like your sense of humor," I tell her. "It's one of my favorite parts of you."

"And it will be one of your new partner's favorite parts, too," Ian says, sounding much more relaxed than when we started this lesson. And happy, too. It seems like he might actually be enjoying his role as a dating coach. "So, your job when you're with someone you think might be a good fit is just to be yourself as much as possible."

"But the most sexy, appealing version of yourself," Harlow adds. "You don't want to tell a guy you just met about the time your Thai curry kicked in halfway through a ten-mile hike and you ended up pooping in the woods and wiping with poison ivy."

Ian laughs. "I don't know. I'd find that story pretty funny."

Jess makes a gagging sound. "Ew, no. Then I would be thinking about the person pooping, and poo and making out don't mix. Also, hiking is the worst. What kind of monster would willingly choose to spend hours tromping around in the woods where he could be eaten by bears or bobcats or really hungry raccoons?"

"Racoons?" I ask with a laugh.

"Racoons are omnivorous and incredibly intelligent," Jess says. "It's only a matter of time before they realize that all they have to do to become the dominant species is team up and pick us off one by one."

"That's it, I'm definitely dressing up as three raccoons in a trench coat for Halloween this year," Cam says. "I want them to know I fully support the raccoon takeover."

"Same," Harlow says. "They can't fuck things up any worse than humans have. And they eat garbage, so...that's good for reducing food waste and stuff." She claps her hands together. "So, what? Are we ready to take this lesson to the streets? I don't know about you guys but I'm ready to ooze my true self all over some tall, dark, and handsome guy who enjoys making ten-year relationship plans and hates sitcoms as much as I do."

"Okay, but you have to do it blindfolded," Jess says. "To make up for the fact that you aren't a clueless virgin. That should even the playing field."

Harlow sniffs. "I haven't been touched by a member of the opposite sex in almost a year. I think that qualifies me as a born-again virgin." She shoots Ian a narrow look and points a finger at his face. "Don't tell anyone about that."

Ian lifts his hands in surrender. "Anything that's said in this room, stays in this room." His eyes shift to the right, locking with mine as he adds, "And anything you wish you hadn't said, consider it forgotten."

But I don't want to forget what I said.

And I really don't want to forget about that kiss.

So, I don't hesitate to hop to attention when Harlow slaps my knee and announces, "Then let's get this show on the road. Cameron, you and Ian head to Spliffy's and get us a table near the back in the less stinky corner before they fill up. Jess, Evie, and I will touch up our makeup and pour Evie into something slutty and be right there."

I'm about to protest that I'll go as I am, so I won't slow everyone down, but then I catch a glimpse of Ian out of the corner of my eye. He looks uncomfortable again, but not in a bad way, more like he's remembering what happened between us at the door and...

Considering it...

As a woman who would really like him to say "Yes, Evie, I will be your one-on-one sex master class teacher," I really have no choice but to give this my best shot.

"I don't want to forget anything we talked about," I say, rising from my spot on the couch. "We've talked the talk, now I want to walk the walk."

"Oh, me, too," Jess says, standing beside me. "Harlow, come reapply that highlighter stuff you put on me this morning. I want to sparkle like a sexy vampire. My friend, Pietro, at work, said glitter is also an excellent way to mark your territory at a bar. Once you've glittered your mark, the other queens know to stay away from your man.

We both think this would hold true for straight men as well as gay ones, what do you think?"

"Totally," Harlow says as we start toward the larger bathroom, the one with enough space for all three of us to get fancy at the same time. "Gay boys and straight boys aren't that different, really. The gay ones are just nicer and funnier and usually in way better shape."

I glance back at Ian, kind of wishing I could tell him that I think he's as nice, funny, and in shape as any of the fabulous gay guys I know.

Who knows?

Maybe, if he says yes, I'll have a chance to tell him all of those things and more.

Preferably, while we're both naked.

CHAPTER 14

Ian

*A*s Cameron plays a round of darts with a woman he picked up with his new flirting mindset not five minutes after we cruised into Spliffy's, the neighborhood dive, I want to bolt out of the darkened bar. I want to jog back across the street to Evie, drag her into a quiet room, and lock the door until we've talked this through like rational adults.

Though, considering the way my cock responds every time she so much as glances my way with her new bedroom eyes, maybe being locked in a room alone together *isn't* a good idea.

No matter what she wants or what I want, sleeping together would be a disaster. There are too many things that could go wrong, too many ways we could hurt each other or damage our relationship with her brother beyond repair. And even if Derrick weren't in the picture, I'm on the rebound. I just ended a three-year commitment.

I'm not ready to jump back into another one, and Evie isn't a casual-fuck kind of girl. She's a virgin who's waited years for the perfect first time, for God's sake, and I can't give her that.

I love her as a friend, but I'm not *in love* with her.

And I've never been anyone's first.

The one time I realized I was dating a virgin, I ended the relationship immediately. I was only twenty-one at the time, stressed about being a rookie, and not in the right head space to take on that kind of responsibility. And things aren't that different eleven years later. I'm older and wiser, but I'm still stressed about where my team is headed—or *not* headed—and wanting to make the most of my last years in the NHL before I'm put out to pasture.

And Derrick and I aren't just best friends. We work together. He's part of team management and technically one of my bosses. I can't afford to alienate or enrage him for a whole host of reasons, not the least of which is that my work life is already a hot mess.

Yes, art therapy went pretty well today, but our group therapy sessions are going nowhere fast and the fighting during practice hasn't slowed down at all. If anything, some of the guys seem angrier after being forced to talk about their feelings and more likely to fly off the handle.

So that's it. My decision is made.

I can't even consider Evie's request.

I'll wait until she arrives and pull her aside. I'll

tell her I'm flattered, but that I care too much about her to put our relationship at risk that way. And if she insists our relationship will be fine, I can always fall back on the fact that I know what it's like to have sex and she doesn't.

I understand how sex intensifies things, confuses things, and leads to all kinds of stupid decisions you'd never make if you'd kept your dick —or your pussy—in your pants.

Yep. That's what I'll tell her, but I'll do it in a way that doesn't make her feel annoyed or hurt or condescended to. I can pull that off. I'm good with things like this. You don't grow up riding herd over seven little brothers and sisters without learning a thing or two about peaceful conflict resolution and Evie isn't an unreasonable person. Even if she's disappointed, she'll see my point.

Now, I just need her to hurry up and get here already...

How long does it take to change clothes and throw on some makeup? I mean, it took Whitney at least an hour but Evie's more low maintenance than my ex and the other women were already dressed.

I'm about to shoot Evie a text asking for an ETA when I hear a voice that sounds like Harlow's shout from the front of the crowded bar, "Stop it, asshole. They're not interested. Get the hell out of our way."

I sit up higher, stomach balling into a cold knot as I catch a glimpse of Harlow's shiny brown

hair just visible over the shoulders of two enormous men.

A second later, I'm off my stool and across the
room.

I'm blocked by a table full of guys watching the
baseball game and a couple making out like they're
trying to leap down each other's throats, but I get
close enough to see Harlow with her hands
propped on her hips, glaring up at the shorter of
the two men. The taller one with the blond buzz
cut has his arm extended to press against the wall,
blocking Evie and Jess into the corner by the filthy
window.

"Don't be jealous, sweetheart," the shorter one
sneers at Harlow. "We just like our girls petite.
Head on back to the pool table, I'm sure you'll
find a guy who likes mouthy chicks with big feet.
We like all kinds here."

"Yeah, I know, this is my local, you stupid
fuck," Harlow says. She doesn't seem to have seen
me, and I don't make a move to shove past the
slobbery couple just yet.

If we're lucky, Harlow will be able to shut this
down without me. I've been in enough situations
like this to know once these meatheads smell
another alpha male in the room, they'll want to
prove themselves by smashing my face in. And
while I'm pretty sure I can take them both, I'd
rather not have the police called on me tonight.
Even with witnesses to confirm I didn't start
anything, you never know who the cops will
decide to believe.

"And Barry and I are tight," Harlow continues. "One word from me and you're both banned for life. So, if you enjoy cheap beer and not having a four-hundred-pound man's foot up your ass, you should get out of our way and stop scaring my friends."

"I'm not scared," Jess says, blinking up at Buzz Cut behind her glasses. "I'm confused. We don't know you, we didn't make eye contact with you on the way in, and we've made it clear we aren't inter-ested. Why are you still...bullying us?" She cocks her head quizzically. "Or whatever this is?"

Buzz Cut laughs. "Your tits look really good in that shirt, especially when your mouth is shut."

Evie glares at the guy but Jess only looks more confused.

Her forehead wrinkles as she says, "See? That's weird. That kind of behavior isn't going to get you laid, so I'm a bit puzzled about the endgame here."

"This *is* the endgame," Evie says, stepping in front of Jess and shielding her with her only slightly taller body. She's wearing the same outfit from this afternoon, but with darker eyeliner that makes her narrowed eyes look decently menacing as she adds, "Some guys get off on harassing women. It makes them feel powerful." She glances between the two guys before she arches a brow and folds her arms with a little smirk. "But with guys like these two, it's usually just a way to deny their deep-seated desire to make out with each other."

"Yeah, right," Shorter Guy says with a bark of a

laugh. "Come over here, little girl, and I'll show you just how straight I am."

"There's nothing wrong or not-masculine about being gay, you know. Even some football players are out now," Evie says, adding to the uneasy feelings spreading through my gut.

If she's not careful, her mouth is going to get her in trouble with these two, but I'm hesitant to step in just yet. If she and her friends are going to make a habit of going out to bars, they'll need to learn how to deal with jerks like these.

Though, honestly, the bouncer should be here by now. Or the bartender.

The music is loud, and the bar is crowded, but surely, I'm not the only one who's noticed this shit.

I glance over my shoulder, but the bartender is at the opposite end of the bar, embroiled in a loud conversation with a bearded-grandpa type with a dirty bandana tied around his neck and the huge, muscled man who was by the door when Cameron and I came in is nowhere to be found.

I get that everyone needs a bathroom break now and then, but where the hell is he?

I turn back in time to see Buzz Cut reach a hand toward Evie's arm, proving it's time to intervene. But if I play this right, maybe we can still avoid a brawl.

"Hey there, darlin'," I shout in a buoyant, slightly slurred voice. I stumble around the panting couple, earning a sharp, "Hey, watch it!" from the woman before the guy's wide, seeking mouth finds hers again and they return to sampling each other's saliva.

I laugh and jab a thumb at them over my shoulder. "I think they have the right idea. Come over here, baby, I've missed you." I reach for Evie, hoping she'll realize what I'm up to and play along.

Her eyes widen, but after only a beat of hesitation, she extends her hand, grabbing mine and holding on tight. "I missed you, too, sugar bear. Did you order apps? I'm starving." Without sparing the meathead mountains another glance, she reaches back, grabs Jess's arm and drags her friend out of the corner as I lead the way toward the back, shouting, "Not yet, but I could go for wings. Who wants wings? Jess, Harlow, do you want wings? And if so, do you like them spicy or sweet?"

But a glance over my shoulder reveals Harlow is still where we left her, glaring up at the shorter, darker-haired guy, though Jess, Evie, and I are now well out of the line of fire.

"Harlow!" I call out. "Come on. We have a table in the back."

But Harlow isn't listening to me. She's wagging her finger at the guy's chest as she shouts, "Now, get out. You aren't wanted here. Fuckheads like you don't get to call the shots anymore. You don't get to make us run away. Now, you run. And you run fast."

"Or what?" Shorter Guy yells back, his voice loud enough to attract the attention of the table of men watching the game, several of whom shoot concerned glances over their shoulders. "You can't make me do shit. I'm not scared of bitches like you. I'm a real man, not some fucking pussy who's going to let a bitch half his size tell him what to do."

"Yeah," Buzz Cut pipes up.

"Shut up, we're trying to watch the game," one of the baseball guys shouts, to which Buzz replies, "Shut your fucking ass, asshole!" which doesn't make a lot of sense, but signals that brawl I've been trying to avoid isn't off the table just yet.

"Harlow, come on!" Evie calls out, but Harlow is already launching into another demand for the men to leave and the bouncer is still nowhere in sight.

Evie starts back toward her, but I squeeze her hand tight and lean down to whisper in her ear, "Take Jess to the back and find Cameron. There's another exit by the bathrooms. I'll get Harlow and meet you there."

"No," Evie says, "you'll get hurt. They won't hurt me."

"You don't know that, and I can take a punch from one of those guys a lot easier than you can," I say, squeezing her hand tighter. "Now, go, Evie. Or I'm going to carry you out first and then come get Harlow, and by then she could be in real trouble."

She glances swiftly over her shoulder and then back at me, clearly torn. But the sound of Shorter beginning to shout over Harlow again seems to convince her I'm right.

She nods. "Okay, but if they jump you, I'm

coming in hard with a beer bottle or a dart or something. I've got your back."

"Me, too," Jess says. "Even though this is all bizarre. Isn't it, Evie? Who knew mating rituals were so...illogical?"

"What's happening?" Cameron asks, appearing beside me. "Is that Harlow?"

"Yeah, and we need to—"

I'm cut off by a deep voice booming, "Back off. Now." A moment later, Harlow shouts, "No! No fucking way. Don't you dare, Derrick, I—"

Her words end in a squeal as she's flipped over a shoulder and toted out the front door by someone I can only assume is Evie's brother.

Evie's. *Brother*.

Evie and I lock eyes, hers widen, and a beat later we're beating a fast retreat toward the back door, Cameron and Jess hot on our heels.

*N*early an hour later, I *finally* get a response to the fifteen texts I've sent Harlow—*Sorry, yes! I'm fine.*

Derrick carried me back to the apartment like a Neanderthal and asked where you were a million times. I told him "I don't know," a million and one before he left.

Argh! I hate him so much.

But I love you. You guys have a good time wherever you end up. I'm going to hit the hay.

Tonight clearly isn't my night.

After texting that I'm relieved she's safe, I sag against the back of the diner booth and announce to the table, "She's fine. She's home, Derrick's gone, and they didn't kill each other. So...all's well that ends well?"

"That did *not* end well," Jess says, taking a solemn pull on her milkshake's straw. She swallows and curls her lip. "That was dumb."

"Yeah," Cameron agrees. "The woman I was

playing darts with was married. She didn't bother telling me that, however, until her husband came in and glared at me like he wanted to peel my skin off with a paring knife."

"Maybe we need to hit a better bar next time?" I suggest, casting a glance Ian's way. But he's still studying his plate of fries like it's an oracle about to reveal the fate of the universe.

He's barely said five words since we raced out of Spliffy's and has been avoiding direct eye contact since...

Well, since I said what I said.

"No, we need a controlled experiment," Jess says. "Somewhere to test our skills where we know there will be lots of single people and zero toxic masculine types."

"Good luck with that," Cam says with a sigh. "Even at the restaurant, we get guys like that every once in a while, and we don't have a single entrée that costs less than fifty bucks per plate." He stretches his arms over his head with a yawn. "And on that note, I'm going to head home, too, guys. I have the lunch shift tomorrow and two of my best guys are going to be out. I want to get there early and do some appetizer prep."

Jess slurps the last of her milkshake. "I'll come with you. But I'm not giving up on this. There has to be a good beginner-flirtation practice venue somewhere in this city. Right, Ian?"

Ian looks up, blinking as if he's been deep in thought. "Um, yeah. Totally. We'll find a place."

"Good." Jess lifts her arm, wagging the small

purse dangling from her wrist back and forth. "And are you sure you don't want us to leave some money?"

He waves a hand. "Nah, it's my treat. Consider it your consolation prize."

Jess and Cam both thank Ian again for the food and slide out of the booth. "You coming, Evie?" Cam asks.

"Soon. I'm going to chat with Ian for a little bit," I say, my stomach palpitating around the handful of fries I managed to force down while waiting for Harlow to confirm that she and Derrick were both alive. "I'll catch you later."

Jess waves and Cam starts toward the door, holding it open for Jess like the gentleman he is before they both start down the street.

When they're gone, I turn back to Ian, not surprised to find him watching me with a more focused expression than I've seen since we arrived at the diner. But then, this is the first moment we've been alone since I asked him to take my virginity.

He pulls in a breath, but I jump in before he can speak, "Two weeks," I say, holding up a hand. "Just until the preseason starts. Then we go back to being friends, you can concentrate on the game, and we both pretend nothing happened." I flip my palm to face the ceiling. "How easy is that?"

He frowns. "Two weeks. You mean—"

"Two weeks of sex," I say, ignoring the way my cheeks burn in response. I had this indecent proposal mapped out in my head hours ago.

But thinking something and actually saying it aloud to a man who's watching you like you're in the process of growing another head right in front of him are two very different things.

"And practice pretending to be part of a fun, functional couple," I hurry on, figuring there's no turning back now. "I realized something during your lesson tonight, Ian. Something important."

"What's that?" he asks, looking vaguely nauseated.

"That I don't need lessons." I lean in to add in a softer voice, "None of what you were saying came as news to me. I know how to flirt and communicate and set boundaries, I just need to work up the courage to actually do it. *That's* what I need help with—testing my knowledge. Practice. But I need to start with training wheels on, so I don't crash and burn. And that's where you come in."

"I'm the training wheels?" he asks, turning to murmur, "Thank you," as our server drops the check on her way by.

"Yes!" I say, forcing what I hope is an easy smile. "A couple weeks of practice with someone I know I can trust—a friend who won't make me self-conscious if I mess up or make fun of my beginner questions—is all I need. Then I'll be ready to leave the nest and you'll have your Whitney rebound out of the way and be ready to get back on the dating horse for real. It's a win-win."

His brow furrows. "Yeah, in theory, I guess, but

things are always more complicated in the real world, Evie. And sex makes them even more complicated. Besides, your first time should be—"

"Special and beautiful and perfect, blah, blah," I cut in with a roll of my eyes. "Yeah, I know. It *should* be all those things, I agree, but I haven't met the man who's up for helping me with all that yet, Ian, and it might be a good long while before I do. Most of the guys in this city aren't looking for a long-term relationship and the few who are don't want to start one with the world's oldest virgin."

His expression softens. "You're not the world's oldest virgin. Cam and Jess are right there with you."

"Cam and Jess are both younger than I am by several months. And that's not the point. The point is that I won't feel comfortable having sex for the first time until I establish trust with my partner. But no one wants to stick around long enough to establish the amount of trust I, as an ancient virgin who's built this virginity molehill into a mountain in her head, need to finally take the plunge. It's a vicious circle, Ian, and there's only one way out."

"A professional matchmaker," he says. "I hear they do good work. I could loan you the money for a consultation if you—"

"No, not a matchmaker. That would be another high-stress situation. I'd have to worry about meeting someone new and whether we like each other and how much money I was wasting on dating instead of concentrating on the part I'm still struggling with. I need a friend with benefits to help me learn the ropes. And you're the only guy friend I have who's super experienced and knows what he's doing." I motion vaguely over my shoulder. "You know. In the bedroom."

"I knew what you meant," he says, a light in his eyes that wasn't there before. "But *I* want to know...what's your plan B?"

I blink. "Plan B?"

"I know you, Evie. When you want something, you don't give up. So, assume I've said 'no,' and there's no way to change my mind. What's next?"

I pull in a breath and let it out slowly. "Well, I guess I'll have to find someone else. Not Cam, of course. Not only do we live together, but as two virgins, that would be like the blind leading the blind. So...I don't know. I could try to track down one of my exes from college, see if they're up for helping me out."

My synapses fire. "Or maybe one of the other guys from the team. I'm really starting to like a few of them, and once I'm no longer their therapy leader, it wouldn't be a conflict of inter-est," I say, warming to the idea even as Ian's scowl digs deeper into his forehead. "And most of them are so busy with their careers and sleeping their way through the puck bunny population that they'd be fine with something casual but honest with a friend. Plus, I already know some of their personal issues, so we'd already have a certain level of intimacy and trust. It could be perfect."

The muscle in Ian's jaw twitches. "Not going to happen."

"It could," I say. "I mean, probably not with Sassy Sven, since he thinks I look like a sheep, but—"

"Stay away from him, Evie. He's the biggest slut on the team and brags about how he never uses a condom. You could get an STD just from standing too close to that guy."

I point a finger at his face. "See! This is why I need someone I can trust, who won't give me cooties or break my heart. Come on, Ian. It won't be weird, I promise."

"It would totally be weird, Evie." He drags a hand through his hair as he mutters, "So fucking weird."

"But I..." I gather my courage and force out, "I thought you liked the kiss. You seemed like you liked it."

"I did like it," he says in a soft, husky voice that sends electricity dancing across my skin. "But Derrick would be so hurt and angry, Evie. If he ever found out I—"

"He won't find out," I jump in, my heart fluttering madly behind my ribs. This crazy plan might actually be working. Ian might actually say "yes"! "How would he find out? We're both adults. We know how to keep private things private. And if we decide to practice flirting in public, we can go to Queens or something. You know how much Derrick hates Queens."

Ian mumbles something unintelligible beneath his breath as his hands ball into fists on the table.

Reminding myself that fortune favors the brave, I reach out, covering both of his hands with mine as I whisper, "Please, Ian. I need you. You're the only one who can help me with this, and who knows... You might end up having an okay time. Maybe I won't be as bad at sex as you think."

His gaze shifts sharply up, locking with mine. "I don't think you'll be bad at sex, Evie. Hell...ever since that kiss..." His tongue sweeps across his bottom lip, making my heart beat even faster. "I've been imagining things I shouldn't be imagining."

My eyes go wide. "Yeah? Like...what?"

"Things like my mouth all over you and what kind of sounds you'll make when you come," he says in a frank voice that does nothing to lessen the impact of his words. "When I *make* you come."

A gulp-squeak escapes my throat and Ian's lips twitch up on one side.

"Not the sound I was imagining," he says. "But okay."

I cough on air and reach for my water glass, but just as quickly decide I'd probably choke on water, too, and set it back down. "No, I don't... At least I don't think..." I clear my throat more forcefully. "I'm pretty sure that's not the sound I make when I...you know."

"Come?" he offers. "Orgasm? Climax?"

I nod quickly, fighting to swallow past the lump in my throat.

Ian lets out a soft laugh. "Yeah, Evie, the fact that you can't even say those words out loud doesn't give me a lot of confidence in this plan. If you're not ready to say it in front of me, then you're not ready to *do it* in front of me."

"Yes, I am," I insist, even as an anxious voice in my head warns he's probably right. "It's just that we're in public. There are people around who could hear."

He glances around the mostly empty diner before turning back to me with a terse nod. "All right." He pulls out his wallet, sets a hundred-dollar bill on top of the check the server left and slides out of his side of the booth. "Come on," he says, jerking his head toward the door.

"Wh-where are we going?"

"You'll see." He tips his head again. "Come on, Feisty."

I slowly inch toward the edge of the booth. "We can't go back to my place," I say. "I don't want Cam or Jess or Harlow to know about our bargain, either. If we do this, then we keep it a secret from everyone. That way it won't be weird when it's over."

He points a finger toward the door and demands, "Outside."

"Okay, okay." I scoot out, keenly aware of how close we are as I slip past him. I glance up at him over my shoulder. "Can you at least give me a hint where—" My words end in a startled yipping sound as he slaps my ass and says, "Walk. Door. Now."

"Fine!" I say, my cheeks flaming as I hurry toward the door, trying to decide what's more mortifying—the fact that Ian just swatted my ass like a toddler in public?

Or the fact that I kind of liked it.

CHAPTER 16

Ian

I hope the cooler night air will clear my head, but by the time we've walked the three long blocks to my friend Chet's building, my thoughts are still a gnarled mess.

Evie might always have a plan B, but right now I barely have a plan A. All I have is a vague hope that calling Evie's bluff will get me out of my present predicament.

I could always just say "no," of course.

At least theoretically I could.

But in reality, some insane part of me is looking for an excuse to do just the opposite, and when I let myself into the building with Chet's key fob, I'm secretly hoping Evie will surprise me again.

"This isn't your building," she says, shooting an anxious glance my way from the corners of her eyes.

"No, it's a friend's building." I punch the

button to summon the elevator. "I'm watering his plants while he's out of town. But he won't mind if you come up with me, and we take in the view from his deck."

"So that's why we're here?" she asks as the doors open and we both step inside. "To take in the view?"

I hit the number twelve and lean back against the elevator wall as the doors glide closed. "No, that's not why we're here. We're here so you can speak freely without an audience."

She swallows, her throat visibly working as her fingers flutter at her sides. "Okay. So what? You just want me to say the word 'orgasm'? Because if so, I can obviously say it. I just said it right now."

I smile and slowly shake my head. "Nope. Not going to cut it, Evie, and you know it. It's not the word I'm looking for. It's the word in the correct...context."

She narrows her eyes on my face. "That's an evil smile, Ian James Fox."

I smile wider and she crosses her arms with a huff.

"Fine," she says, nodding as if psyching herself up to jump off the high dive as the doors open and I lead the way out of the elevator and down the hall to Chet's place. "I can do context. You just wait and see. I'm going to give you more context than you can handle."

I stop in front of his door and turn to her with an arched brow. "I don't know, Feisty. I can handle a lot of...context."

"I don't like that nickname," she says, her breath coming noticeably faster as I open the door and motion for her to lead the way inside while I turn on the lights. "I'm not feisty, I'm... Oh, wow. This is..." She glances back at me as she wanders deeper into the large open loft with the floor-to-ceiling windows that take up one entire wall of the apartment. "What does Chet do for a living? Because I think I might want to do that."

"He's a photographer but not for a living. Mostly, he just thoughtfully invests his trust fund and collects rent from the properties he inherited from his grandmother," I say, laughing as Evie blows a breath out through her lips. "Though he swears life as a trust fund baby isn't all it's cracked up to be."

"Right, poor rich boy with his poor-rich-boy view." She steps closer to the windows with a sigh. "Wow. So pretty. Sometimes you forget how beautiful the city is at night, all lit up."

I stop behind her, studying the way the soft lamplight reflects off her curls. I've always wondered if Evie's hair is as soft as it looks, and I might be mere minutes from finding out. If...

"What are you?" I ask softly.

She turns, her arms still locked tight across her chest. "What?"

"You said that you aren't feisty, you're..."

"I'm determined," she says, lifting her chin. "And braver than you give me credit for. And I'm going to prove it. Right now."

Lips turning down at the edges, I nod. "Okay. Lay it on me. I'm ready."

Pulling in a breath, she drops her arms to her sides and breaks into a long, breathy fit of laughter. "Sorry," she says after a bit, clearly fighting to pull herself back together. "I don't know why this is funny all of a sudden."

"Me, either," I say, grinning as she continues to giggle. "This is very serious. This is your shot, Olsen. Your one chance to convince me you've got what it takes to make all your kinky dreams come true."

"They're not kinky dreams," she says, still laughing. "I don't want you to tie me up and put umbrellas in my butt. I just want to have some nice, normal, fun sex with a friend."

"Umbrellas in your butt?" I ask, laughing now, too. "What the hell? Did someone try to do that to you? No wonder you're scared of sex."

"I'm not scared of it, I'm unfamiliar with it and intimidated by it. There's a big difference," she says, sniffing as she presses her fingers to her cheeks. "And no one tried to umbrella my bum. That was one of Harlow's college boyfriends. He had a very active butt fantasy life. She let him put a finger in there once and apparently it was all umbrellas and shampoo bottles and chocolate bars with the wrapping still on after that."

I wrinkle my nose. "And she let him do all that? No, don't tell me. I don't want to know. I'll never be able to look at umbrellas, chocolate bars, or Harlow the same way again."

"No, she didn't," Evie says, grinning. "But she did keep dating him for a few more weeks, just to see what he would come up with next. Cam printed up Butt Stuff Bingo cards and we had a group chat every Sunday night to see what Trip had suggested the night before. It was pretty fun actually. But then Harlow ended it because it was just getting too weird and she was a little traumatized by the time he suggested sticking a frozen cob of corn up there."

"Valid," I say. "But there was nothing wrong with him asking for what he wanted in the bedroom, either. How else was he going to learn they weren't on the same page?"

She frowns. "You're not into weird butt stuff, are you?"

"Define weird," I say, biting back a laugh when her face pales, but she sees through me and swats my arm.

"Stop. This is hard enough without you teasing me. I don't know how to do this. Just...launch into dirty talk out of the blue."

"It's not out of the blue. We were just talking about fantasies. So, why don't you tell me one of yours." I hold her gaze, part of me praying that she'll chicken out and make backing away easier for both of us, but the other part...

Well, the other part is holding its breath and ready to hang on every word that comes out of her pretty little mouth.

She bites her bottom lip and shifts back onto her heels. For a moment, it looks like she's about to make a run for the door, but then she leans forward again and says, "All right, but you have to close your eyes." She waves a hand toward my face. "Go ahead, close them. And keep them closed until I say it's okay to open them. Those are the rules."

With a sigh, I close my eyes.

"Once upon a time there was a girl," she starts, before amending quickly, "a woman. A woman who loved art so much she was pretty sure it could heal the world. Art was her favorite thing to do, her favorite thing to talk about, and she was also pretty sure that art could be pretty sexy."

I arch my brows and Evie says, "Keep them closed!"

"They're closed, they're closed," I mutter. "Might this girl have watched Titanic a few too many times as a kid?"

"And developed a 'draw me like one of your French girls' fetish?" she asks. "Not really. But she probably did watch that scene a few thousand times on repeat before she realized that she didn't want to be Rose. She wanted to be Jack."

I almost open my eyes, but she touches my shoulder and whispers, "Don't open them. I'm not done yet."

"Okay," I murmur, very aware of her touch and how it makes my entire body feel warmer. "You want to draw me like one of your French boys. And then?"

"No, you're rushing past the best part," she murmurs, her fingers tracing slowly down the center of my chest. "First I'm going to pose you just so. I'm going to fuss with the lighting and your position and where to drape the sheet. And I'll have my eyes on you the whole time."

I bite my bottom lip. "Go on."

"And when I finally have you where I want you, I'll settle into my chair in front of my easel and start to sketch," she says. "But I'll only get a few lines drawn before I start to feel too warm to concentrate. So, I'll have to unbutton my blouse."

"Yes, please, you should—"

"Hush." Her free fingers brush across my lips as her other hand continues to skim over my abs, tracing each one through my shirt as she adds, "I'll keep undoing the buttons until you can almost see my bra, and every time I look up, your gaze will be locked on that place, like you can pop that final button through the hole with your eyes if you stare at it hard enough."

I hum my appreciation for this fantasy against her fingers.

"My nipples will get hard," she adds, making my already thickening cock swell fatter behind the fly of my jeans. "And I'll be dying for you to touch me, but I won't stop until I've trapped you on my canvas. Until every dip and hollow and angle of this beautiful body belongs to me in a way it's never belonged to anyone else. And no matter how many women you're with after me, you'll never, ever forget me and the things I made you feel."

My eyes flicker open, my heart lurching as my eyes lock with hers.

"You opened your eyes," she whispers.

"Have you ever told anyone else that fantasy?" I ask in an equally soft voice.

She shakes her head slowly back and forth. "No, I told you, I need to be with someone I can trust. And if I'm with someone like that, I know I'll be able to say those other things without getting embarrassed, too. Eventually."

I lift my hand, brushing my fingers gently across her forehead and over her hair, chest tightening as her silky curls brush against my palm. "It's even softer than I thought it would be."

She steps closer, tilting her head back. "Does that mean what I think it's means?"

"That I've been wondering if your hair is as soft as it looks?"

She arches a challenging brow.

I let my hand fall to my side as I let out a long breath. "All right. But we keep this top fucking secret, like you said. And when it's over, we're still friends. You don't get to stop being my friend just because I made you come a few hundred times. Deal?"

Her lips press together as she seems to fight a smile. "Shouldn't that be top secret fucking? Instead of top fucking secret? Because...you know."

I grin. "Right. Project TSF. Highly classified. Don't ask, don't tell. The first rule of Top Secret Fucking Club is that we don't—"

"Talk about TSF Club, got it," she supplies with a small roll of her eyes.

"Why the eye roll?"

"Because you make Fight Club jokes all the time," she says. "You have since you were like...seventeen."

"Well, thanks," I say with a huff. "Are you saying I'm an old man who repeats himself without realizing it and should get some new material? You could find someone younger, you know. You don't have to settle for a guy eight years older than you are with a bunch of bad dad jokes."

"I like your dad jokes," she says, "but I also like to tease you about them. But mostly, I'd like to circle back around to that 'few hundred' comment you tossed out. In my experience, getting the um... train to the station isn't that easy, mister. You might want to revise that goal down a few notches."

Now it's my turn to roll my eyes. "Oh, please, Feisty. Give me some credit."

"I am, I just—"

"Hush," I say, pressing a finger to her lips. "It's not going to be a problem. I promise."

"But what if my parts aren't like other women's parts?" she asks, just her mouth moving against my finger enough to make me even harder. Or maybe it's the fact that we're talking about orgasms that's doing it. "Some women are train station challenged. It's a thing."

I smirk. I can't help it. "Yeah, still not worried."

"And why's that?" she asks. "You're just cocky as hell?"

"I have two major talents, Feisty. One is being an excellent hockey player. The other is...train station related." I pull my hand from her lips to point an accusing finger at her face. "Now you've got me doing it. Orgasm related. Coming related. Climax—"

"I get it," she says. "And I'll work on finding a word I like before we..." She glances around the apartment, a mixture of anxiety and anticipation on her face. "Unless we... We aren't starting *now*, are we?"

"No," I say, even though several body parts are loudly demanding I reconsider. "I think we should sleep on this. Make sure we still think it's a good idea in the cold light of day. I'm also pretty sure Chet would frown on me hooking up in his place when all I was invited to do was water the plants and lounge on the balcony if I need to work on my tan before autumn sets in."

She nods. "Understandable. But I'm not going to change my mind. I'm actually even more into this kind of thing in the cold light of day. I wake up ready for the train to leave the station. If you know what I mean."

"You're horny in the morning?" I bite my lip as I hum softly beneath my breath, doing my best not to imagine a warm, sleepy Evie rolling over and asking to ride my cock and failing miserably. "Good to know."

She giggles. "You really do seem pleased. Is that the kind of thing guys like to hear?"

"Absolutely." I shrug. "Well, any guy worth your

trouble. Most of us are horny all the time and desperate to get in your pants. The easier you make that for us, the happier we are. Same applies to telling us what you like in bed. We like to make you come. It makes us feel like victorious gladiators kicking ass in the arena." I pause, grunting as I add, "It's kind of like hockey that way. The two might have more in common than I realized."

Evie crosses her arms again, worry creeping in to banish the light in her eyes.

"What's wrong?" I ask.

She shakes her head. "Nothing, I just... Vince didn't seem very keen on being a gladiator. Once he realized how hard it was to get me there, he kind of lost interest. I mean, we only did hand stuff mostly, so maybe that was what bored him but still..."

I rest my hands lightly on her shoulders, giving them what I hope is a reassuring squeeze. "Vince was a selfish shit. We won't have any problems. I promise. Assuming we don't change our minds, of course. If you do, that's completely fine, by the way. We can just forget we had this conversation and move on."

"I'm not going to change my mind," she says, stubbornness flickering in her gaze again. "And unless I get a message from you telling me to stay away, I'll be at your place at seven tomorrow night. I have class until five, and then I'll need to run home and change out of my grungy paint clothes."

"I don't mind your grungy paint clothes," I say,

adding before I can stop myself, "You won't be wearing them for long anyway."

She bites her lip, sending a jolt rocketing through me as I realize how much I'd like to do the same. "We're really going to do this. Aren't we?"

"I fucking hope so," I confess, "no matter how much we'll probably regret it later."

"We won't regret it. We can do this, Ian. And who knows, we might end up even better friends on the other side."

As I lock up and lead the way downstairs, saying goodbye to Evie at the entrance to the subway that will whisk me uptown, I hope like hell that she's right.

But deep in my bones, where all my most trustworthy instincts live, a choir of voices is singing the "You're Going to Be Sorry" chorus. At top volume.

CHAPTER 17

Evie

I don't know who I am anymore.

The woman who propositioned Ian and seductively confessed her sexy art fantasies *isn't* Normal Evie.

But she's part of me, I realize, as I find myself sketching a pencil drawing of a man's hand threaded through a woman's hair in Studio the next afternoon instead of working on my series of baby animals in teacups. I still love baby animals in teacups, but there's something so sexy about the contrast of the man's rough skin and the silky curls wrapping around his knuckles.

And I'm not the only one who notices.

My faculty mentor, Ellen, encourages me to keep exploring the "gritty sensuality" of my new style, and not long after, a deeper voice murmurs from over my shoulder, "Wow, that's really good."

I jump in my chair as my breath rushes out in surprise.

I spin to see Derrick standing behind me, an uncomfortable expression on his face. I have to fight the urge to whip my drawing pad closed and cover it with my arms the way I would when I was little, and he'd pop into my room to see what I was drawing before dinner.

Instead, I clear my throat and stand up, forcing a smile even though my overprotective big brother is the *last* person I want to see a mere two hours before my first sex lesson with his best friend.

Ian's right. Derrick will kill him—and maybe me, too—if he finds out what we're up to. We're going to have to keep this deep undercover. Like, all the curtains closed, every door locked, and no cell phones anywhere close by on the off chance that the FBI is listening in, and Derrick is a spy.

"Thanks." I wipe my pencil-smeared fingers on my overalls. "To what do I owe the pleasure? I thought you were crazy busy at work this week."

He sighs and drags a hand through his hair, but the carefully cut brown strands fall instantly back into place. Derrick isn't just a handsome guy; he's a handsome guy who knows how to groom and dress himself, which is rarer than I realized growing up with a fashion-savvy big brother.

It also makes it even weirder that he goes so long between girlfriends. Maybe he's just picky. But I would think a guy like Derrick would pull mad tail based on his looks alone, and he's also actually a very nice guy.

He saves the bossy stuff for his little sister.

I'm just lucky that way, I guess.

"So busy," he says. "The new PR team is in my office every ten minutes. They seem to think fixing the team's reputation is my job, even though we made it clear when we hired them that we need *them* to run damage control."

I wince sympathetically. "I'm sorry. Hopefully the team-building camp will help. My session with the guys yesterday actually went really well."

"Yeah, I heard," he says, casting another curious glance at my drawing before his focus returns to my face. "Upper management is very happy about that, by the way. I'm pretty sure you're off probation."

"Oh good. That's great news." I shift a few inches to my left, hoping to block the drawing from Derrick's view. I googled pics of Ian to get inspiration for that hand. On the off chance my brother has the shape of his best friend's fingers memorized, I'd rather he not study it too closely. "Is that why you stopped by?"

He blinks and shakes his head. "No, sorry. I just wanted to check and make sure you had a gift picked out for Dad's birthday weekend. If you don't, I can order some extra paving stones when I order mine and we can say the gift is from both of us."

I nod. "Yes, please, would you? I'll pay you back. I just never know what to get him. He's the hardest person to buy for."

"He is," Derrick agrees, glancing down at his feet. "But he doesn't seem to have seen the video from the other night. Or the meme. So that's good. Hopefully it will all blow over before he's in the mood to get back on social media."

"Fingers crossed," I say, my shoulders feeling lighter. It would be nice to skip the drama with Dad regarding my public meltdown. Knowing Dad, we'll get around to fighting about something or other before his birthday is over anyway, but the less fuel for the fire, the better.

I expect Derrick to say his goodbyes, but he lingers, his gaze still fixed on his shoes.

"Is there something else you wanted to talk about?" I finally ask.

"Yeah, I... I also wanted to..." He shifts closer before adding in a softer voice, "Did Harlow say anything to you? About last night?"

"No, she didn't. Why?" Propping my hands on my hips, I ask, "Did you do something awful? I know you two don't get along, but she's my best friend, Derrick. I need you to be nice to her."

"She calls me Satan," he says, but not in the frustrated tone he usually uses when discussing Harlow. "And all I did was save her from getting pounded by a pair of meathead assholes at a bar. I think you should be lecturing her on being nice and not going to bars alone."

"She should be able to go wherever she wants alone. It's the meatheads that were in the wrong, not Harlow," I add before pushing on, "And if you're so innocent, why are you asking me if she said anything to me about last night?" I don't mention the fact that I saw him carry Harlow out of the bar or that she might be pissed that he scooped her up like a sack of potatoes first and, knowing Derrick, bothered asking her if that was okay much, much later.

He assaults his hair with his fingers again and gives a rather unconvincingly innocent shrug. "No reason, I just... I'd like to bury the hatchet with her. This feud or whatever it is has gone on long enough."

"Agreed," I say, softening toward him. Derrick's such an overbearing, self-assured person that sometimes I forget he also has a soft side.

But he does. When I was little, I always had beautifully wrapped presents waiting for me beside a big stack of pancakes when I woke up on my birthday. And my dad sure as hell never did anything to help. Every stuffed animal and collection of art supplies was selected, paid for, and wrapped by my big brother.

Derrick was also the one who watched over me when I was sick and made sure I had Children's Tylenol every six hours when I was fighting a fever. He'd get up in the middle of the night to check on me, even when he was exhausted from hockey practice and had school the next day.

Warmed by the old memories, I give his shoulder a squeeze. "I can talk to her for you if you want. Let her know you'd be interested in a fresh start?"

He shakes his head. "No, that's okay. You have enough on your plate, and I don't want to come between the two of you. I'll figure something out on my own." He glances around the room. "Sorry to interrupt you, by the way. I thought your class let out at five."

"It does, I just stayed late to tie up a few loose ends." I glance at the clock on the wall and curse beneath my breath. "Wow, it's almost six. I completely lost track of time. I have to go."

As I turn back to my drawing pad, flipping it closed and carefully slipping my supplies back into my art case, Derrick asks, "Why? Hot date?"

I laugh harder than I should. "Nope. Just a bunch of homework. And I need to get my lesson plan sorted out for the team tomorrow. I want to make sure I show up with something great to build on the progress we made yesterday."

All of which is true, but I'm already done with my homework and have my lesson plan prepared aside from printing out the worksheets I intend to use for the first project of the day. I rolled out of bed early this morning to burn through my to-do list so I wouldn't be distracted during my first practice session with Ian.

I have no idea if he plans to get straight to the de-virgin-izing or ease into this a little, but either way I figured I wouldn't be in the mood to write a paper on the therapeutic benefits of play for adults afterwards.

Doing my best not to let my terri-citement—a mixture of terror and excitement I've been feeling so often today that I decided to give it a name— show, I turn back to Derrick with a grin. "But catch up later? Maybe we could have coffee later this week and brainstorm ways to get in Harlow's good graces? I know she seems locked into her loathing of you but she's not as rigid and inflexible as she seems. Honestly, a sincere apology for leaving her stranded at that bonfire when we were in high school would probably be all it would take."

"Except that's not what happened," he mumbles so softly I can barely hear him.

But I do hear, and it throws everything I've ever heard about why Harlow thinks my brother is Satan into question. "What?" I ask. "What do you mean that's not exactly what happened?"

He shakes his head. "Nothing. Never mind. I'll let you go and figure this out myself. Have a good night." He turns to leave, but spins back a second later, his forehead furrowed. "Oh, and if you see Ian before I do, tell him I'd like to talk to him about last Friday."

Panic dumping into my bloodstream, I squeak, "Why would I see Ian before you? You're best friends. And Ian and I?" I let out an unconvincingly derisive snort. "We barely know each other. I mean, not compared to the two of you."

"Yeah, I know," Derrick says, suspicion tightening his expression. "But he's in your class tomorrow afternoon."

"Oh, right," I say, forcing another laugh as my inner voice warns that I need to get away from my brother before my poor lying skills ruin my chances of ditching my hymen this century. "Right. Totally. I'll tell him, but why can't you tell him yourself?"

"He's not answering my texts," he says with a sigh. "I thought about stopping by his place later, but—"

"No!" I shout, my tongue practically leaping out of my throat as I hurry to cover my mistake. "You should give him space. I mean, you know how much *you* hate it when people stop by without calling first. That's practically grounds for assault charges, right? I thought you were going to kick me down the stairs the last time I popped by to borrow your crockpot."

He winces. "You don't really mean that, right? You know I would never hurt you. Like...never. No matter what you did or how upset I was about it. You're my baby sister, my family. I just want to protect you, Evie."

"I know," I say, aching at the genuine pain in his words. "Of course, I know." I frown. "What's going on with you? Did something happen at work or—" I break off with a sigh as I connect the dots. "It was Harlow, wasn't it? She said something to you last night about me."

He takes another step back. "No, she didn't. Well, she did, but I promised I wouldn't say anything." His breath rushes out. "I shouldn't even be here. Just remember that I love you, okay? Even when I'm being grouchy? And I'll try to do a better job of conveying my concern for you with a little less...intensity."

"Okay," I murmur. "That sounds good. And remember I love you, too. So much." I want to say more, but Derrick is already lifting a hand goodbye, and if I don't hurry, I won't have time to change.

I don't care what Ian said about liking my overalls. I want to feel confident and sexy tonight.

Tonight, I'm not animals-in-teacups and baggy-overalls Evie. Tonight, I'm the woman who drew that sexy-as-hell picture and who was bold enough to set this plan in motion in the first place.

Tonight, I am Brave New Evie and by tomorrow...

By tomorrow I might not be a virgin anymore, a prospect so momentous I tell myself it's okay to get to the bottom of the Harlow and Derrick mystery later.

Tonight is for me and Ian and a whole world of sexy new possibilities.

CHAPTER 18

Ian

I pace back and forth across my living room, torn between excitement and dread. I'm eager to see Evie again—to touch her, taste her, and see if my hunch about her knowing far more than she thinks she knows about sex is correct.

She's just innately sexy, so much so that I can't believe I didn't notice it before.

Hell, just the way she drags a French fry through ketchup and pops it into her mouth makes my pants tighter. The way she tucks the rogue curl on her right side behind her ear, the way her eyes dance with mischief when she smiles, the way her voice goes soft and husky when she talks about wanting to draw me—any one of those things alone would be enough to turn me on.

Altogether, they're enough to make me positive she doesn't need these practice sessions. She just needs to find a partner she can trust.

If I were a good friend, I would help her find that guy instead of taking advantage of her belief that I'm the only man she can be at ease with.

I almost text her as much a dozen times, but I don't, and when the buzzer sounds a few minutes before seven, I don't hesitate to punch the button and say, "Come on up."

I don't ask who it is—I'm not expecting anyone except Evie and the timing is right. She said she'd be here by seven. But when I open the door a minute later and glance toward the elevators, it isn't Evie who steps out onto the tightly woven gray carpet in the hall.

It's…Whitney.

The greeting on the tip of my tongue fades away as I scramble to think of a way to get rid of my ex before Evie arrives. Whitney is a gossip hound to the core of her delicate bones, and she's still friends with the girlfriends of several guys on the team. If she sees Evie show up to my place at this time of night, she's going to get suspicious. She was already jealous of Evie. Seeing her here will all but ensure a rumor that Evie and I are hooking up starts circulating by tomorrow morning.

Thinking fast, I start coughing. Hard.

Whitney's steps slow as she lifts a hand to hover in front of her face. She's also a germaphobe and once bailed on me halfway through a meal at a fancy restaurant because I cleared my throat one time too many.

"Sorry, I thought you were the pharmacy delivery," I say in a deliberately rough, scratchy voice. "I think I have a little end-of-summer cold. But I'd love to talk later if you want. Could I call you tomorrow? Or maybe this weekend, if I'm better by then? I just—" I break off in a tortured round of hacking, squeezing my eyes shut as I pretend to struggle to regain control.

When I finally wheeze in a breath and open my eyes, Whitney is back by the elevator, furiously punching the down button with her knuckle. "I just came by to get the rest of my things, but fine. I'll text you later and you can bring them by my work or something."

Trying not to let my relief show, I nod. "Of course. Will do. Maybe during your lunch break?" I ask, regret swirling through me.

I'm not sad that it's over between us—it should have been over a long time ago—but Whitney and I have been close for a long time. I don't want to lose that, not if there's any chance that we can still salvage what was good about our relationship. "I could take you for salads at the place you like, and we could talk. I'd really like to be friends, Whit. How will I know how to dress myself without you?"

She sniffs and lifts her nose higher in the air. "You'll do just fine. Just ask a salesgirl. Or your new girlfriend."

"I don't have a new girlfriend," I say. "We just broke up last weekend. I'm not ready to start anything new."

I'm not, which is just another reason I should

call this off with Evie before it's too late. No matter how many times she assures me she's down for a low-key, friends-with-benefits situation, my gut insists I'd be a fool to believe that and an asshole to take advantage of her innocence about things like this.

But after Whitney says, "Okay, then maybe we can talk. Hope you feel better soon," and disappears into the elevator, I don't text Evie to cancel.

In fact, I'm still standing in my doorway when Evie steps out of the elevator a few minutes later and starts toward me in a black mini dress with white stripes down the sides that clings to her curves. Paired with white-and-red rose-printed Vans on her feet and simple star earrings in her ears, she shouldn't reduce me to a puddle of lust, but...she does.

I'm still trying to pull myself together when she says, "Sorry I'm late. I got busy drawing and lost track of time." She stops in front of me, a mixture of uncertainty and flirtation in her tone as she adds, "I was drawing your hand and it turned out really sexy. If you're good, I might show it to you later."

"And if I find myself unable to be good?" I ask, my voice husky for reasons that have nothing to do with my fake coughing fit. "Because this dress..."

She smiles. "Better than overalls, right?"

"So much better." I push the door open behind me. "You ready for this?"

She swallows before letting out a soft laugh.

"As ready as I'll ever be, but there's one thing we should discuss first." She takes a bracing breath and takes my hand. "Come on. Best if we talk about this inside where no one can hear you scream. Or me scream, when you say there's no way you're going to indulge my insanity."

"All right," I say, pulling her inside and shutting the door, already knowing I'm going to say yes, no matter how insane her request.

Her hand feels *that* good in mine.

Looking back later, I'll see this as the first warning sign of trouble. But at the moment all I feel is happy to see her and even happier to finally have her all to myself.

CHAPTER 19

Evie

*T*his should feel weird.

I'm here for a *booty call*.

Or booty call practice, anyway.

I have never done either of those things, Ian and I have spent very little time together one-on-one and none of that has been while we were naked, and despite all my big talk about not needing sex lessons...I might actually need sex lessons.

I'm a good kisser and decent at flirting, but I've never given a man a blow job. I almost did once, for Vince's birthday, but I chickened out at the last minute. It just didn't feel right to get down on my knees and put his penis in my mouth when I'd never even seen it before that night. We were still making out a lot at that point but always with our clothes on. Vince had said he was happy to take things slow, and I was naïve enough to believe him.

And now, here I am, facing the sexiest man alive across his coffee table with very little idea what to do with him. In addition to the no-blow-job factor, I can also count the number of hand jobs I've given on...

Well, one hand.

Vince was so unimpressed with my technique that on one occasion he fell asleep in the middle of my sweaty-palmed attempts to make him feel good. He said it was his fault for staying up late at a concert the night before and skipping his afternoon coffee, but it took my ego a long time to recover from that one.

By the time it had, Vince wasn't kissing me nearly as much anymore. If I had to guess, I'm betting that was around when he started dating his fiancée. And even with another woman taking the edge off behind the scenes, Vince still found my sexy-time efforts so unsatisfactory that he started cutting our kissing sessions short and heading home instead of spending the night on the couch so we could grab breakfast the next morning the way he did when we started dating.

Any one of those things should be enough to have me shaking in my tennis shoes right now, but shockingly, I'm not nervous.

At least, not about the intimate stuff.

My other request is a source of anxiety but hopefully Ian won't think I'm crazy. Or not *too* crazy.

"What's on your mind, Feisty?" he asks, using that nickname I can't decide if I love or hate.

Before recently, I wouldn't have described myself as "feisty," but obviously that's changing or I wouldn't be sitting here right now.

"Right before I left Studio, Derrick showed up. He mentioned something about swinging by your place to talk. I convinced him not to," I say, when Ian's eyes widen, "but it was a close call. And then, I'm pretty sure I saw Whitney heading into the subway station as I was on my way out. Does she live in the area?"

He exhales. "No, she doesn't. But she was here a few minutes ago. She stopped to get her things, but I managed to put her off until next week. I knew if she was still around when you showed up, any chance of keeping this under wraps would be over."

"Exactly." I nod, hopeful that this ask will be easier than I anticipated. "That's why I think we should find an alternate location, a place where we won't risk running into people we know." I fish my phone out of the front pocket of my backpack. "I did a little googling on the way here. There's a hotel in the Bronx that's affordable and has decent reviews. Maybe we could meet there, next time? I know it's kind of a hassle, but if we plan a few days ahead, I'm sure I can get a room. And I'll pay for it, so you don't have to—"

"You'll do no such thing," he cuts in. "And we're not going to a cheap hotel in the Bronx. I'll get us something nice for Friday night."

"Are you sure? I mean, this is my idea, and I don't mind paying."

"No way. I think it's a good idea, too, and I have more disposable income than you do. I'm happy to make that happen, but..." He leans forward, his forearms braced on his knees as he asks in a softer voice, "Does that mean you want a rain check for tonight?"

I shake my head. "No. I think we're safe for tonight. Don't you?"

"I do," he murmurs. "And I've been looking forward to playing hangman with you. Like we used to. Remember?"

I frown even as a smile stretches across my lips. "Um, yes, I do. But..."

He arches a brow. "But what?"

"I was expecting something a little sexier than hangman."

His eyes dance. "Are you saying you don't think I can make hangman a sexy experience?"

"I bet you can make just about anything a sexy experience," I say, my skin beginning to tingle again, just from holding his gaze across the coffee table. "Okay, hangman it is. I have paper and pencils in my art bag."

"Nope, I've got that covered," he says, bouncing to his feet and crossing to the desk against the far wall. "I've already prepped the first word." He turns back to me, yellow legal pad and pencil in hand. "But first, we should go over the rules."

"I know the rules to hangman."

"But this isn't ordinary hangman, Feisty," he says. "This is strip hangman. Every time you guess a wrong letter, an item of clothing has to come off. The first one down to their underwear is the loser."

I bite my lip, delighted by this twist on our old childhood game. "All right. I'm game. What's the category?"

"Foods to lick off of your lover." He turns the pad to face me as he sits down a few inches away from me on the couch, making me keenly aware of the warmth of his big body and how amazing he smells. I don't know if it's just the soap he uses or what, but Ian always smells so damned good.

The combination of his yummy scent and the thought of licking something tasty off his skin is enough to make my nipples tighten, making me wish I'd worn something thicker than the bralette I threw on in the studio bathroom.

I'm pretty sure my nipples are visible through my dress, but before I can discreetly glance down to check, Ian says in a husky voice, "And if you're interested, I might have a few lick-worthy foods in my fridge we can experiment with later."

"I am *very* interested," I say in a voice that makes Ian's eyes darken.

"Are you sure you need seduction practice?" he asks. "Or is this just your way of driving me crazy for your pussy?"

I bite back a smile as I shrug. "I don't know. But we should definitely find out."

"Hell, yes, we should," he says, holding my gaze as he says, "Two words. First word is five letters, second word is six."

I glance down at the pad he's holding up for me to study, even though I'm suddenly finding it hard to concentrate on anything but him.

His silky brown hair hanging down nearly into his eyes in that way that makes me want to brush it to one side and kiss his forehead. His eyes burning into mine, making promises I know he'll keep if I'm brave enough to let him. His powerful body with those big hands that bring me to life in ways no one else ever has and he hasn't even touched any of my "sexy zones" yet.

If he does...

When he does...

I'm not backing down from this challenge, and neither is he. He wants me. I can see it in his eyes. Maybe not as much as I want him—he's experienced, after all, and already knows what sex is all about—but he's definitely interested. He isn't doing this because he feels sorry for me.

He's doing this because he wants to touch me, which gives me the confidence to shift closer to him on the couch as I lean in and whisper, "I."

He grins—wickedly, sexily. "There is no I, I'm afraid."

"You're not afraid," I say, toeing off my shoe. "You're happy about it."

"I am," he says with a laugh. "Though I'll be happier when you're out of those shoes and socks and the real clothes start coming off."

"Not as happy as I'll be when I'm sitting here fully dressed and you're in nothing but your boxers."

"Big talk for a little girl who's already lost a shoe and gained a stick body," he says, making a scratch on the paper, just below the noose already on the page.

I snort. "I expect more than a stick body, mister. I've seen your art skills now. I know better than to buy that 'I can't draw' line anymore. And I'm about to make a comeback, wait and see."

He smirks. "Lay it on me. What's your next letter?"

"E," I say, pumping a fist as he shifts the pad to fill in the three Es in the second word.

When he turns the pad back, I see _ _ _ _ _ _ _E E _ E and my wheels turn. Almost instantly, a possible answer pops into my head.

But surely not...

"Nacho cheese?" I ask, wrinkling my nose as he groans in defeat. "Are you serious?" I ask as he fills in the rest of the letters. "Nacho freaking cheese? You lick that off your lovers? What's wrong with you?"

He laughs. "I've never licked it off of anyone, but you *could* lick it off someone. It's drizzle-able."

"First, that's not a word. Second, nacho cheese would not only smell disgusting, but you also could burn someone." I shake my head, shooting him my most judgmental look. "Are you sure you're qualified to speak on this topic?"

"I didn't want to make it too easy," he says, a hint of defensiveness in his tone. "If I'd put whipped cream on there, you would have had the answer in two seconds."

I can't resist smirking a little. "I had the answer in two seconds anyway."

"Okay, Sassypants," he says, thrusting the pad my way. "Your turn. Let's see what you've got."

"The nickname is Feistypants." I flip the paper over to reveal a fresh sheet. "And from now on, all lickable items must be things you'd actually enjoy licking off your lover. No funny business."

He rolls his eyes, but he's grinning as he says, "Fine. Hit me with your best shot, woman."

I do. And ten minutes later, Ian is down to his jeans. His sweatshirt, undershirt, and both socks are already on the floor and not a single correct letter has been guessed on my hangman board.

"Oh dear," I say, tsking beneath my breath. "Looks like I'm about to find out whether you wear boxers or briefs."

"Assuming I wear underwear," he says, glancing back at the paper. "But you're going to have to wait to find out. I'm about to make a comeback. Y."

I shoot him a faux pitying expression and coo, "So sorry, but there is no Y. Time to take off those jeans, mister."

"There has to be a Y," he says. "If you chose a word in a foreign language, you forfeit your win. You know the rules. Words have to be in English *and* recognized by Merriam-Webster."

I hum low in my throat. "Wow, you didn't use to be such a sore loser. Does this mean I should assume you aren't wearing boxers and are afraid to pull a Full Monty so early in the competition?"

"I fear nothing," he says, making me snort-laugh. He jumps to his feet, striking a superhero pose before reaching for the top button on his jeans, making me giggle as he opens the flap of his zipper just far enough to reveal the top of a pair of dark red underwear of some sort.

But then he pauses, his eyes locking with mine as he says in a softer voice, "You really want me to take these off?"

I nod, my smile fading. "Yes. I do."

"Tell me the word first."

I shake my head, gaze still locked on his. "No. I'm in it to win it. And I don't win until you're wearing nothing but your birthday suit."

"I forfeit," he says, adding in a husky voice that is maybe the most butterfly-inducing thing I've ever heard, "And I think we're both going to win tonight."

"Yeah?" My cheeks warm and the rest of me begins to tingle in that increasingly familiar way only Ian seems to inspire.

"Yeah. I just...have a feeling."

"I have that same feeling," I say, "but I'm going to need you to take off those jeans before I reveal my hangman secrets."

His lips hook up on one side. "As the lady wishes."

"Thank you," I say, my tongue slipping out to dampen my lips. He really is mouthwatering, looking so damned good in jeans and nothing else that it's hard to imagine him getting any hotter.

But then he shoves the denim down around his

ankles, moving closer as he steps out of the puddle of fabric, exposing the very firm, very thick, very *long* ridge beneath his boxer briefs.

My breath catches and my lips part. "Well, then," I say, fighting the urge to squirm as my nipples tighten until they begin to sting with the need to be touched. I finally drag my eyes from his arousal up to his face, awareness zipping through me again as his heated gaze locks with mine. "Is that for me? Or do you just really like losing at hangman?"

"I don't like losing at anything. Now, tell me the word."

"Molasses," I say, dry panties a thing of the past as he puts his hands on my shoulders, urging me to lean back into the couch cushions.

He straddles my hips, arousing my body and my curiosity, as he says, "That's a diabolical selection."

"I know. I'm very diabolical," I say, distracted by his fingers teasing into my hair. "Are you giving me a lap dance?"

He grins. "No. I just felt like I wanted to straddle your smug little body and trap you on my couch, so I did. Is that all right?"

"Very all right." I trail my fingers over his pecs and down the ridges of his abs. "I feel like I want to lick you right here, in between every tight muscle. Is that okay?"

"That's not only okay," he says, his voice deepening as I continue to explore him with my fingers, "it's our practice for today."

I glance up, feeling weirdly powerful in my current position, even though he's huge and hovering over me and I couldn't get up if I tried. "What's that?"

"Following your sex muse," he says, "and making sure what you like is cool with your partner."

I bite my lip. "I'm not sure I've ever been in touch with my sex muse. Usually, I'm so busy worrying about whether I'm doing it 'right' I'm all in my head about..." I trail off, distracted by his fingers wrapping around my wrists. "What's this?"

"This is me pinning your arms and kissing your neck." He shifts until his knees are on the floor, which—thanks to the height difference—brings his lips even with my shoulder. "One second."

He releases my wrists to grip the backs of my thighs. He jerks my hips a few inches closer to the edge of the cushion, sending a lightning bolt of arousal surging through me at the assured way he handles my body.

"There we go," he murmurs, recapturing my wrists and pressing them into the cushions above my head as he bends to kiss my neck, which is now in the perfect position.

I draw in a shuddery breath. "My sex muse likes it when you jerk me around a little. Like that with the... With the... That body part I can't remember the name of because you're very good at kissing."

"Your hips?" His lips curve against my throat, where my pulse is throbbing faster.

"Yes, those." My lids flutter closed as his mouth settles over mine, kissing me slowly, almost carefully, making it clear he's in no rush.

"You taste so good," he whispers in between kisses. "Your skin, your lips."

"You, too," I say, wrapping my legs around his waist as he presses closer, intensifying the kiss until my head is spinning. "But I want to feel you. More of you. Without...fabric in the way."

"I think we can make that happen." He reaches for the bottom of my dress, pulling it up and over my head, his breath catching as his gaze settles on my bralette. "Wow, that's sexy as hell. Your nipples through that lace."

I swallow hard, my pulse going crazy as he cups my breasts in both hands and drags his thumbs over both tight, aching tips. The sensation is so intense, so much more electric than anything caused by my own hands or even Vince the few times he touched me here, that my body bows, pressing my hips into his chest, knocking him back into the coffee table.

"Oh no, I'm so sorry," I say in a rush, mortification threatening to banish the delicious feelings.

"Don't you dare apologize," he says, scooping me up in his arms and guiding my legs around his waist as he carries me over to an empty patch of carpet beside the windows and lays me down, lengthening himself on top of me. "I love that you're so responsive. It makes me crazy."

He kisses my nipples through my bra as I pant, "Yeah, me, too. God, that feels so good, Ian."

"So sweet," he murmurs as he pulls my bra up and over my head. And then his tongue is on my bare skin, sucking and licking and teaching me just how much crazier I can get.

"Holy shit," I gasp, clinging to his shoulders as he continues his wicked, wonderful torture. "I feel that everywhere. How can I feel it everywhere?"

"Magic. And nerve endings. But mostly magic." He holds my gaze as he hooks his thumbs into the sides of my panties. "Is this okay? Can I take these off?"

"Yes, please," I breathe, as he draws my panties slowly down my legs before guiding my thighs farther apart.

I guess I should feel embarrassed—no one's ever seen me like this, so open and exposed—but I don't. I feel alive. Electric. And so beautiful I don't worry for a second that Ian doesn't like what he sees. The hungry expression on his face as he presses a kiss to the side of my knee is all the confirmation I need that he's enjoying this as much as I am.

Well, maybe nearly as much.

"Are you about to do what I think you're going to do?" I ask.

"Devour your pussy until you come all over my face?" he asks, his thumbs digging lightly into my thighs in a way that makes the electric, lightning-filled feeling inside of me crackle hotter. "Hell yes, I am."

"Thank God, I was hoping—" My words end in a groan as he drags his tongue from my aching entrance to my clit. And then he starts to suck—drawing my clit into his mouth in deep rhythmic pulls—and the world explodes in a rainbow of colors and light and sensations so intense all I can do is arch into his mouth and pant for air.

And then he pushes two fingers inside me, summoning a ragged, hungry sound from deep in my soul. Before I'm aware that an orgasm is on the horizon, it crashes over me like a tsunami. My heels dig into the floor as pleasure sounds rip from my throat and Ian continues to suck and lick and moan against my skin like I'm the most delicious thing that's ever happened to his mouth.

"Told you I wouldn't have any trouble making you come," he says, but I'm too high on pleasure to be bothered by his smug tone.

In fact, right now I'm finding that smugness hella hot, so sexy I'm ready to beg him to take me to his bed and finish what we started.

I can't imagine waiting another second to be as close to him as two people can get. To be...his.

The request is on the tip of my tongue when a knock sounds on the front door and my brother's voice calls out, "Ian? Can we talk?"

Ian's head jerks up from between my thighs, a panicked expression on his face that I'm positive I'm mirroring right back at him.

CHAPTER 20

Ian

*a*t the sound of my best friend's voice, my mouth goes dry and a vision of my murdered corpse bleeding out on the carpet beside Evie's gorgeous body flashes through my head.

Cursing softly, I call out, "Um, yeah, just a second."

Derrick probably won't *literally* kill me if he catches me with my head between his sister's thighs, but I'd rather not tempt fate. Or my best friend's notoriously short fuse.

"I can let myself in," he calls through the door. "I have my key."

"Okay, but just a second, I was um..." I tug on my t-shirt, shove our hangman pad under the couch, and reach for my jeans. "Asleep. I was asleep on the couch."

"Asleep?" he replies, concern in his voice. "At eight o'clock? Are you okay?"

Evie snatches her dress, underthings, back-pack, and shoes off the floor before she jumps to her feet. "The bedroom?" she hisses, clutching the collection as she points to the right side of the apartment.

"No, other side," I whisper. I hook a thumb to the left. "I'll get rid of him as fast as I can."

With a frantic nod, she dashes barefoot and naked as the day she was born across the room and down the hall. And even though I can hear Derrick fitting his key into the lock and I'm still not wearing pants, I can't help taking a moment to soak in the view.

Fuck, she's gorgeous.

Sexy. Fun and playful. Everything I've ever wanted in a lover.

The thought sends an uncomfortable stabbing sensation through me, but there's no time to analyze the feeling. Derrick is on his way in, giving me just enough time to button my jeans and collapse back onto the couch with a rush of breath before he's closing the door behind him.

"Hey." He shoots a narrow look my way as he tucks the keys back into his jacket pocket. "Are you sick? We can get you in to see the team doctor first thing tomorrow morning."

I shake my head as I smooth a hand over my hair, hopefully calming the strands disturbed by Evie's fingers tugging at them while she came all over my face. The thought makes me brush my sleeve across my mouth just to be safe. "Nah, just beat from a rough week at practice."

"It's Tuesday," he says, clearly still suspicious.

"Yeah, well, you know how things are with the team right now." I force a laugh as I discreetly glance around the couch, my heart leaping into my throat when I see one of Evie's tiny white socks on the carpet by the coffee table.

I stretch, making a big show of flexing my fingers to hopefully distract Derrick as I cover the sock with my foot and drag it closer to the couch.

"Yeah, that's part of what I wanted to talk to you about." He settles into the leather couch across from the upholstered couch where just moments ago I was sucking his sister's nipples.

God, this was too close. Evie's right. We need a safer location.

Maybe the Bronx is a good idea after all. Or Connecticut. Or Outer Mongolia. Could we get there and back in a day?

"Okay," I say, forcing my thoughts back to the here and now. The sooner I talk through whatever's bothering Derrick, the sooner I can get him out of here. "What's on your mind?"

"Would it be cool to grab a beer?" he asks, nodding back toward the kitchen.

"Yeah, sure, grab me one, too," I say, cursing inwardly as he rises from the couch. Beer means at least twenty minutes until I can rescue Evie from her hiding place. But at least Derrick's back is turned long enough for me to tuck her sock between the cushions and assure myself the rest of the living room is all clear.

By the time Derrick settles back into his seat

and passes a Brooklyn brewery IPA across the coffee table, I'm feeling a little steadier. I can do this, and hopefully Derrick will assume any weirdness on my part is due to a combination of our recent fight and the fact that I allegedly just woke up from an exhaustion-induced nap.

"Senior management called me in for a talk today," he says, twisting the cap off his bottle. "They're already considering the team-building camp a wash."

"It's only been three days," I say, surprising myself. I don't feel all that hopeful about the camp solving our problems myself, but I hate to see other people giving up on us so quickly. "And we had the weekend in there breaking up the momentum. They have to give everyone time to find their footing."

Derrick takes a pull on his beer. "I agree, but they're at the end of their ropes, Ian. They knew starting a third NHL team in a city with two already established teams was a risk, but I don't think anyone thought the call would be coming from inside the house."

I grunt and drink deeply from my own bottle. "Yeah. It's pretty fucking disappointing. The first few years were so good and then..."

"And then things started going to shit," Derrick says with a defeated sight that isn't like him. He's a problem solver, the guy who always has a new tactic or alternate approach. "Maybe group therapy and art therapy were a bad idea. Maybe we should have just focused on running plays and docked anyone caught fighting even more of their pay than they're losing already."

"I don't know about that. I think Evie and Sandra are both doing a great job, but..." I shrug. "Maybe the damage runs too deep for some of these guys, both in their past and with their history with the team."

Derrick nods, studying the label on his beer for a beat before he adds in a softer voice, "Senior management agrees with you, but they aren't on the same page about what to do about it. Some of them want to push through a bunch of last-minute trades, giving up some of our better, more expensive players for a few promising drafts and hope a year out of the headlines for fighting will be worth the possible mediocre performance on the ice. But the others, especially those with partial ownership..." He brings his free hand to his face, rubbing at the tops of his eyes before he adds, "They're talking about selling the team, Ian. At a loss if they have to, just to get out from under it."

My throat goes so tight my beer has to fight its way down to my stomach. "What? You're kidding."

He shakes his head and takes another drink, his gaze still fixed on the coffee table. "They're fed up. A couple of them even think the team is cursed."

"That's ridiculous."

"Pro-sports people are superstitious, you know that. And season ticket sales are at an all-time low for this time of year." He picks at the top of the label, peeling it away from the glass. "Some of that could be the economy and how damned hot it's been lately—maybe no one's in the mood to think about hockey yet. But it could also be a sign that the people who loved to watch you guys fight it out on the ice are getting sick of the same old bullshit. That they're going back to their old hockey team or looking to another sport entirely for their loyalty fix. Fans are tribal, and once they've found another tribe, it's hard as hell to win them back."

I set my beer down and lean forward, my hands clasped together. "Should I set up a meeting with management? Try to talk it out? Convince them I can bring the team around by the end of the camp?"

"No, you can't," he says. "I'm not supposed to speak a word about this to anyone outside the inner circle. I could get in big trouble if they find out I leaked anything to you. But you're my best friend and you've worked so hard to help build this team. The Possums wouldn't be worth fighting for without you. I thought you should know where things stand so you can make the decision that's best for you. It might not be too late to switch things up, find something better. And my gut says they'd let you go without a fight. They respect you and your salary is one of the larger ones, so..."

I let out a long, weary breath, shocked by the misery flooding through me. I've already been considering what he's saying—I even set up a meeting with my agent for next Monday to discuss my options—but now that leaving New York is an even more likely possibility...

"I didn't realize how much I wanted to stay," I mutter.

Derrick's shoulders hunch closer to his ears. "Yeah, me either. I'm sorry about last Friday. I was out of line. I shouldn't have yelled at you or Evie like that. It was uncalled for."

I look up, guilt mixing with the misery pumping through my veins. "Don't worry about it. I know you were just trying to look out for her. But I would never hurt Evie or put her in danger. I care about her. A lot."

"I know you do," he says, "but that's the one thing I promised myself I would never fuck up, Ian. That I would always watch out for her and take up the slack for our shitty parents." He glances up, an uncertainty in his gaze that isn't like him. "But I don't know if I've pulled it off. She's still so..."

"So what?" I finally ask, torn between being there for Derrick and the knowledge that Evie could be hearing every word of this conversation.

Hopefully she's out of earshot, but I can't know that for sure.

"So young, so naïve," he says. "Childlike in a lot of ways. I don't know, maybe I did the wrong thing by protecting her the way I have. Sometimes I worry that if something happened to me, she wouldn't be okay and that's...scary."

"I don't think that's the case, Derrick," I say, my stomach going sour as I tread into even trickier territory. "As far as I can tell, she has her shit together better than most people in their early twenties. She was great with the team yesterday."

He tips his beer back, making a non-committal sound.

"And she kicked us both out of her apartment last Friday with a firm hand," I remind him. "I'd say she's doing just fine." I reach for my bottle, spinning it to the right, leaving a wet trail on the marble top. "It's the pair of us we need to worry about. What are your plans? If they do end up selling, I'm sure a management shake-up is inevitable."

"No clue." He drains the last of his beer and sets the empty down with a sharp click. "I have a couple of options, but I don't want to give up on the Ice Possums yet. Landing this job straight out of college and knowing I was going to get to work with my best friend...it was one of the best days of my life."

I nod, defeat slumping my own shoulders. "Yeah. Me, too. It was all our high school dreams coming true."

Derrick's lips curve into a crooked smile. "Except in the original dream, I was good enough to play for the NHL, too." He huffs. "High school me would never believe I'm actually happier in management."

"And your head would have exploded by now if you'd been forced to deal with all the bullshit on the ice the past few years. Or you would have been arrested for murder."

Derrick laughs. "Murder for sure. The first time Pete and Sven started hitting each other instead of the other team, I would have knocked their heads together and let them bleed out on the ice." He lets out a soft growl of frustration. "Where's their sense of loyalty? Players used to fight to stand up for our own. That's the world I want to live in. Not this free-for-all bullshit." He exhales another weary sigh and lifts his beer, frowning as he studies the empty bottle. "You want to grab another somewhere? I know you're not supposed to be drinking during camp, but…"

"Actually, I should jump in the shower and get to bed soon," I say. "Big day tomorrow. But I'll take a rain check. Maybe Saturday night?"

He nods. "Sure. I have to head to Jersey on Sunday for my dad's birthday, so I can't stay out all night like we used to, but a wild-ish Saturday sounds good. I'll touch base with you about a time later in the week. Maybe I'll have good news by then. I'm going to do everything I can to convince the higher-ups to give things a little more time."

"And I'll try to get the rest of the guys in line without saying anything I shouldn't. Hopefully it's not too late to save this team. I'd hate to see it go down like this."

"Me, too." He collects his empty and stands, but pauses before he heads to the kitchen, a frown wrinkling his forehead. "When did you start drawing in your spare time? That art bag looks just like Evie's."

"What?" My heart catapults back into my throat again as I lean forward, following his gaze to see Evie's black portfolio bag leaning against the side of the couch I'm currently seated on. "Oh, that." I stand, waving a dismissive hand. "I picked it up last weekend. Just thought I should practice a little, so I won't let Evie down with my stick figure portraits."

His frown deepens. "You know she doesn't care about that kind of stuff, right? When she's in therapy mode, it's about how drawing makes you feel, how it helps you process emotions, not what it looks like."

I take his bottle as I start toward the door, needing to get him out of here before he realizes that bag doesn't just look like Evie's, it actually *is* Evie's, and that his little sister is currently naked in my bedroom.

"Yeah, I know, I just wanted to give it my best effort," I say. "And sketching is kind of relaxing. I might keep it up after art therapy is over."

Derrick makes a surprised sound.

"What?" I ask. "Don't see me as the artsy type?"

"No, I don't," he says with a laugh as we stop in front of the door. "But people can surprise you. I've been reminded of that a lot lately." He reaches for the door, but hesitates with his hand on the knob, making me pray Evie's intending to wait for me to fetch her before she emerges from my bedroom. "What do you think about an age gap? Between you and the women you date? Is eight years too much? It feels like a long time to me, but...maybe it's not anymore, now that we're in our thirties."

I clear my throat and will an innocent expression onto my face. "Yeah, I think that's fine. Eight years is mid-twenties, and I'm pretty sure our moms were married and had us by then."

Derrick's expression sours. "My mom isn't a great example of successful adulting, but that's a good point. Something to think about." He claps me on the shoulder. "Thanks for the talk. And sorry to show up out of the blue. The train got held up in the station right by your stop and it felt like a sign."

"No worries," I say, opening the door. "Catch you later, man."

"Later," he says, and finally steps out into the hall.

I wait until I hear the elevator ding outside and Derrick is presumably on his way down to the ground floor, before I spin back to the kitchen. I drop the beers beside the sink before I call out, "All clear!"

Almost instantly, Evie—now, *sadly*, fully dressed—explodes from my room. "That was way too close," she says, bustling out to grab her portfolio bag. She holds it up to me, revealing the giant "E" painted on the other side. "If it had been turned the other way, we would have been toast. We're playing with fire meeting up here."

"Agreed," I say, moving around the island to meet her as she shrugs on her backpack. "I'll definitely book a hotel for Friday night."

She exhales. "Are you sure you still want to do this? I mean...what with everything going on with the team?" Her expression softens with sympathy. "I heard what Derrick said. Everything he said. I'm so sorry."

"Yeah, it's...not great." I rub at the tight muscles at the back of my neck. "But I'm not giving up yet. And hell yes, I still want to meet up on Friday. It'll give me something to look forward to."

Evie nibbles her bottom lip. "Yeah. Me, too. I um..." Her cheeks flush as she nods over her shoulder toward the couch and the carpet on the other side. "I had a nice time tonight."

I grin. "Me, too. You are...so sexy."

"You, too," she says, her shy smile widening. "Next time, I promise I'll return the favor."

"You don't have to. I enjoy making you feel good."

"I know I don't have to," she says. "I *want* to. It makes me feel...powerful. Knowing I'm driving you crazy."

"You certainly do that," I say, my cock thickening again as she stops in front of me, tipping her head back for a kiss. "Are you sure you can't stay a little longer?"

"I'd be too stressed about Derrick coming back," she says, humming against my mouth as I kiss her soft and sweet. "But Friday, I'm all yours."

"Sounds good."

"It does and I mean it, Ian," she says softly, resting her hand on my chest. "I want to be all yours. I'm ready if you are. I think we should take care of this V-Card."

"All right. Then that's what we'll do," I say, the thought of being Evie's first filling me with a mix of anticipation and an odd, unsettled feeling that has me so distracted she's been gone nearly ten minutes by the time I remember the sock I tucked under the cushion.

I fish it out and sit staring at it for way too long, wondering if it's a bad sign that I kind of want to keep it. Even her socks are...weirdly adorable.

"Trouble," I mutter to myself. "You're headed for trouble."

But am I going to change course?

Hell, no.

CHAPTER 21

Evie

*W*ednesday's art therapy goes even better than Monday's, but I overhear the gossip as the players work on their "found family trees"—a tree filled with people they trust to be there for them, whether they're blood relatives or not.

Seems the two Svens got into it not once, but twice, during practice and Pete broke his stick in a fit of rage after the assistant coach called him out for repeatedly making dangerous passes through center ice.

This is pretty much business-as-usual for the Possums at this point, but I can feel how heavily the continued conflict is weighing on Ian. He's the only one who knows how high the stakes are for the team and how much they all stand to lose if they can't find a way to work together.

We leave separately after the session—the better not to be seen together by my brother—but

I can't resist shooting him a text when I get home —*Sorry today was another rough one. I'm rooting for you and the team. Let me know if there's anything I can do to help.*

Just a few seconds later, he texts back—*Thanks, Feisty. Just keep being you. You're helping those guys, whether they realize it or not. You've got a gift for this stuff. You picked the right career. No doubt.*

Warmth spreads through me, making me grin as I type—*Thanks. That means a lot from a guy who was pretty eye-rolly about art therapy at first.*

He shoots over an embarrassed emoji and—*I'm not nearly as smart as I think I am sometimes. My pep talk in the locker room this morning proved that. I'm not sure anything I say will get through to them at this point, not even if I could spill the beans about how much danger we're really in. But I'll keep trying.*

That's all you can do, I assure him, *hang in there. I'm sending good vibes your way and studying up on how to give a quality blow job for Friday.*

He sends a gif of a balding man in saggy under-wear doing a victory dance in a greeting card aisle that makes me laugh out loud.

"Show me," Jess says from the kitchen table behind me. "I need funny to get me through this code cleanup without attempting to drown myself in the toilet."

I shift to shoot her a sympathetic look over the back of the couch. "Another rough day with the new team?"

"They're either imbeciles or fucking up on purpose to make me look bad and take my shiny new boss job," she says with remarkable calm. "I'm not sure which yet, but I'll let you know when I do."

"Poor thing. Do you need cookies? I hid some so Harlow couldn't eat them all."

Jess's eyes light up, but she doesn't look up from her screen. "Oh, yes, please. Even though I read an article about sugar causing nerve damage last night while I was insomnia scrolling that was pretty disturbing."

"No good comes from insomnia scrolling or reading articles about sugar." I head into the kitchen, fetching the stepladder from beside the fridge so I can reach the back of the cabinet above the microwave.

"And what about withholding funny texts from one of your best friends?" Jess tosses casually over her shoulder. "Any good come from that?"

"It was nothing," I say, collecting the small Tupperware container from under the pile of empty coffee bags we're collecting to earn a free sock cap. "Just a goofy thing. Not worth sharing."

She hums thoughtfully. "Right. And I wasn't secretly hoping to be teacher's pet and get Ian's monster cock to sledgehammer through *my* V-Card."

I tumble off the stepladder in surprise, sending the cookies flying as I reach out to catch myself on the lower cabinets before I crush my tailbone on the tile.

"You okay?" Jess calls out.

"I'm fine," I say, my heart still racing.

"And the cookies?"

I glance over to see the Tupperware container still closed though it *has* rolled halfway into Cam's giant tennis shoe. "Also fine, but what are you... How did you..."

"Nothing gets past me," Jess says. "You should know that by now. I appear to see nothing, but I see all. Like the Eye of Sauron. And no, I haven't told Cameron or Harlow and I'm not too disappointed. Ian would have been a means to an end for me. I mean, I like the guy and he's undeniably hot, but he's not my type. Too interested in sweating and sports and being outdoors. But you two...well, it could be something special, I think."

"I—no," I sputter as I collect the cookies. "We're just friends. With benefits. Some benefits. Not all of them."

"No sledgehammering yet?"

"No," I say, dropping the open cookie container beside her swiftly tapping fingers. "And how did you know he has a...you know."

"Giant penile protrusion?" She chuckles as she reaches for a cookie without slowing the tip-tapping of her other hand. "Sweatpant shots, my dear. They're all over the internet. Apparently, there's a group of women who lie in wait outside his gym in Midtown in the colder months to catch The Fox in his most tempting ensembles."

"Sweatpants. Huh...who knew?" I mutter, snatching a cookie before Jess can reach for another one.

"Everyone, my dear," she says, chewing. "Even

I knew sweatpants were a thing. Gray ones, in particular. Probably because they're a lighter color and it's easier to see the protrusion that way than with say...black or navy."

"You don't call it a protrusion for real, do you?"

"Why?" she asks, grabbing another cookie. "Is that weird? I thought guys would find that sexy."

I nudge her shoulder with my hip. "You're fucking with me."

"I am," she says with a happy sigh. "I'm sorry. I shouldn't tease you after you were sweet enough to share your cookie stash."

"It's okay, I don't mind," I say, perching on the seat beside her. "But back to the other stuff. I'm so glad you guessed what's going on because I could really use some advice."

"You do remember that I'm a virgin, too, right? And I'm pretty sure I'm even less experienced than you are. I've never been to third base with anyone but myself. Though I *am* pretty great in bed. Just FYI."

"I bet," I say with a laugh. "But not that kind of advice. Feelings advice." I study my cookie, trying to find the bite with the most chocolate chips. "We're supposed to meet up on Friday for the sledgehammering but Ian's under so much stress right now. I can't go into details, but things are really rough for him at work. I'm wondering if maybe we should put the first-time stuff on hold until that's resolved. Maybe that's just too much drama on top of all the drama he's dealing with already."

I realize the tapping has stopped and look up to find Jess starting at me with a dubious expression. "What?" I ask, pulling my cookie closer to my chest. "I'm looking for the bite with the most chocolate. I like to save it for last."

"Not that," she says. "You're doing it again—putting everyone else's needs before your own and finding excuses not to go after what you want."

"I don't do that," I say, chomping one buttery edge before I mumble around the bite of cookie, "At least not with friends. Just new school acquaintances and clients because I want to make friends at school and clients need extra patience and understanding. That's like...my job."

"Then why do I get three cookies and you only have one?" she asks. "And I know you let Harlow have at least seven before you hid the rest."

"She's on her period," I mumble. "She needs chocolate more than I do."

Jess's expression softens. "Your sweetness is sweet and always has been, but there comes a time when you need to put yourself first and let other people worry about setting their own boundaries. If Ian's not feeling up to punching your V-Card on Friday, I'm sure he'll let you know. He's a grown man." She arches a brow. "But he's also *a man,* and from what I can tell, they really enjoy putting their protrusions in other people. Aside from myself, of course."

I squeeze her knee. "Stop it. You're gorgeous and sexy and fun and you're going to find a guy who sees all that. You just may have to look a little harder to find one who gets your sense of humor."

"Because I'm weird."

"Because you're unique," I say. "And brilliant and one of a kind. So...you're going to need a guy who's as special as you are. Like Sam. You remember Sam? From high school? He always reminded me of you. I mean, not physically since he's a massive Sasquatch person, but your spirits vibrated on the same wavelength, I think."

Jess laughs. "That's so funny you say that. Sam and I made a bargain at coding camp junior year that if we hadn't lost our virginity by the time we were twenty-four, we'd meet up and help each other 'solve the problem.' All the other campers were banging like bunnies after lights out and we were the only ones without a boinking partner."

I narrow my eyes, nodding as I consider this revelation. "Interesting. You do realize twenty-four is only a year away."

"Nine months, actually," she says. "I'm a June baby, remember?"

"That's right." I grin. "Huh. So...maybe you should slip into Sam's DMs and see what's up."

She snorts. "No way in hell. And even if I wanted to mortify myself by bringing up a bargain from when I was seventeen, I have no idea where Sam is. He dropped off social media after high school and never popped back up again. He's probably working for the CIA as a code cracker or something and has to stay deep undercover."

"Or he just realized he feels happier spending

his time doing real life stuff." I pop my perfect last bite between my lips with a happy sigh. "Mmm, so good. The chocolate is caressing all my best taste buds."

"Speaking of caressing," Jess says. "Do you need birth control for Friday? I have boy condoms, girl condoms, three different kinds of spermicidal lube, and a couple of morning-after pills I've stockpiled, just in case."

My eyes go wide. "I'm still on the pill for cramps, and I'm sure Ian will bring condoms, but thanks. Also, should I be worried about you? That's a lot of precautions."

"Don't ever assume a guy will bring condoms," she says firmly. "They don't get pregnant; we do. I'll give you some of mine. That way you're totally prepared."

"Okay, but—"

"And I'm fine." She drops the last of her third cookie into her mouth, chews, and swallows before she says, "The women in my family are just really fertile. And my mother will murder me with a rusty chopstick if I get pregnant before I'm married, thirty-five, and hopefully a billionaire."

I wince. "That Tiger Mom thing is for real, huh?"

She snorts. "Oh my God. So real. So very, very real."

"But your mom always seems so sweet."

"She is sweet, but she has high expectations, and I don't want to find out what happens if I don't meet them."

"She'll still love you, is what will happen," I say gently. "Because you're a wonderful daughter and person and you deserve love and support from your family even if you aren't perfect all the time."

She wrinkles her nose. "Gross. Way too many feelings and hard conversations down that road. I'll just stick to meeting expectations and hiding the things I don't want her to find out about. But you're good at the therapy stuff. If I were your student, I would feel very supported right now, and reveal my squishy inner world to you with a drawing of a wet cat drowning in noodles or something."

My lips hook up on one side. "Ian said the same thing. Without the cat part, but..."

"See, I told you. This could be more than a hookup for you two," Jess says, a smile in her voice as she turns back to her computer. "Now I have to focus. The sugar rush has activated my genius centers and I'm pretty sure I see how to fix Dick-head's screwup. And I'm also positive he did this on purpose, the little shit. I'm going to have a long talk with him tomorrow."

"Should you ask for a meeting with HR and chat there, maybe?" I ask, concerned for her. "If this guy is sabotaging your project, that's a big deal. He should, at the very least, have that added to his record."

She shakes her head. "No. I don't want it to seem like I can't control my team. There are already enough stereotypes about Asian women being timid and submissive. I need to show the powers that be that I can handle these guys. And if a hard talk doesn't do the trick, I'm tracking all my work. I can go to HR and show them exactly what's up at a later date if necessary."

"You're smart," I say. "But I'm sorry that you have to worry about stereotypes instead of just doing your work."

"All part of the fun of being a lady in a male-dominated profession," she says. "But it's okay. I love my job, and no one can take that from me, no matter how hard they try."

"Same." My heart fills with a warm, proud feeling. "We've come a long way from the little girls who were always picked last in gym class."

Jess grins as she whispers, "Yeah, we have. I want you to have so much fun Friday. You deserve a sexy, romantic first time with a gorgeous guy who adores you. And don't say he doesn't adore you because he so does. It's written all over his face every time he looks at you. He's smitten."

"I would stay here and explain again that Ian and I are just friends," I say, "but somebody I know said they had to work."

"I do. But I'm also right. We've been over this. I see all and I—"

"Right, Sauron." I pat her shoulder as I hop to my feet. "Good luck with your work. I'm going to go write a paper about the beneficial effects of play for the adult brain."

Jess looks up, blinking as if she's emerging from a fog. "Oh, that reminds me, I won't be able to make it to sex tutoring tomorrow night. We have a mandatory work team-building thing. We're going to a trampoline park."

"That sounds like fun."

"If you enjoy having your internal organs rearranged, I guess." She shrugs. "Can you let Ian know?"

"I won't be here tomorrow night, either," Cameron says, poking his head out of his room, making us both jump and cry out in surprise. He grins and rubs his puffy eyes. "Sorry. Didn't mean to scare you."

"I thought you were at work," Jess says.

"Nope, I'm off today, so I decided to load up on naps. Just woke up a few minutes ago." He runs a hand through his sleep-mussed hair. "Did I miss any good gossip? You two have your gossip faces on."

"Not really," Jess says, proving she's still the same trustworthy vault she's been since we were in middle school. "Just work drama, but I'm on top of it." She glances back to me, pushing her glasses up her nose. "So, I guess we should tell Ian not to bother coming over tomorrow night?"

"Or give up on Sex Class altogether," Cam says, with a yawn. "I hate to be Danny Downer, but I don't think Ian is going to be able to help us. His experience is skewed by being a hot, famous professional athlete. Our dating lives aren't really comparable, if you know what I mean."

"You're hot, Cam," I say, arching a brow as he yawns again, showcasing his tonsils. "When you remember to cover your mouth when you yawn, of course."

He chuckles. "Sorry."

"And you can cook," Jess says. "I know tons of girls who would date you for the gourmet meals alone. You just need to find a woman who's food motivated and likes nice guys."

"Or I could embrace my dark side," he says with a sleepy grin that makes his dimples pop.

Jess and I both laugh.

"Hey, I have a dark side," he says, glancing down at his pajama pants with the sleeping cats on them. "Though I can see your point. I'd need a wardrobe change."

"And a personality transplant," I say. "You're a sweetheart, Cam. And that's one of the best things about you. You shouldn't change that to pull tail, especially if you want the tail to stick around long term. You want to find someone who's smart enough to adore you just the way you are."

Cam sighs. "That's the dream, anyway. Thanks, Evie." He glances back and forth between us. "What do we think? Should we tell Ian we'll find our way on our own? I vote yes."

"I think so, too," Jess says, turning back to her screen. "He means well, but you're right, he's not on our wavelength. Will you text him for us, Evie? Tell him it's not him, it's us, or whatever gentle breakup thing you should say to your amateur sex therapist."

"Yeah, I will," I say, backing toward my room.

"But is that okay with you, Evie?" Cam asks. "I

mean, you get a vote, too, and I think it should be unanimous. Otherwise, I'm happy to resume class next week or whatever."

"I agree with you guys," I say. "I think this is a journey we each have to make on our own."

But once I'm tucked away in my room, I don't text Ian right away. Instead, I sit staring at our text thread, wondering if I should cancel *our* meeting, as well, and not for the reasons I gave Jess. If I'm honest, it's not worry about all the stressful things on Ian's plate that's tempting me to cancel; it's the way I felt last night.

Like I never wanted our co-ed naked play time to end.

Like I would be perfectly happy if I died right there on the floor of his apartment, as long as I got to come again on his wickedly talented mouth first.

Like I wanted to stay and sleep in his big, cozy-looking bed with him, wake up with his arms around me, and share our plans for the day over breakfast. I want to be with him, enjoy him, support him, and not just as a friend.

"Looks like you're as bad at casual as you are at trying to start something serious," I mutter to myself, while my gut quietly, but insistently warns that this longing I'm feeling will only get worse if Ian and I seal the deal Friday night.

But when I craft my final text, all I say is—*Sex Class is off for Thursday and on pause for the indefinite future. Jess and Cam are busy tomorrow, and we all agree this may be the kind of thing we'll have to figure out on our own. Even if it's hard. But we all appreciate your offer and all the work you did for us.*

Bubbles fill the screen and then—*I get it. I've been having fun with my research but you're probably right. There are too many variables at play. And if teaching people to find a great sex partner or true love were easy, someone smarter than I am would have figured it out by now.*

I sigh and reply—*I think you're very smart, but yeah...relationships are hard.*

He shoots back a smiley face emoji and—*But at least we're easy. Looking forward to Friday with you. And not just because kissing you is fun. I really enjoy your company, Feisty.*

Throat going tight, I text—*You, too. Off to tackle homework, sleep well!*

I add a gif of a cartoon kitten covering another cartoon kitten with a blanket that's cute and playful, but I don't feel either of those things.

I feel...torn. Worried.

And excited, so excited I'm going to be at our meeting place on Friday with bells on, no matter how dangerous my feelings for Ian are becoming.

CHAPTER 22

Ian

Friday morning practice starts off strong. We're actually running new plays without anyone bitching and moaning about it, and Sven the Dick is clearly hungover, despite the ban on drinking during the week, and doesn't have the energy to cause his usual level of trouble.

I feel hopeful that we might be turning a corner as a team until we settle in for our eleven a.m. group therapy session and Braxton, of all people, has a meltdown, tells Sandra, our therapist, to "respectfully, fuck off," and storms out of the room.

Braxton is one of the few guys I can usually count on to be a team player and put the game first. If he's getting sucked into the drama, I'm not sure how much hope there is for the Ice Possums in their current incarnation.

And maybe that's okay.

Maybe this is what we deserve.

Thousands of players would kill for a chance to be part of an NHL team. If these guys are too angry and childish to realize how lucky they are, then maybe they're going to reap what they've sown and be out of a job sooner than some of them expect.

But as one of the few players who have been with the Possums since the beginning, I've proven that I can be part of a functional team. Those first few years, we were good. Not great, but we had promise. But I can't bring that promise to fruition on my own. I'm just one man and maybe it's time to admit that I can't solve this problem, no matter how much I want to.

It's like with Evie and her friends. You can only take another person so far, no matter how pure your intentions.

But at least Cam, Evie, and Jess were invested in giving my suggestions a shot. These men stopped listening to me a long time ago and you can't help people who refuse to help themselves.

After another shitty afternoon practice, I text my agent—*Looking forward to our Monday meeting. I'm about ready to admit defeat and get out before it's too late.*

Fred texts back almost immediately—*So happy to hear that, buddy. You have no idea. Want to swing by my office now? I have an opening at four and some very exciting news to share with you.*

I can't, I shoot back, not even stopping to consider it, *I have plans this afternoon, but I'll be there with bells on come Monday.*

All right, he replies, *but be ready to pull the trigger by then, okay? We're running out of time to make a deal before the preseason starts. And I'm not sure how long the interested parties will stay interested. And yes, I did say parties. Plural. The Badgers aren't the only ones looking for an experienced defender with a great rep. You've got options, good ones, and I, for one, can't wait to see you finally get the kind of respect and support from a team that you deserve.*

Stomach churning, I assure him I'll be ready to decide by Monday and tuck my phone back into my bag before I head into art therapy, where the guys are once again on their best behavior.

Watching them happily collect collage supplies from Evie and chat freely about their various phobias—apparently exploring fear is the topic for today—you'd never guess they're incapable of acting like grown-ups for more than a day or two at a time.

Maybe if Evie were our coach, she'd be able to get through to them on the ice, too. But she isn't. And I'm tired. So tired.

Tired of looking on the bright side, tired of hoping for the best, tired of pretending that things are going to be better tomorrow. My optimistic nature has always served me well in the past, but there's a difference between being optimistic and straight-up crazy. Repeating the same behavior and expecting different results is the definition of insanity.

"How about you, Ian? Any phobias?" Evie asks as I approach her desk to collect my packet of materials from the cutest teacher I've ever had, and one I'm not eager to leave behind.

If Fred works out a trade, I could be gone by early next week. Once these things are set in motion, they move fast. This could be one of my last classes with Evie and tonight...

Well, tonight might be the only night we ever have.

Which...sucks.

"You don't have to share if you don't want to," she adds in a softer voice, clearly misunderstanding the reason for my slumping shoulders. "And you don't have to share this project, either. Sharing is optional today."

"Thanks." I force a smile as I accept the manilla envelope. "But I don't mind sharing. I've always had a thing with heights. Not a fan."

"Then you should probably get off your high horse," Sven the Dick mutters from behind me.

I turn, my temper flaring—fast and hot, like a pile of dry leaves hit with a blowtorch. "Shut the fuck up, Sven. Now. If I hear another fucking word out of your mouth today, you're going to regret it."

His eyes widen, but he doesn't look intimidated.

He looks...pleased, like he's finally gotten what he's wanted from me for so long. "Oh, yeah? What are you going to do to me, Boy Scout? Report me to management? Because I'm pretty sure they already know I'm twice the player you'll ever be. That's why I'm still here. Even though you've been trying to get rid of me since the day I was drafted."

"I have no idea what you're talking about," I seethe, my jaw so tight my molars are grinding together. "And as far as I can tell, the only thing you're good at is throwing tantrums like a fucking two-year-old."

Pete laughs. "Nah, my nephew has more self-control than Sven."

"You have no room to talk," I say, my voice rising as I spin to glare a hole in Pete's five-inch forehead. "You act like a toddler, too. Half the players in this room do, and it's ridiculous. Where's your pride in yourself? In the game? Do you know how many men out there would kill for your job?"

"And how many would kill for yours," Sven shoots back, surging to his feet, pointing his scissors at me across the table. "We're a fucking incredible team, but instead of being grateful for our talent and every kick-ass comeback we made last year, you bitched and moaned about sportsmanship and how things look in the press. You're a pussy team captain, Boy Scout. A whiny pussy. That's why this team is failing. It's not us, it's you, you condescending son of a bitch."

For a moment, I think I'm going to hit him. I want to so badly I can almost feel the explosion of pain across my knuckles as my fist connects with his face.

But then I feel Evie's hand on my elbow and

the rage melts away so fast it leaves my skin ten degrees colder.

"I can't do this anymore," I say, turning to drop the packet back on Evie's desk. "I'm sorry."

"Ian, please," she says as I start toward the door. "Stay and let's talk this out. We might be able to make some progress if—"

I don't know if she stops talking or if I'm just out of earshot, but by the time I reach the end of the hallway, I can't hear anything but the blood rushing in my ears and the resigned voice in my head saying this is it.

This is the last time I'll ever push through the double doors leading out onto the street as the captain of the Ice Possums.

CHAPTER 23

Evie

*A*s soon as Ian's gone, the room explodes in deep, angry shouts.

Most of the players seem to be on Ian's side, but the ones who aren't are louder and meaner.

I try to reestablish order, but tempers are running way too hot. I'm starting to worry they might actually start punching each other when an even louder voice booms, "That's it. Get out. All of you."

I glance over to see Derrick standing by the door, circling a frustrated arm. "Get out," he says again, his voice rough and raw sounding in the sudden silence. "Get the fuck out. Go home. And know everything that's waiting for you on Monday morning is exactly what you deserve. Including the pay you'll be docked for missing art therapy this afternoon."

"I'm not missing shit," Pete shouts, the veins standing out on his neck. "I'm right here."

Derrick shoots him a look that could drop a charging rhinoceros in its tracks and whispers, "Out. Now. If you make me tell you again, you aren't going to like the consequences."

"Come on," Laser says, putting the cap back on his glue stick and standing with a firm glance around the room. "He's right. We've proven we can't have nice things. Whatever happens now is on us." He turns to me, what sounds like genuine regret in his tone as he adds, "Sorry, teach. You did a good job. Thanks for trying your best. And for that thing with the fire. It really helped a lot of us. Even if we won't all admit it."

A few of the other players mumble their agreement and even Sassy Sven—whose nickname is officially being changed to Shithead after this class—keeps his mouth shut. One by one, they gather their bags and leave the room, slinking past or stuttering apologies to Derrick on their way out, depending on where they are in their personal "taking responsibility for my actions" journey.

When they're gone, I sag back into my chair, ready for Derrick to tell me how disappointed he is in me for being too weak to retain control over my class.

But he surprises me. "You've done a great job, Evie, but these guys are just..." He shakes his head. "They don't deserve you. Consider your contract fulfilled here. We won't need you next week. Management has decided to take the camp in another direction."

I sigh. "I'm sorry to hear that. Sorry but not really surprised."

"But they're going to write you a glowing recommendation for your work so far," he adds as he wanders over to pick up another abandoned glue stick and pops the top back on. "And Gina in publicity wants to connect you with a friend of hers who works with at-risk youth in Soho. They're looking to add art therapy to their calendar once a week and she thinks you'd be a great fit. If you're interested."

"I'm very interested," I say, torn between excitement at the chance to work with teens—my preferred demographic—and worry for Ian and the rest of the team. "But I'm also sad. I know Sven is an ass and Pete can be a lot sometimes, but some of the guys just need therapy and support. And they've needed it for a while. Some have been through a lot of intense stuff, Derrick."

"I know," he says, surprising me again. "But we're running a professional sports team, not a rehab center or an anger-management program. And we need to prove this team isn't cursed before things get even worse than they are already." He clears his throat and nods toward the tables. "Want me to help you clean up in here?"

"No, I'll get it," I say, "but I do have a favor to ask, if you don't mind."

"Shoot."

"Could you send out an email with my contact information, letting the guys know I'm happy to continue working with them off the clock if they'd like? I think Laser, especially, was finding art therapy really helpful. I'd like to keep that going for him if he's interested." My lips curve. "And he's a really great artist. I actually enjoy his pieces."

"You don't have to do that, Evie," he says softly. "You don't have to go out of your way for people who don't appreciate you. And I don't just mean the team. I've been thinking and maybe we should skip the birthday visit to Dad's on Sunday. I'll still send him our gift and a card but...maybe that's enough."

My brows shoot up my forehead. "But he's our dad, Derrick. Flawed or not, he's the only family we have left."

"Not true. We have each other. And you have Cam and Jess and Harlow. And I have Ian. We both have people who really care about us, even though they don't have to. Maybe that's enough. More than enough."

I pull in a deep breath and let it out, but the tight, fearful sensation locked around my ribs remains. "Can I think about it? And give you a decision tomorrow?"

"Yeah, of course. Sure thing." He exhales as he nods toward the door. "I should get back to my office. A lot of work to do to revamp our entire camp plan before Monday morning."

"I bet," I say, adding as he turns to go, "And, Derrick?"

He glances back. "Yeah?"

"Thanks for asking me about Dad. Being asked

feels a lot nicer than being told what we're going to do. You know?"

His mouth tightens and his chin dips closer to his chest. "Yeah. I bet. I've um...been talking to someone. A professional someone."

Thank God I haven't stood up yet or I would have fallen over in shock. Derrick has been militantly anti-therapy since we were kids and my school counselor pressured Dad into family therapy for a few months not long after Mom left.

I try to conceal my surprise as I say, "Oh really?" but I must do a lousy job.

Derrick laughs and rolls his eyes. "Yeah. I know. Not my usual, but it's been good so far. I always thought I was protecting you by being a hard-ass, bossy big brother, but... I was really trying to protect myself from losing another person I cared about. Guess Mom leaving and Dad being Dad fucked me up more than I wanted to admit."

"It's okay. Sometimes it takes time and distance to realize how our family of origin shaped us."

He sighs. "It didn't for you. You've been deep into the therapy stuff since the day you left that house."

I shrug. "Well, I was gifted with exceptional emotional intelligence, so..."

He grins, proving a joke was the right choice. He's in the early stages of his journey of self-discovery. There will be time for more in-depth discussion about everything he's working through later.

And I guess I need to do some more work, too, I realize after Derrick heads back to his office and I'm left alone to tidy up the art room for the last time.

I know my relationship with my dad isn't healthy. I've known that for a long time. Until very recently, my relationship with Derrick wasn't super healthy, either. But the thought of leaving both Dad and Derrick in my past was too much of a blow.

Human beings are wired for connection, for family, for tribe. And yes, I have three amazing friends I can count on, but no matter how much I love them, Harlow will never be a father figure and Cameron is my buddy, not my brother. So even though cutting ties with people who've treated me like an inconvenience (Dad) or a problem to be managed (Derrick) might have been the emotionally healthy thing to do, I've never let myself seriously consider that option. I've always assumed I would establish a healthier, grown-up relationship with both of them. Someday.

Meanwhile, the years ticked by, and nothing changed until now.

Why is that?

Is it because I finally laid down the law with Derrick last week?

Because I stood my ground with the team and insisted on their participation?

Because I stepped *way* outside my comfort

zone by propositioning a man who, if I'm honest with myself, is completely out of my league?

Or is it all—or maybe none—of the above?

Maybe Derrick would have come to this place no matter what, but I can't help but feel like I'm in the middle of something big, a major transition I couldn't stop now if I tried.

No, that's not true. I could stop it. But I don't want to. I have to find out what this brave, bolder me is going to do next. I need to see what she draws, learn how she connects with her new clients at the teen center, and discover what it feels like to fall asleep in Ian's arms, even if it's just for one night.

Even if it breaks my heart.

With that in mind, I pull my cell from my bag and shoot Ian a text.

CHAPTER 24

Ian

*T*he text from Evie comes through just as I'm finishing up at the car rental in Midtown.

Want me to bring your packet with me? We could work on collages together later tonight. I'm no expert, obviously, but I don't think people can have sex for twelve hours straight. But please correct me if I'm wrong, and I will pack cold compresses for my nether regions.

My lips twitch.

It isn't a smile, but for the first time since I left the stadium, I can stretch my neck to one side without my jaw cracking. It's a start. And it's because of Evie. In just a few days, she's become one of my favorite people.

I guess she always has been, but now she's more than a surrogate little sister. She's my friend, part of my support system, and increasingly the first thing on my mind when I wake up in the morning.

And I'm going to betray her.

Tonight.

We only agreed to two weeks of "friends with benefits," and I won't be skipping town much earlier. But if I'm honest with myself, I haven't been thinking short term about this thing with Evie, not since our hangman session. Being with her is so easy, so natural, so right in a way being with Whitney never was, not even when we were in the golden days of our relationship.

Evie just gets me. And I get her. She likes me for who I am, not how many goals I score or how much money I make, and I feel the same way about her. She could become a world-famous artist or spend the rest of her life sketching things people refuse to hang in their guest bathroom and what I feel for her wouldn't change. I would still respect her integrity, her creativity, and her innate goodness.

If things were different, if I wasn't about to leave town, maybe we could have found a way to break the news to Derrick that didn't end in disaster and seen if we could make it as a couple.

But I am leaving. And I can't keep that from her. No matter what promises I made to Derrick, I have to be honest with Evie. I have to tell her the truth, and if she decides she'd rather not keep our date tonight, then I'll go to the hotel alone... even though I did spring for the suite with the mountain view with her in mind.

We should talk before we head out, I text back, my stomach balling into a stress knot. *There are things*

*you should know. About me and how much time I have
left in New York.*

My phone rings, making me jump and earning
me a dirty look from the woman behind the
counter as she pushes my paperwork closer and
points to the elevator. "P3. Choose any car from
row five."

"Thanks," I say before taking the call, "Hello?"

"Hey, it's me," Evie says, sounding breathless.

"Yeah, I know," I say, smiling again as I start
toward the elevator. "Your name popped up when
you called."

"Right. Duh. Sorry. I'm a little frazzled," she
says, her breath still coming faster. "I'm running
up to grab my suitcase before Harlow gets home
so I don't have to answer any questions about
where I'm going until we get back. But I still want
to go with you tonight, okay? No matter what.
Even if you do end up moving to another team."

I blink. "How did you know?"

"The writing's on the wall, Ian," she says gently,
"and I'm not stupid. And you aren't either. You're
going to come to the decision that's best for you as
a person and a player, no doubt in my mind. But I
bet you could use a friend right now, to help you
talk through your options. And it just so happens
I'm an excellent sounding board."

"You are," I agree, touched. "And that sounds
great. Thanks, Evie."

"My pleasure," she says, before adding in a
softer, but still breathy voice, "And it *will* be my
pleasure, buddy. You're not getting out of that part

so easily. If you don't want your bones jumped, you're going to have to come up with a compelling argument against sexy times."

The elevator dings. "Noted. I'll be at the rendezvous point in twenty minutes. Be ready to roll."

"I was born ready," she says with a giggle that's nearly as cute as she is. "Okay, that's totally not true, I was born overly cautious and odd but I'm ready now. And so are you. Whatever life has lined up next, we're going to crush it."

"We are," I say, emotion making my throat tight as I add, "Elevator's here. I'm on my way. See you soon."

I end the call and step into the elevator, my usual optimism rising inside of me again.

Evie's right. We're both ready for whatever comes next.

I just wish we wouldn't be crushing our future goals on opposite sides of the country while leading separate lives.

CHAPTER 25

Evie

I'm early to our rendezvous point on Avenue B, but Ian is already waiting for me, leaning against a snazzy silver convertible wedged between a delivery van and an ancient Oldsmobile covered with parking tickets.

I pause, my brows lifting. "Wow."

"I told you I was renting a car."

"A car," I say, laughing as I wander closer, "not a down payment on a house. How much does this cost in real life? Like…a hundred grand?"

"About a hundred and fifty," he says, nodding toward the duffle bag on my arm. "May I take your luggage, miss?"

"Yikes," I say, anxiety making my pulse race as he takes my bag and tucks it into the back seat. "What if we wreck it?"

"We're not going to wreck it," he says, seeming remarkably relaxed considering his life is about to be turned upside down. "But if we do, it's covered under my insurance."

I exhale. "Oh, good. That will make it easier to enjoy, though I confess I struggle with fancy things. I still refuse to eat off the china Harlow inherited from her grandmother. I get so stressed worrying that I'm going to break it that I can't enjoy the meal."

He wraps his arms around my waist, drawing me against him, sending a warm rush of gratitude and excitement zipping across my skin. It just feels so good to be close to him—energizing and comforting at the same time.

"It's probably a good thing you're leaving," I say with a wobbly smile. "Before I get hooked on your hugs." I clear my throat and force an upbeat tone. "So, when do you leave? And where are you going?"

"Not sure on the where yet," he says. "My agent and I are going to hash it out on Monday. But if I make a decision quickly...I could be out of here as early as Tuesday or Wednesday."

My eyes bulge and my heart shrivels. "What? That fast?"

His brow furrows but his eyes never leave mine. "Yeah. We're already so close to the preseason. My new team will want me in practice ASAP."

I nod and swallow past the lump forming in my throat. "Right. That makes sense."

"And if that changes your mind about tonight, I

get it," he says. "I already know I'm going to want a hell of a lot more than one night with you, but...that might be all we get. There's a good chance I'll end up in Oregon or somewhere else on the West Coast."

I hitch my chin up, pushing aside the misery inspired by the thought of Ian thousands of miles and a long-ass plane ride away from me. I'm not going to ruin the present by stressing out about the future. I'm going to treasure every minute with Ian, burn every memory into my brain, and make the most of the time we have left.

"All right," I whisper, "then we'd better make tonight a good night."

His eyes narrow. "Are you sure?"

I smile. "Yes. There are millions of women in the world who will never know what it's like to be with a sweet, sexy man who makes them feel like the hottest girl in the city. I'm not going to let them down by skipping out on my chance for one amazing night just because I can't have more."

"You're going to bang me for the sex-starved women in Saudi Arabia?" he asks, his lips twitching.

"Yes. And Idaho and Orlando and Southern California. We have sex-starved women right here at home, Ian," I say as I wrap my arms around his neck.

He bends his head closer to mine. "Sorry. My mistake. Thanks for setting me straight."

"Anytime," I murmur as his lips meet mine. The kiss is a tame one—closed lips, no roaming hands, and just the slightest teasing brush of his tongue against mine—but it still makes my head spin and my body burn all over. By the time he pulls back, my breath is coming faster, and dry panties are a thing of the past. "Shall we get the heck out of here?" I ask. "The sooner we leave, the sooner we're going to be naked in whatever hotel room you've booked."

"Yes, ma'am," he rumbles before pressing a kiss to my cheek and adding softly, "I'm glad I make you feel like the sexiest woman in the city. Because you are. And the sweetest. I'm glad you're in my life, Evie. I hope you always will be."

"Of course, I will," I promise him.

And I mean it.

Ian's like family to me, except better.

He's like the families I watched on television growing up, someone who supports me, cares about me, and forgives me when I screw up without even being asked. He's my fan, not my critic, and one of the few people who love me unconditionally. Nothing can come between us, especially not something as relatively silly as whether or not his penis has been in my vagina.

I laugh as Ian shuts my door and circles around the front of the car to the driver's side.

"What?" he asks, his blue eyes crinkling and gorgeous against the backdrop of the clear blue, late afternoon sky.

I shake my head. "Nothing. I just... Sex is kind of weird if you stop to think about it. I mean, we smoosh our parts together with a little panting and sweating and then it's over and you go back to talking and eating snacks and doing normal stuff."

He buckles his seat belt with an arched brow. "Well, yeah, when you put it like that, it does sound kind of weird. And a little gross."

"You're welcome."

He grins. "There's a little more to it, though, I think. When it's done right."

"Huh," I say with a shrug. "Guess I'll have to wait and see."

"You will have to wait." He squeezes my thigh, sending more tingles dancing along my already fizzing nerve endings. "But not for much longer. Should only take us a couple of hours to reach the hotel."

"Perfect." I twine my fingers through his and tell myself it's okay that we're holding hands. That we'll be able to shut off these feelings as soon as we get back to the city and that eventually it will feel normal to be "just friends" again.

I tell myself all sorts of pretty lies, not realizing how naïve I'm being until it's far, far too late.

CHAPTER 26

Ian

$\mathcal{W}$e arrive at the massive, Victorian hotel carved into the mountains outside of New Paltz just as the sun is setting behind the blue hills, making the few trees already turning red at the tips look like campfires scattered across the horizon.

"Oh my God," Evie murmurs as the property comes into view at the end of the long, winding drive, the elegant architecture reflected in the still lake in front of it and framed by stunning bluffs. She jerks her head my way, laughing as she adds, "Oh my God, Ian. What is this place? It's magical."

"It's the only five-star property in town," I say, her obvious delight making the twelve-hundred-dollar-a-night price tag worth every penny. "Only the best for you, Feisty."

She takes my hand and squeezes it tight. "You didn't have to go all out like this, but..." She lets out a happy squeak. "I'm glad you did. I'm never going to forget a second of this trip." She sighs happily as her gaze flicks back and forth across the horizon. "It's so beautiful. I'm going to burn this view into my brain so I can do a watercolor when I get home."

"I'd like a picture of that when you're done."

"Don't be silly. I'll do an original watercolor for you, too. It's the least I can do," she says, her eyes wide as she soaks in the scene with an appreciation that makes me appreciate it even more.

That's one of Evie's many gifts. She sees the beauty in so many things, and she makes sure you see it, too.

"Remember that summer you kept borrowing my phone to take pictures of the bugs in your backyard?" I ask. "And begged me to print them out on the good printer at my house?"

"Yes," she says, casting a fond look my way. "You were very patient, as always, but not nearly as impressed with my bug paper dolls as you should have been. I mean, they had tiny bug ball gowns and tuxedos and everything."

"I was a stupid teenage boy. I'm sure I'd appreciate their brilliance more now. But even back then, I was impressed. You made me look at bugs differently, see how alien and cool they were. I still think of you every time a roach crawls across my toe while I'm waiting for the subway."

She laughs. "Oh, good. And you're welcome. That's the magic of art. It makes you see things differently, feel things differently."

I almost tell her that *she* makes me feel things differently and that I increasingly want to share those feelings with her first, before anyone else. But I keep my mouth shut.

That kind of talk is only going to make it harder to say goodbye.

I still can't believe I'm leaving the East Coast. I've spent my whole life and career here. There were times when I was tempted by the thought of changing teams, changing scenery, but my family and friends are all here. And Mom would have killed me if I'd transferred to Arizona because I thought it would be cool to live near a desert for a while.

The thought makes my ribs clench.

I guess I must make a face or something, too, because Evie asks in a concerned voice, "Are you okay?"

"Yeah," I say, forcing a tight smile. "Just thinking about my mom. She's going to be sad. I know she'll understand, but she's always been so happy that all her kids settled close to home."

Evie releases my hand to press her palm to my face. "She will understand. And you'll come back to visit all the time."

"But it won't be the same."

"No," Evie admits, her hand dropping back into her lap, "but that's okay. Change is part of life and it's unavoidable in your current situation. Either you're going to change teams so you can work with people who share your values, or this team is going to change you. And probably not for the better."

I cast a narrow look her way as we approach the circular drive in front of the hotel. "How did you get so smart?"

She arches a wry brow. "I watched you have a shouting match with your teammates this afternoon, Ian. You don't have to be a rocket scientist to see that they aren't bringing out the best in you."

"No, they aren't," I say as I brake in front of the valet station. "But you do."

Her smile is shy, but her eyes burn brightly into mine as she whispers, "Ditto."

Before I can say anything else, a man with a handlebar moustache and a notepad in hand appears at the driver's side window. "Checking in with us?" he asks, giving the car an appreciative once-over.

"Yes, Mr. and Mrs. Jenkins," I say, giving the fake names I used to book the reservation. The man welcomes us, hands me a ticket, and assures me our bags will be waiting in our room by the time we've finished check-in.

I circle around the back of the car, taking Evie's hand as the valet pulls away from the curb. "Ready?"

"To pretend to be your wife?" she whispers with a soft laugh. "Um, no. I've never been in a serious relationship, let alone a marriage."

I shrug. "Sure, you have. You and your roomies are in serious relationships."

"That's different," she says, her fingers tightening on mine as we start toward the large, rotating doors leading into the lobby.

"Not really. A husband or wife is just a best friend you like to bang, right?" I pause as we push through the doors, lowering my voice as we emerge into the lobby on the other side. "And the way you look at me makes it obvious how much you want to ride my pony, Mrs. Jenkins."

She glares up at me, but she's fighting a grin. "Oh yeah? Well, it's pretty obvious you feel the same way, Mr. Jenkins. I bet you're fighting the urge to squeeze my ass right now."

I reach down, copping a quick feel of her irresistible backside through her linen shorts, loving the way her jaw drops in response. "Nope," I say. "I'm done fighting battles I can't win."

Amusement and compassion mingle in her gaze. "Good. But if you do that again, I'm going to return the favor."

I frown and add in a soft, dry voice, "Oh, no. Not your hot little hands all over me in public. Anything but that."

She wrinkles her nose as she hisses, "Really? You're into that? Public groping?"

"When it comes to you? Hell, yes. I'm into any kind of groping I can get."

"Well, then." She fights another smile, but her dimples pop through. "That's okay, I guess."

"So much better than okay," I murmur as we approach the back of the short line to check in and I stand behind her, my hands lingering at her waist. "But I'll do my best to control myself until we get upstairs."

Evie looks up at me over her shoulder, the heat in her eyes making my jeans tighter. "I can't wait to be alone with you."

"Me, either," I say, ignoring the voice of doom whispering away at the back of my head, insisting I'm going to regret this, maybe for the rest of my life.

CHAPTER 27

Evie

We step into our room just as the last of the sunset light fades behind the mountains, casting the valley below in soft purples and blues. The view through the floor-to-ceiling windows on one side of the enormous suite is stunning, but it's the massive four-poster bed in the bedroom—clearly visible through the open door to my right—that catches and holds my gaze.

There it is.

The bed where I'll finally learn what it feels like to make love.

It isn't going to be just laid-back sexy times between Ian and me, I know that already. But the realization doesn't make this moment scarier, the way I would have assumed even a few days ago.

It just makes it feel...inevitable.

This may have started as friends with benefits, but it's already so much more. Ian is my destination, the safe, but oh-so-exciting place I didn't realize I was looking for until I ended up in his arms and realized I never wanted to leave.

I never want *him* to leave, either, but I understand why he has to. He can't stay here. This team is damaging something inside of him, that bedrock of kindness and optimism that make him the wonderful person he is. I would rather go through the pain of saying goodbye than have him stay and watch the light go out inside of him.

I care too much about him for that.

I'll make the most of our one night, wish him well, and set him free.

Ian reappears in the doorway of the bedroom, nodding over his shoulder as he leans against the frame. "Our bags are in the closet. As promised. Are you hungry? Should I order room service? Or we can go down to the restaurant for dinner. They're supposed to have a killer polenta."

"I don't want polenta," I say, stepping out of my Vans and padding slowly across the thick carpet in my socked feet. I stop a short distance from the gorgeous man watching me with a look of tenderness and desire that makes me feel so special, that I know I'm never going to regret this choice.

How could I? When all I feel as I hold out my hand to him is hope and happiness and...love.

I love him, I realize as he pulls me into his arms, crushing his lips to mine with a grateful groan that hums through my bones, making me want him even more. I'm in love with this beauti-

ful, sexy, perfect man, and I have been for a long
time.

As he hugs me tight, lifting me off my feet
before he turns and sways slowly toward the bed,
memories from all the years that came before flash
behind my closed eyes. Memories of the kindness
he showed me when we were kids, the faith he had
in me as I chased my dreams after high school, and
all the ways—big and small—that he showed me I
was lovable.

Maybe Derrick's love and support would have
been enough to help me grow up strong, but
maybe not. I don't think I've realized until right
now how much Ian's support and care meant to
me, how much he helped me become the person I
am, someone I'm proud of, who has the confidence to not only know and love herself, but to
help other people do the same.

As he lays me down on the bed, lengthening
himself on top of me, I can't help cupping his face
in both hands and saying, "Thank you. For being
my friend and caring about me. I don't know who
I would have grown up to be without you, but I'm
pretty sure she wouldn't have been nearly as
awesome. Or emotionally stable."

Something moves behind his eyes, a feeling I
can't name, but that makes my heart beat faster as
he says in a husky voice, "Don't thank me, Feisty.
You're one of the best of us. And you were always
going to be who you are, with or without my help.
You should be so proud. I know I am."

Tears pressing against the backs of my eyes, I

confess my last secret, the one I have a feeling he already knows. Because he knows me. *Really* knows me, nearly as well as I know myself. "I love you."

His throat works and his body tenses against mine. For a moment, I think he's going to pull away, but instead he says, "I love you, too."

Willing my soaring heart to keep its feet on the ground, I add in a softer voice, "And not just as a friend."

His lips curve. "Yeah, I figured, since you're grinding on my cock and all."

"I'm not..." I trail off as I realize I *am* grinding on his cock and will my hips to still and sink into the mattress.

"Don't stop," he says, a smile in his kiss as he murmurs against my mouth, "I like feeling how much you want this, want me." He deepens the kiss, his tongue stroking against mine as his warm hand slips beneath my sweater, just the feel of his fingers molding to my ribs enough to make it hard to breathe. "And I like knowing this isn't casual for you, either. It sure as hell isn't for me."

I shiver against him, my nipples so tight it's painful. "I need you to touch me," I say, arching into the hand lingering beneath my breast.

"Here?" he asks, brushing his fingers over my nipple through the satin of my bra, making my pulse leap and my hips rock against his erection again.

"Everywhere," I say, tugging at the bottom of

his shirt. "And I need you naked. Five minutes ago."

"Yes, ma'am," he rumbles against my mouth before pulling back just long enough to jerk his shirt over his head, revealing the perfection of his chest.

But I want more than his chest. I want all of him, every gorgeous inch bared to my hungry gaze.

I reach for the close of his pants, but his hands are already there. Our fingers tangle as we battle for the privilege of popping that top button. He lets me win, watching as I drag his zipper down and curl my fingers around the top of his jeans and the boxer briefs beneath.

Taking a bracing breath, I pull the fabric toward me and then push it down, freeing the hot, heavy length of him. His cock is so thick I can barely fit my fingers around him as I stroke him tentatively up and down, but it's the length that's truly intimidating. As he rolls to lie beside me, kicking off his shoes and shoving the rest of his clothes off and onto the floor, I have several uninterrupted seconds to study his erection again, long enough to cool the lust galloping through my blood.

When he turns back to me, I'm pretty sure I look like I've seen a ghost.

He arches a brow and glances down at my torso, where I've crossed my arms protectively over my breasts. "Everything okay?"

I gulp and shake my head. "Um, I'm concerned... Uh, worried—" I break off with a rush of breath and jab a finger toward his lower half. "That's not going to be an easy fit, is it?"

He grins. "It'll be fine."

"Don't patronize me," I order. "I'm inexperienced, not stupid. I've watched porn and I know not even the big ones are usually that big. That's an outlier."

"My cock?" he clarifies with an arched brow. "My cock is an outlier?"

I nod. "Yes. Or possibly a mutation. Have you looked into that? Consulted any of your doctors? Had them study your DNA to make sure it isn't compromised in some way?"

He rolls onto his side, propping up on one arm as he continues to study me with a bemused expression. "It's not a mutation. It's not even the biggest dick in the average locker room. And we aren't going to have any problems with fit."

"Why's that?" I ask, torn between relaxing into the feel of his fingers squeezing my hip and the panicked voice of my vagina, insisting she's too young to die.

He leans closer, brushing his lips over mine before his says, "Because I'm going to make you come so hard, make you so damned wet, that I'll sink into you like a hot knife through butter."

"You realize comparing your cock to a knife isn't comforting, right?" But my arms are already around his neck and my skin hungry for more of his touch.

"A finger through butter?" he says as he pulls

my sweater over my head and rolls back on top of me.

"Sounds gross. And messy," I say, sighing as he kisses his way down my throat.

"Got it." He smiles against the curve of my breast as he asks in an innocent voice, "An umbrella through butter, maybe?"

"Sick bastard," I say, but I'm grinning as I give his hair a tug. "You're a sick bastard."

"So sorry," he murmurs as he pops the front clasp on my bra and guides the cups away from my breasts and tight, tingling nipples. "Let me see if I can make it up to you."

And then he lowers his lips to my breast and proceeds to do just that.

CHAPTER 28

Ian

$\mathcal{I}$ flick my tongue over her nipple, and she arches into my mouth with a sexy moan, making me want to spend hours feasting on her sweet, responsive skin.

I want to memorize every sound she makes and store them away for when I'm on the other side of the country, wishing she were still in my bed.

Wishing she were mine.

"God, Ian," she pants, writhing beneath me, bucking into my hard-on through her thin satin panties, making some deviant part of me want to wrench the drenched crotch to one side and sink into her without a condom.

I've never had unprotected sex—never wanted to—but I want to with Evie. I want to feel her body tight on mine with nothing between us, want to come buried to the hilt in her sweetness and mark her with every gush of come. Some savage, territorial part of me has been activated, a primal beast I didn't realize existed until Evie was nearly naked beneath me.

It's crazy enough—sobering enough—to make me reach for the condom I pre-positioned on the bedside table and rip it open, sliding it on before things go any further. Just in case.

"Yes," she breathes, reaching for the top of her panties and shoving them down. "I'm ready."

"No, you're not." I strip the satin fabric down her legs and toss it to the floor before lengthening myself on top of her again. "Not until you come for me, I want your pussy dripping for me."

"It already—oh, Ian." She breaks off with another turned-on gasp as I suck her nipple into my mouth, nibbling at her swollen tip with my teeth, making her whimper and dig her nails into my ass.

And then she pulls me back to her lips, kissing me like she can't get enough of my mouth, my taste, her tongue branding mine with her sweet, innocent heat. She sets me on fire, this woman, her hunger making my own burn even brighter.

Dragging my lips from hers, I kiss my way down her throat, loving the way she shudders beneath me. I press her breasts together and lick the seam between them and then her nipples, imagining how good it would feel to stroke my dick through the velvet softness between her breasts, but I'm too turned on to risk it.

I need to make her come with my mouth, then

I need her to come on my cock, need it so bad I'm quickly losing what's left of my sanity.

"Please," she says, her hands trembling as she squeezes my shoulders. "I need you inside me."

I groan against her belly in response. "Fuck, Evie, you're killing me."

"No, you're killing *me*," she says, panting beneath me. "I'm ready, I promise. I'm past ready. I'm so wet, Ian, so crazy wet."

"Spread your legs for me," I demand. "Wide. Show me. Every inch."

I sit back on my heels, gripping my cock at the base and squeezing, using the hint of pain to retain control as Evie obeys me, hooking her hands behind her knees and opening herself to me without an ounce of hesitation or shame.

"Fuck, baby." I drag my finger up the center of her slick, swollen pussy, tracing every delicate, hungry inch before I circle her clit with my thumb. "You're so damned beautiful. So sexy."

She jerks beneath me, proving her clit is every bit as sensitive as her nipples, and that the men who had trouble "getting her train to the station" were fucking clueless idiots.

My girl was built for pleasure and made for my mouth.

Scooting lower on the mattress, I kiss her pussy like I kissed her lips.

Like I mean it. Like I love her. Because I do, no matter how shitty the timing or how many times I promised myself I wouldn't get attached, I love this woman.

She leaves me no choice, and I'm already in too deep to turn back now.

Not that I would, even if I could.

Not for anything in the world.

Evie

"IAN. GOD, IAN. PLEASE." I press shamelessly against his face, his tongue, so desperate to come I can barely think straight.

But he keeps the pressure light and teasing, building my hunger to such a fever pitch that when he finally suckles my clit into his mouth, my eyes roll back in my head and I'm pretty sure I *literally* see stars. Supernovas explode behind my closed eyes as he spreads me even wider, murmuring, "So sweet, baby. Fuck, you're so sweet. You taste so good."

I gasp and cling to the sheets as his hands smooth up to my breasts, squeezing them, sending another jolt of lust straight to my core.

But I don't want to come. Not yet.

I want Ian inside me, want to reach that dazzling, perfect place together, with him as close to me as two people can get.

"Your cock," I pant. "Please, Ian. Now."

He drives his tongue deeper into where I ache, making me moan. "Need your orgasm first, Feisty. Need you coming all over my face, screaming my name. Fuck, sweetheart, I need it so damned bad."

Pulling in a breath, I open my eyes and look down, my heart surging into my throat as I watch Ian kiss my most intimate places with a blissed-out expression on his face, as if he's truly never tasted anything better. I watch him rub his stiff tongue over my clit, the heavy, dragging sensation between my hips growing even more intense.

And then he looks up.

Our eyes lock as he glides two fingers into me as his tongue moves faster, pressing more insistently into my clit.

"Come for me, Evie," he demands, his fingers stroking deep, making my inner walls pulse and throb. "Come for me and I'll give you this cock. Come and I'll be buried in your pussy so deep you'll feel me everywhere, baby."

I spiral out, bliss igniting in my core and swallowing me whole. Suddenly, I'm drowning, dying, burning up and rising from the ashes as Ian fits his cock to my entrance with reverence and...love.

I don't know how I ever thought it would be anything else between us. It seems so clear now, so obvious. I love Ian and he loves me and after tonight nothing will ever be the same.

I reach up, digging my fingers into his shoulders and pulling his lips down to mine. I pour everything I feel for him into my kiss, telling him with every brush of my lips, every stroke of my tongue that I'm ready and that I love him and that I'll never, ever regret him being my first.

I wrap my legs around his waist, shivering as I feel his thick, burning shaft press against where I'm wet and eager. "I love you," I whisper against his mouth. "So much."

The words are barely past my lips before Ian sinks into me with a long, low groan, changing my world forever.

CHAPTER 29

Ian

I grit my teeth and try to slow down, to give her time to adjust, but I can't.

I need her too much, need to possess her, to join with her, to eliminate as much of the distance between her heart and mine as I can without slipping inside her skin.

But thank God, I don't seem to be hurting her.

"Yes, Ian, oh yes," she whispers, hugging me close as I push all the way to the end of her pulsing channel, tunneling deep.

I can feel her inner walls stretching to welcome me in but she's still so tight, so incredibly, fiercely tight. "You okay?" I ask, holding still at the end of my first thrust, hopefully giving her time to adjust.

"No," she says, sending regret rushing through me only to banish it as she adds, "I need more. More of you. All of you. Moving. Inside me. Now."

"As the lady wishes," I whisper, pulling back

and stroking more slowly into her this time, loving the way she shudders, and her legs wrap tighter around my hips. "I like this greedy side of you."

She bites her bottom lip only to release it with a gasp as I rock my hips forward at the end of my next thrust, grinding against her clit. "Sorry, but I'm not sorry. Wow, Ian, that feels..."

"Good?" I ask, doing it again.

"Magnificent. Resplendent. Superb," she says, lifting her hips to intensify our connection. "And all the other words for wonderful I can't remember because this feels so crazy good."

"And no pain?" I ask, shocked, but grateful when she shakes her head, "No. Just a tiny stinging feeling and then... You. This. All of this." Her breath rushes out. "I can't talk anymore. I just have to feel. Feel you. Feel everything."

"Everything," I echo, because it makes perfect sense.

She is everything and her body is heaven and I never, ever want this moment to end.

I hold on for as long as I can, but soon we've found a deep, urgent rhythm that has lightning dancing up my spine as we cling to each other, writhing and fucking and shamelessly taking each other where we need to be like we've been lovers for years not minutes.

"God, Ian," she says, lips parting as her arms begin to tremble. "I'm going to come again. Going to come so hard, so... Oh my God!"

She breaks off with a cry I smother with my lips, kissing her hard as her pussy practically squeezes me in half. Wetness reaches the base of my cock below the condom, drenching my feverish skin.

"Fuck, Evie, fuck," I growl. Realizing that all of that wet heat is for me is enough to banish the last of my control.

I hammer into her, deep and hard, as she squirms and makes more unspeakably sexy coming sounds. The fire burning low in my body flares hotter, hotter, until finally I can't hold on another second.

I come with a roar, shoving deep as my balls tighten and my soul pours out of my cock and into Evie. Into the condom between us, of course, but that isn't what it feels like.

I feel so connected, so consumed, so grateful and blissed out that it takes several minutes for me to realize the wetness I feel on my cheeks is tears.

I pull back, heart stuttering as I search Evie's face. "You okay?"

She grins. "So much better than okay." Her forehead furrows and her smile drops away as she cups my face in her hands. "You?"

I sniff, realizing with a start that the tears are mine, not hers. "Um, yeah," I say with an awkward laugh. "I don't know why I'm... I'm not sad. Not even close."

She lifts her head, pressing a soft kiss to my cheek. "Sometimes unexpected emotions rise to the surface during therapy."

I smile. "This isn't therapy."

"Isn't it, though?" she asks. "We just got close,

got honest, and...got off. It's like therapy but with a big bonus at the end." She exhales a happy sigh. "I'm a fan."

Laughing I pin her wrists to the mattress and stare down into her flushed, satisfied face. "Me, too. But I don't think I've worked through all my issues just yet. I'm going to need another session."

She studies me from under her lashes. "I think that can be arranged."

And it is and our second time is even better than our first.

The third isn't too shabby either and by the time we fall asleep—exhausted and oh-so-satisfied —in each other's arms, I'm pretty sure I want to be in "therapy" with Evie for the rest of my life.

But you only have one night, and that night is almost over.

Ignoring the inner voice of doom, I cuddle Evie close and drift off with my face buried in her silky soft hair, pretending we have all the time in the world, knowing morning—and reality—will intrude soon enough.

CHAPTER 30

Evie

I wake with a smile on my face and a warm, glowing feeling inside.

Then I turn over to see the most beautiful man in the world asleep beside me and my chest overflows. My heart just spills over until it feels like love is rushing out of me like a waterfall.

And then Ian opens his eyes and smiles like I'm the best thing he's ever woken up to and the waterfall becomes a flood.

"Hey, you," he says, his voice rough.

"Hey to you, too," I say, grinning as he wraps an arm around my waist and pulls me closer. "How'd you sleep?"

"Shitty," he says, still grinning. "I kept waking up hard and dying to be inside the sexy little blonde in my bed."

"You should have woken me up."

"Nah, you needed your rest. And you're pretty when you're sleeping."

"You, too." I prop my arms on his pecs, studying the stubble on his chin. "And I really like your morning whiskers."

"You're not going to like them once you feel how scratchy they are," he says, taking my hand and bringing my fingers to his cheek. "See?"

I hum thoughtfully. "Yes, they are scratchy. But what if I like scratchy whiskers against my thighs first thing in the morning?"

"Do you?" he asks, the last of the sleepiness fading from his expression as he squeezes my bottom beneath the covers.

"I don't know," I whisper as I press a kiss to his chest. "But I'm dying to find out."

Less than three minutes later, I'm crying Ian's name as I come on his mouth, proving scratchy whiskers paired with soft lips and a firm tongue are as riveting a combination as I suspected. And then Ian is rolling me over onto my stomach and gliding into me from behind, sinking into me with the same ease, the same perfection as last night.

There's a hint of soreness at first, but by the second long, languid thrust, there's only pleasure, only bliss, only Ian, the lover who could quickly become the biggest piece of my heart if I let him. I come again, clinging to the arm he's wrapped around my ribs and arching into the thick cock jerking inside of me, telling myself over and over that this is beautiful, but temporary.

This is the end, not the beginning.

And that's okay. I can survive this. I can enjoy our last few hours together and then let him go.

But no matter how firmly my inner voice lectures on the importance of perspective, there are tears in my eyes by the time we're finished. Thankfully, however, he's behind me, and I have time to wipe them away while he removes the condom and wraps it in tissues from beside the bed.

When he turns back to me, I'm smiling and solid again.

I'm also starving.

"Breakfast," I say, my stomach snarling its agreement. "I want some of that, don't you?"

He nods, a somber expression on his face as he says, "Absolutely. We should hit the buffet and eat until we can barely stand."

I grin, but it fades away a beat later. "That sounds great. So why do you look so serious all of a sudden?"

He smiles, but it doesn't reach his eyes. "No reason. Just hungry, I guess. You want first shower? Then I can jump in and get dressed and we'll be ready to go grab food in thirty minutes or so?"

"Fifteen minutes," I say. "I'm a very fast shower-er, especially when I'm jonesing for waffles."

"Fifteen, then." He kisses my cheek before rolling out of bed and shrugging into one of the thick robes hanging on hooks beside the entrance to the bathroom. "I just need to make a quick call and I'll join you in the shower. If that's all right with you?"

"Fine with me." I sit up, swinging my legs out

from under the covers. "Assuming we can keep from getting...distracted while we get clean."

"Sorry, that's a non-starter," he tosses over his shoulder on his way into the living room area of the suite. He stops in the door, turning to shoot me a wicked grin. "I *will* be fucking you against the wall in the shower. Not even going to try to control myself."

"Fine," I say, heaving a melodramatic sigh as I slink toward the bathroom, loving the feel of his eyes devouring me with every step, "twenty minutes, then. But don't stay on the phone too long or I'll be out before you get in. I'm telling you, I'm speedy in the shower. Especially for a girl."

"Noted," he says. "I'll be quick."

"You do that." I disappear into the bathroom with a giddy grin, close the door, and quickly pee and wash my hands before turning on the shower.

I'm about to step in when I remember how worried I was about possible morning breath a few minutes ago and head for the sink instead. I brush my teeth and smooth on a coat of Chapstick—Ian's whiskers left my lips a little chafed—and then set out Ian's toothbrush and toothpaste beside the soap dish.

I stick my head out of the bathroom to teasingly suggest he clean his dirty mouth for me before he joins me in the shower to see him pacing back and forth in front of the window in the other room.

Even with his back turned, I can tell something is wrong. His movements are too stiff, his shoulders too tight.

My nosy side getting the better of me, I wrap up in a towel and creep softly across the carpet to the doorway, but Ian's listening at this point in his conversation, not talking. I can't hear anything but an occasional frustrated sigh as he paces.

I'm about to sneak back into the bathroom like I should have from the beginning when he says, "No, I'm not going to change my mind. I'm going to stay in New York and on the team. I don't care if it's bad for my career. There are more important things on my mind right now." He sighs again. "Yeah, there are more important things than hockey or my career. I've met someone, okay? Someone amazing and her entire life is here. So, I'm going to stay here, too, and...make the best of things. Who knows? Maybe I'll figure out a way to get through to the others and turn the team around."

As the meaning of his words hit, my heart splits in two, one part soaring into the clouds on wings of happiness because Ian feels it, too. He feels how special this is, how right, and how worth fighting for, and a selfish part of me couldn't be happier.

But the not selfish part is sinking in my belly like a stone, dragging at me with a weight I know I won't be able to bear for very long. Maybe a year if all goes well with our budding relationship, maybe two. But eventually watching Ian's love for the game fade with every miserable practice and lackluster game will become too heavy. Too much. Eventually, I'd come to hate myself for letting him choose me, and maybe he would, too.

But he's right—my entire life is here. My school, my work, my friends and my family. I love Ian, but I also love living with my three best friends, the way we always dreamed we would. Even if Ian wanted me to go with him, if that didn't feel like way too much, way too soon, I would feel so torn.

I'm not ready to give up this life I've worked so hard for, and my art therapy program is the best in the country. I might be able to transfer to a school wherever Ian goes to play but it wouldn't be the same, and I'd always wonder what I missed out on by following my man instead of staying fixed on my own star.

I back away, my throat so tight I can barely breathe as Ian continues to argue with whoever is on the other end of the line—his agent, I'm guessing. He's probably cancelling that meeting he had scheduled for Monday. But that's okay, he can always reschedule it, as soon as he sees...

As soon as he understands...

Hurrying into the bathroom I take the fastest shower of my life, ensuring I'm dressed and running curling gel through my hair by the time Ian sticks his head into the lightly steamed-up space.

"Hey," he says, disappointment in his voice, "sorry. My call took a little longer than I thought."

"It's fine," I say, forcing a smile. "I'm just

hungry." I rake my toiletries into my bag with one smooth sweep of my arm and move around him to the door. "Enjoy your shower. I'll wait for you in the sitting room."

"Okay," he says, seeming to sense that something's not quite right, but he doesn't pry.

Because he's Ian. He lets people come to him. He doesn't push or expect intimacy you're not ready to give. It's one of his best traits, but it also gives me plenty of time to throw my toiletries in my duffel bag, write a quick note, and slip out of the room while the water is still running in the shower.

Downstairs, the woman at the front desk informs me there's a free shuttle to the Amtrak station in the next town over and that if I hurry, I can catch the van before it leaves.

I plop into the last free seat, accepting a hospitality box from the driver before he slides the van door shut and circles around to get into the driver's seat. Inside the box are a water, an orange juice, and a fresh-baked blueberry muffin, but my appetite is gone.

My stomach is a sour pit, and my heart is still overflowing but with pain now.

Ian is the last person I ever wanted to hurt, but I had no choice. I did what I had to do, I tell myself, a miserable mantra that offers no comfort as the van drops us at the train station and I buy a one-way ticket back to my old life, the one with no Ian in it.

CHAPTER 31

Ian

I know something's wrong the second I shut off the water.

The air is too quiet, too still, too...empty.

That's what a world without Evie in it feels like now. Empty. Lacking in the meaning and vibrancy it has when I'm with her.

But I guess that emptiness is something I'm going to have to get used to, I realize as I step into the sitting room to see no sign of Evie except a piece of hotel stationary on the coffee table with her writing on it.

Heart in my throat, I collect the note and read—

Dear Ian,

Thank you for a wonderful night (and morning), but I think it's best I leave before things get any more confus-

ing. I will always love you and be so happy you were my first but I'm not ready for a relationship right now. I'm focused on school and my friends and trying to grow into the best version of myself.

Even if you were staying in town, the timing just isn't right.

For either of us.

This would end up being a rebound for you and a mistake for me and not worth the drama it would cause with Derrick. I think we both know, deep down, that the two of us were meant to be friends, nothing more.

But that doesn't mean I won't always be your biggest fan. No matter where you end up moving or what team you play for, I'll be here cheering you on and wishing you well. There's no doubt in my mind that you're on your way to great things.

Much love and good luck on your next adventure,

Evie

PAIN EXPLODES BEHIND MY RIBS, followed quickly by more explosions in my throat, head, and deep down in my gut where I know that Evie's wrong. We weren't meant to be just friends, the timing isn't wrong, and she's the farthest thing from a rebound. She's the one I've been waiting for, the only woman I want to build a life and a family with.

I'm more ready to get down on one knee after a week with Evie than I was after three years with my ex.

But she doesn't feel the same way.

How can she not feel the same way? After last night, I was so positive, so certain... And so wrong.

Fuck, how could I have been so wrong?

I fetch my cell, but after letting my thumb hover over Evie's name for a long beat, I tap my agent's number instead. Fred doesn't answer—he's probably still pissed off about our conversation before I got in the shower—but he'll be less pissed once he gets this message.

"Hey, it's me again," I say, my voice hollow and sad, but already resigned. This is what Evie wants and there's no point in staying here now. Living so close to her, but being outside her inner circle, a spectator to her life as she grows and evolves and eventually starts dating other guys, would be too painful. "I've changed my mind. You're right. I need to get out of here before I waste another good year on a bad situation. I'll be at the meeting on Monday, and I'll be prepared to make a decision. So, guess I'll see you then."

I end the call and sink into the soft couch cushions, gazing out the window at the beautiful view and feeling...not much. The landscape isn't as stunning without Evie here to share it with, and I suddenly find I can't stay here another second.

Now that she's gone, I can't stand to be in this place where she was so close, so *mine*.

She *was* mine, even if it was only for a night.

I try to let that make me feel better, but it doesn't, and by the time I've dressed and packed up my things, I'm lower than I can remember being in ages.

But that's all the more reason to get out of here, get a fresh start, and put the stress and angst of the past year behind me. That's the only good part about that note and everything Evie said in it —it's going to make leaving easier than I ever imagined.

And that, no doubt, is exactly why she wrote it.

"Dumbass," I say aloud, the word echoing through the empty room. "You're a fucking dumbass."

I am, but at least I realized the truth before it was too late.

Now, I just have to figure out what to do about it. Because there's no way I'm giving up on this thing with Evie, not without one hell of a fight.

CHAPTER 32

Evie

I cry behind my sunglasses most of the train ride home, producing enough snot that the woman across the aisle buys me a bottle of water from the refreshment car.

"You'll get dehydrated, sweetheart," she says as she settles back into her seat. "Drink that and try to eat something. And remember, men are rarely worth crying over."

I sniff and thank her for the water before adding in a tear-ravaged voice, "But he is. He was. He's a really great person." And then I start crying again, so I'm not sure what she says back, but I think it was something about finding a girlfriend to talk to when I get home.

Which, I absolutely do.

* * *

BACK ON OUR COUCH, I spill everything to Harlow and Jess—Cam is at work—and they pet my hair and feed me chocolate in between crying jags and ask if I'm sure I did the right thing.

"Yes," I say, as sure of that as I am that I'm never going to feel this way about another man. There's only one Ian for me. Every other guy will always be second best. "He'll be miserable if he stays here. It will ruin his life."

Harlow shoots me a gentler version of her usual "don't bullshit me" look. "There's more to life than work, babes. And from what you overheard, it sounds like Ian's pretty crazy about you. Why do you automatically assume you're less important to him than what he does for a living?"

"Well, to be fair, he is an NHL superstar," Jess says, "with a chance to make even more money and become more famous if he gets away from his problem-child teammates." She lifts her arms in surrender as Harlow shoots a more murderous gaze her way. "Hey, I would pick true love with Evie if it were me, but it's not like he has a regular job. And it's not like he can do his job forever. He probably only has four or five years left, tops. The number of players still in the NHL in their late thirties is higher than it used to be, but it's still pretty small."

"Exactly," I say, motioning toward Jess. "And if he stays here another year, he might not get another chance to join a better team. They might decide he's too old or too tainted by being an Ice Possum for too long or just not their favorite flavor anymore. These things are mercurry... mercurni...mer—"

"Mercurial," Harlow cuts in, saving my tongue from itself. "You're right, they are, but so is love. It's hard to find and even harder to keep. So even if it shows up at the wrong time or with someone you *never* would have expected you'd fall for... I don't know, I think it seems foolish to throw it away without thinking long and hard about it first."

"I'm not throwing it away," I insist, tears making the back of my nose sting again. "I'm doing what's best for him. I'm putting him first."

"Without talking to him about it," Harlow says, "or making sure this is what he wants."

My lips part, but no words come out, just a faint squeak that does nothing to make my case. Finally, I shake my head and pull my knees in, "Can we not talk about this anymore? I need to give my brain and eyeballs a rest."

"Of course." Jess puts her arm around my shoulders, giving me one of her signature stiff and awkward, but still perfect hugs. "Want to change into our soft pants and watch the drag makeover show?"

I nod. "Yes, please. Especially the soft pants. These jeans are dumb."

"Speaking of dumb, I have to head out to another study session," Harlow says, rising to her feet. "Dingus and Dongus are having trouble understanding what they need to do for the group project. Are you two going to be okay until I get back?"

"We'll be fine," Jess says with a firm nod. "But please get ice cream on the way home. I have a feeling we're going to need ice cream once the chocolate runs out."

I nod and reach for a caramel truffle with a sniff. "Yes, we're definitely going to need ice cream. And maybe dill-flavored pickle chips? And peanut butter pretzels?"

Harlow's upper lip curls, but she gives a weak thumbs-up. "Got it. And I'll pick up some antacid, too, just in case." She turns to go but spins back before she's taken a step. "I love you guys."

"We love you, too," Jess says.

I nod my agreement, seeing as my mouth is still full of caramel.

"You're the best people I know," Harlow continues in a rare show of squishy feelings. "And I know you're going to find happily ever after some-day. You're too good not to. And the good guys are going to win in the end. No matter how cynical I can be, sometimes, I believe that. I really do."

Her words echo in my head as I change into sweatpants and a t-shirt and snuggle with Jess on the couch, watching ten gorgeous men dressed as women lip-sync their hearts out to see who will advance to the next round. I hope she's right, and I hope Ian finds an amazing new girlfriend wher-ever he ends up next.

No matter how much it hurts to imagine him with someone else, he deserves a wonderful woman who realizes how special he is, that he isn't just a famous athlete, but an all-around incredible human being.

In between episodes, while Jess is fetching tea to calm our stomachs before Harlow returns with more junk food, I close my eyes and send out a silent wish for Ian's happiness.

And for mine.

But the universe is clearly not in the mood to do me any favors, at least not when it comes to *my* well-being.

No sooner has my wish left my brain than my cell dings with a message from Derrick—*Have you made your decision about tomorrow? Dad texted me a few minutes ago to ask if he should eat lunch before we take him out since "you two always pick places with tiny-ass portions." Honestly, he'd probably be as happy as a clam if I just drop off his paving stones and order pizza for him before I leave. So don't feel like you have to come.*

Pulling in a breath, I search my heart, a little shocked to find that I actually want to see my dad. I want to see him through my new, bolder Evie lens and maybe even talk to him about some of the hard things in our past.

Maybe, if we clear the air, we can move on from our old patterns and find a better way to be family. And if not, at least I can say I tried my best to keep my father in my life.

I want to come, I reply. *What time should I be ready? Eight? Nine?*

Derrick says he'll pick me up at nine and Jess and I return to our drag queen binge. Harlow returns in time for the start of the fourth episode and Cam rolls in smelling of delicious restaurant smells not long after. We all crowd onto the couch, sharing our snacks the way we did when we were kids and for now it's enough to soothe my savaged heart.

I know there will be more pain to face tomorrow, but this is what's best for Ian. There's no doubt in my mind about that and that's what I'll hold on to if he calls or stops by before he leaves next week. I'll remember how much I love him and want good things for him and stand firm, even if it hurts.

But the night melts into morning and there isn't a single text from Ian, not so much as a "got your note" or "message received."

Derrick picks me up and we head over the bridge into New Jersey and still there isn't so much as a peep from my phone, aside from an alert from my coupon app that I can save big on fall gourds next week at my local health food store.

I'm beginning to think I was wrong about Ian —maybe he was relieved to read that note—when Derrick turns right, instead of left, at the first turn leading into our old neighborhood.

I glance his way and jab a thumb over my shoulder. "Wrong turn, right? Or have I forgotten the way to Dad's house?"

"You haven't forgotten," Derrick says, his gaze still fixed on the road. "We're just making a quick detour. Or maybe a not-so-quick detour, depending."

My forehead bunches. "Depending on what?"

"Oh, a lot of things, I guess," he says vaguely. "I don't presume to know much about love, but I know Ian is head over heels for you. He'd give his life for you. Which he almost did last night when I threatened to kill him for seducing you."

My lips part to explain that *I* seduced Ian, not the other way around, when Derrick beats me to it. "But he explained that you were the one who started things as well as the one who finished them." He glances my way. "But I have a strong feeling you were pushing him away for his own good. Is that right?"

I gulp and press a hand to my chest, where my heart is thrashing against my sternum. "Yes, but what... Where are we going? What did you do?"

"I'm giving him a chance to convince you that *you're* what's good for him. I figured it's the least I could do after giving him a black eye."

"What?" I shake my head. "No, this isn't right. I can't, Derrick. He has to go to Portland or wherever else he decides to go. He can't stay here for me. I can't be responsible for ruining his chance at making the most of his talent."

"Love and commitment are scary. I get it," he says, slowing as we approach Ian's family home to see all the Foxes out in the front yard. The adults are drinking beers around a firepit while the grandkids jump in the bouncy house inflated on the front lawn. As soon as I see Ian's mom's warm, welcoming smile, so many memories come rushing back.

She was like my second mom after mine left and always there when I needed help from an older, wiser woman. Kay is the one who bought me my first box of pads and who explained how to use tampons when I decided I couldn't stand to keep sitting on the sidelines while my friends splashed in the community pool. She was the one who helped me take in the prom dress I found at the thrift store and took pictures when Jess and Harlow came to pick me up in the limo.

I love her so much and I know she loves me, but will she still love me if I set off a bomb in her son's career?

As I emerge from the car, my knees unsteady and my pulse even unsteadier, Kay envelops me in a big, hard hug and whispers, "No matter what, you're still one of my girls. You always will be. Even if you say no." She pulls back, beaming down at me as she adds, "But I hope you'll say yes."

"Yes to...what? Exactly?" I ask, my voice trembling nearly as hard as the rest of me.

Kay smiles. "You should ask Ian about that. He's in the backyard waiting for you. But if you're hungry, I can get you a hot dog before you head back. He won't mind waiting a few more minutes."

"I could probably fly easier than I could eat right now," I confess, making her laugh.

"Understandable," she says, giving my arm an encouraging squeeze. "Then head on back. We'll be here when you're finished, but we won't bother you unless you want to be bothered. If you want, you can jump right back into the car with Derrick and head off, no stress, no mess."

Right.

No stress or mess...

I adore Kay, but she's always been almost delusionally optimistic. Though, to think of it, his dad, Jack—who waves and booms, "Hey there, Evie!" as I pass by the firepit—is pretty upbeat, too.

Clearly, Ian comes by his hopeful streak honestly.

I don't want to dent his spirit any more than the team has dented it already, but I don't see a way forward for us. I may have made my decision quickly when I wrote that note and ran, but that doesn't mean I made it casually or didn't think things through.

I'm preparing to explain that to Ian, while hopefully holding myself together, when I step through the gate into the backyard and all my good intentions evaporate in a rush of emotion.

CHAPTER 33

Ian

*I*t took ten hours and every last bit of spray paint in my parents' garage—and I'm not sure when I'll be able to feel my "spraying finger" again—but the moment I see Evie's face, I know every second was worth it.

"What..." She trails off with an awed shake of her head as she wanders closer to the painted sheet pinned to the clothesline. "What did you do?"

"I wanted to show you that I could take art therapy seriously." I force myself to remain beside the tree that supports our old tree house, giving her space. "So, I redid the iceberg assignment. With a few changes."

Her hand comes to hover in front of her lips and her eyes begin to shine. "It's a love berg," she murmurs, her throat working as she swallows.

"I wanted to prove to you that this isn't a flash in the pan or a rebound," I say. "I may have just woken up to the way I feel, but that doesn't mean this feeling is new or shouldn't be trusted. Just look at all the stuff lurking beneath the surface, Feisty. I basically had no choice but to fall in love with you."

She blinks, sending tears streaking down her cheeks and that's it, I can't keep myself from her for another second. A beat later, she's in my arms, hugging me tight as I drop kisses over her sweet curly head, praying harder than I've prayed in years that she won't pull away from me again.

"I love you, Evie," I say, "more than I've ever loved anyone. Please don't push me away. We can figure this out. I know we can. Assuming you feel even half of what I feel."

She pulls back, gazing up at me with wide, tear-filled eyes. "You painted a giant love mural. For me."

"And it has all my favorite things about you," I say, pointing toward the very bottom of the berg. "Down there is the way you make ordinary things feel magical. Even when you were a little kid, you had this way of seeing the world that just...blew me away. It made me want to be around you, to be a part of your world."

"Like the Little Mermaid," she says, more tears streaming down her cheeks.

"Exactly like that," I say, swiping them away with my thumbs. "I would comb my hair with a fork with you any day. And that's not even my favorite Evie thing. I love the way you face your problems, even when they're hard or confusing, the way you're always there for the people you love, and how warm and open-hearted you are, even when it would have been so easy, and so understandable, if you'd grown up bitter instead. So many people have let you down or underestimated the incredible person you are."

"But not you," she whispers.

I shake my head. "No, I'm guilty, too. I was so busy telling myself you were still a kid I needed to protect that I didn't see the strong, smart, savvy woman you'd become. And I'm sorry for that. My only defense is that telling myself those things made it easier to deny the way I was starting to feel about you."

"That makes me so happy but..." Her brows pinch closer together as she adds, "But I don't want you to stay in New York for me, Ian. I mean, of course I selfishly want you close, but that isn't—"

"What about New Jersey?" I ask. "Would that be close enough?"

She blinks and her mouth opens and closes a few times before she stammers, "You think you can get a spot on the team?"

"They haven't offered yet, but I have my agent on the case, and all my fingers crossed. But if I do end up in Portland or on the West Coast, I can fly home every month and plan to do my summer conditioning in the city next year so we can have as much time together as possible. I know long distance isn't ideal, but—"

"I didn't think you'd want to," she cuts in, her

breath hitching as she fights another wave of tears. "I never imagined you'd... Not when this is so new. I mean, some crazy part of me thought you might ask me to come with you, but never that you'd go to so much trouble just for me."

"For the woman I love?" I ask, cupping her face in my hand. "Hell, yes, I will. I'd crawl all the way here on my belly if I had to."

Her lips tremble at the edges. "That wouldn't be necessary. I'd meet you halfway."

"So, does that mean you want to meet me halfway? For real?"

She bites her lip, worry creeping back into her eyes again. "On one condition—if the long-distance thing starts interfering with your ability to succeed with your new team, then we take a break. I love you too much to get in the way of your dreams."

I brush my thumb over her cheek. "You're my dream, Feisty. Don't you know that by now? I don't stay up all night painting giant ugly pictures for just anyone, you know."

She leans into my touch, a real smile finally stretching across her sweet face. "First, that painting is gorgeous, nothing ugly about it. Secondly...yes, I am starting to suspect that you may have it pretty bad." She reaches up, touching tentative fingers to the eye Derrick punched last night. "Speaking of bad, that doesn't look great. Should you get it checked out?"

"Nah, it's healing fast. It just looks ugly while it's swollen, but it doesn't hurt much anymore." I exhale. "Nothing hurts right now. I'm just...so grateful. I promise, you won't regret this. I'm going to make damned sure of that."

"And I'm going to do the same for you," she says with a happy sigh. "We should probably make out now, right?"

"Most definitely," I say, bending and pressing my lips to hers, the last corner of my heart splitting wide open as she kisses me the way I hoped she would—like she's as grateful to officially be "us" as I am.

We're still kissing, swaying, and softly murmuring all the things you say when you're crazy in love when Derrick shouts from the other side of the fence. "Should I go get my dad and bring him over? I'm assuming we're in for a happy celebration?"

"Yeah," Evie calls out, grinning up at me. "We're in for a happy...everything."

Her words prove prophetic. Not only do my parents freak out with excitement that Evie and I are a couple, but even Mr. Olsen seems pleased.

Well, as pleased as that grouch of a man ever gets, anyway.

"A smart choice for once," he barks at me as I hand him a non-alcoholic beer. "Not like when you joined the Possums. Could have told you that was a bad fit if anyone had bothered to ask. But my Evie...well, you can't go wrong there. Unless you hurt her and then you'll be fucking sorry."

"He's not going to hurt me, Dad," Evie says,

tucking herself against my side. "But thank you. I didn't realize you thought I was such a catch."

He bristles and runs a rough hand over his balding brown hair. "Yeah, well, this bozo could do a lot worse. You're a good kid. Always have been. Probably should have told you that a little more often but I'm a shit father. Everyone in the neighborhood knows that."

I'm too stunned to reply—I had no idea Mr. Olsen was aware of how shitty he was, let alone dreamed that he'd ever own up to it and offer anything close to an apology to the daughter he neglected or bullied for most of her childhood.

But Evie, as always, knows exactly what to say, "You were a shit father," she says with a smile, "but you don't have to keep being one. I can leave the past in the past if you can, Dad. Because I love you, no matter what, and I'd love to find out what it's like to really be your daughter."

The old man actually looks like he might cry for a moment before his features knit into a scowl and he grumbles, "Well, I guess that's a good idea. You're all grown up now. And you can't help that you look so damned much like your mother. You never could."

"No, I couldn't," Evie says, "but I can understand why that was hard for you. So...truce?"

"Truce," he says, taking a long pull on his nonalcoholic beer before pointing a finger at me. "But I've got my eye on you, son. Don't hurt her. She's had enough of that already. You understand?"

"I do, sir," I say. "And I don't plan on doing

anything but loving her. With all my heart and then some."

"Sappy," he says, his lip curling slightly, "you and Derrick, both. But I guess that's the fashion nowadays. Guys talking about their feelings like a bunch of little girls."

"Stop, Dad," Evie says pleasantly. "Quit while you're ahead. And maybe consider a little sappy yourself now and then. I bet the ladies at the Elks Lodge would love that."

Mr. Olsen turns a deep shade of red, mumbles something about wanting to check with my dad about his fertilizer schedule, and hustles away, leaving Evie giggling beside me.

"I think that means he has a girlfriend," she whispers. "Or a lady friend he wishes were more. I'll have to ask Harlow's mom to activate her spy network, see if she can suss out the identity of Dad's crush."

"I'm just glad he seems to be softening a little in his old age," I say.

"Me, too," she says, hugging me closer with the arm wrapped around my waist as she adds in a softer voice, "How long before we can get out of here and find a place to get naked?"

"An hour?" I suggest, my cock already thickening in response to her words. "Then we hustle back to my place as fast as the traffic will allow and stay in bed until I leave for my meeting tomorrow afternoon?"

"I can miss my class tomorrow morning, and I no longer have art therapy with stinky hockey boys in the afternoon so...yes. I think that sounds doable."

"You're doable," I say, reaching down to squeeze her ass.

She laughs. "And you're shameless."

"Only with you, baby," I promise. "Only with you."

* * *

TWO AND A HALF HOURS LATER, we finally close my apartment door behind us and come together.

Her hands are busy with my clothes and my hands are even busier with hers, and by the time we reach my bedroom, we're both naked, nothing between us but heat and emotion and the deep knowing that clicks into place every time she's in my arms.

This is my person, my one, my girl, and I'm so grateful to have found her. Even if I have to spend the next two years zipping back and forth across the country while she finishes her master's, I won't regret it for a second.

She's worth the long-distance hassle. She's worth just about anything, a fact she proves as we tumble onto the bed and she says, "On top. I want to be on top this time. I feel like I need to show this cock who's boss."

Grinning I roll over on my back, drawing her on top of me. "Please do. I like Evie boss energy."

"Yeah?" she asks, her grin fading as I cup her breasts in my hands and pinch her tight nipples between my fingers. "Oh wow... That's... Why is that so good?"

"Because you're mine and I'm yours and everything feels good." I lift my hips, bringing my cock into an even more intimate connection with her sweet, slick pussy. "Fuck, baby. I love how wet you get for me, love knowing I'm going to be inside you."

"Without a condom," she murmurs as she reaches between us, gripping my erection in her hand. "I'm on the pill and I want you bare. I want to feel you without anything in between us."

"I've never had sex without a condom," I say, hurrying on when she looks like she's about to change her mind. "But I'm disease-free and I want to with you, too. Just don't be mad if I can't last as long."

Her mouth lilts up on one side. "Well, I do enjoy getting mad about things like that, but I'll try to control my primal rage."

The answering joke on the tip of my tongue vanishes as she fits my aching cock to her entrance and drops her hips, not stopping until she's taken every inch of me, until I'm buried in the paradise of her body, and everything is finally right with the world again.

"Fuck, baby," I breathe as she begins to rock slowly on top of me. "You feel so good, so perfect. I love you so much, Evie."

"And I love you," she says, gasping as I pull her forward, guiding her nipples to my mouth. "Can you do both... Oh my God, you can do both at the same time. Oh my God, Ian, oh that feels so good. I love being the boss of your cock."

I hum my agreement against her soft skin as I suckle her deeper, loving the turned-on sounds dropping from her lips and the way her pussy grips my dick so much that I almost regret the moment she tumbles over the edge, her slick heat gripping me so tight that I have no choice but to spin out right along with her.

Almost regret...

But then I remind myself that we aren't on borrowed time, and that I'll get to make her come for me—on top, from behind, and everything in between—for the foreseeable future and snuggle her closer with a happy sigh.

"Am I crazy?" she finally asks, lifting her flushed face from my chest. "Or am I super good at sex for a virgin?"

I grin. "Well, you're not a virgin anymore, but yeah, I'd say you're pretty fucking great. A sex prodigy even." Her smug little grin makes me laugh so hard my cock ends up slipping out of her and then I'm sad, but only for a few minutes.

Soon, I'm hard again and reminding her how good it can feel to let my cock be the boss. We roll around like teenagers until nearly dawn, only stopping to sleep when the first pink light teases at my curtains.

Five hours later, I'm up and in the shower, crossing all my fingers that this meeting with Fred goes my way.

Spoiler alert—it doesn't. New Jersey isn't interested in a trade, but the Badgers have upped their offer, ensuring I'll have plenty of extra cash to spring for plane tickets every chance I get.

And for two years, that's exactly what I do.

Until the day Evie graduates and answers the question I've been almost afraid to ask. "I've already packed my things," she says. "And lined up three interviews for art therapy positions in Portland. So...when do we leave?"

"Are you sure?" I ask. "If you want to stay in the city, I—"

"I want to be with you," she cuts in, her eyes shining with conviction and that fierce, unwavering love I hope I never take for granted. "All the time. From when I wake up in the morning to when we go to sleep at night and as many minutes as I can beg, borrow, or steal in between."

"I'm never going to make you beg, baby," I promise.

And I keep my word, right up until the night she tells me she's off her birth control and begs me to start trying for a baby. To which I say, "After we're married."

"Tomorrow?" she asks, a mischievous light in her eyes. "Courthouse? You and me?"

"It's a date," I promise.

It ends up taking three days—there's a mandatory waiting period after we get our license—but on the Friday before the Stanley Cup finals, we're saying our "I do's" at a rooftop restaurant, surrounded by my new friends from the team, their wives and girlfriends, and the ladies from

Evie's art therapy practice, who have miraculously transformed the space with hundreds of paper flowers.

Early the next week, I help lead the Badgers to victory and land the first Cup title of my career. Against the Ice Possums, no less.

After a management shakeup and some well-timed trades, the Possums eventually got out of their slump and became a team to be reckoned with. But they still wouldn't be the team for me, even if I'd stayed. We just didn't have the right chemistry.

But my new team? Well, we kicked ass, took names, and shook Possum hands with grace in our victory.

And I'm so damned happy about that, but not nearly as happy as I am that the little blonde running to hug me at the edge of the ice after the final game is now my wife.

My heart. My everything.

And she always will be, no matter where our adventures takes us next.

Keep reading for a sneak peek of
SCREWED Harlow and Derrick's story!
Available Now!

SNEAK PEEK

Please enjoy this sneak peek of
Screwed!

Prologue

From Harlow Raine's
TOP SECRET Diary

Dear Diary,

It's just a penis. A cock. A dick.

There are literally *millions* of them in this city and it's not like I'm looking for Mr. Right. I just want a dude bro who knows what he's doing in the bedroom, with a personality *just* obnoxious enough to keep me from falling for the guy.

You would think that kind of casual bang-buddy situation would be an easy thing to find.

You would, sadly, be wrong.

Let's look to the dating log for all the depressing details, shall we?

Brad One: Emotional. Cried easily. Allergic to synthetic fabrics. Or possibly was using his "fabric allergy" to excuse his second crying fit. Wanted to hold my hand fifteen minutes after meeting and kissed my forehead *twice*.

My thoughts: Feelings are not on my radar right now, tears make me nauseous, and forehead kisses are creepy on a first date.

V-Card Status: Still Un-punched

Steve: Referred to breasts as "tiddies." Kept wanting to talk about fishing. Hit the bathroom right before the check arrived and stayed there until I paid, making me think he was waiting to return until the bill was taken care of.

So, yeah, this douchebag was in the running... right up until he gave his leftovers to a homeless man outside the restaurant and offered to buy drinks and dessert at the bar across the street since I covered dinner.

My thoughts: These small kindnesses weren't much, but they were enough to make me fear falling prey to First Dick Fever like so many of the Raine women before me.

What is First Dick Fever you may ask?

First Dick Fever (aka FDF)—Noun—*falling stupidly and irreversibly in love with the first man to* *put in more than "just the tip." A malady that slowly kills your single hopes and dreams and for which there is currently no known cure.*

My mother married her first dick and has remained locked in fractious matrimony with my father for nearly thirty years, despite the fact that they can't go more than an hour without shouting at each other until they're red in the face.

She says "verbal sparring" is their love language.

I say she's got a bad case of FDF.

First Dick Fever also came for my cousin, Sheila, who followed her first cock to the Philippines, where she now lives in a tiny apartment with Joshua and his big sister, Jane, who hates Sheila like a lollipop covered in dog hair and keeps trying to scare her off by putting hissing roaches in her shoes.

Ditto for my big sister, Lauren, who was knocked up by her first dick at seventeen and subsequently gave up her scholarship to Cornell to stay in New Jersey and help her now husband, Chuck, run his family's plumbing business.

And, sure, Lauren seems happy enough for a woman with three kids under the age of ten—albeit permanently exhausted—but I can't help but wonder what her life would be like if she hadn't let Chuck's dick shape the course of her future.

This is why I have to be careful.

I have big dreams and none of them include

settling for the first trouser snake that slithers along. I'm one of the only women in the most challenging forensic accounting master's program in the country. I'm determined to graduate top of my class and land an incredible first position, one I'll choose based on my own preferences, not the needs of a partner who wants to stay close to his family or his own (likely lower paying) job.

And when it comes to significant others, I want my future husband and I to have a top-notch sex life, and how the hell will I know if it's The Stuff if I have nothing to compare it to?

Nope.

One and done isn't the path for *this* Raine woman. I'm glad my mom and sister are happy with their lots in life, but I refuse to be derailed by a case of FDF.

Which brings us back to **Steve**, and why he had to go.

His flicker of human decency wasn't much, but it was enough to be dangerous. On the off chance that a close encounter with his dick would be enough to convince me that "tiddies" was an acceptable term for breasts, I had to make a swift escape.

I thanked him for a nice night, pretended to have tragic diarrhea, and left.

Useful takeaway: Mention of diarrhea—especially a tragic case—on the first date is an excellent way to ensure a man never calls again.

V-Card Status: Un-punched.

Carl: Picked his nose in public. Twice.

V-Card Status: Grossed Out.

Kyle: Called me Snow White, presumably because of my pale skin and dark brown hair. Spanked my ass within five minutes of starting our walk around Central Park, told me I smelled like asparagus, but in "the good way," and then picked *his* nose in public.

V-Card Status: Disturbed by the number of grown men who seem to think sticking a finger in a nostril is acceptable behavior at any time aside from when they are alone in the bathroom and intend to wash their hands promptly after.

James: Skunk Breath.

V-Card Status: Barfing.

Brad Two: Announced he had always dreamed of "settling down with a girl like me" ten seconds into coffee. Verdict—even more off-putting than the first Brad.

Note to Self: Don't date Brads.

V-Card Status: Losing hope, probably also shrouded in cobwebs, infested with spiders, and suffering from a mild case of depression.

Matthew from the gym who said sweat is his religion and who is probably on multiple steroids: Called off due to freak snowstorm.

V-Card Status: Relieved for an excuse to stay home.

I *am* relieved, Diary.

Hunting obnoxious but sort of sexy men is exhausting.

But sadly, I'm also running out of time.

My ancient V-Card can wait—she's clearly in no hurry to vacate the premises—but I need to find a boyfriend. Stat. Gram might not be with us much longer. This could be her last Raine family reunion and all she's ever wanted was to see me settled down with a "good" man.

Though I suspect a "good enough" man would also do at this point.

Argh!

If only I hadn't confessed all my romantic daydreams when I slept over at her house as a starry-eyed teen. If I hadn't fantasized to Gram about finding a best friend who slept over every night, one who would make me laugh and think and feel all the glorious things girls felt in '90s rom-coms and be my partner in love and mischief for life, maybe she would believe me when I say I don't have any urge to settle down.

But Gram knows better. She's the only one who does. I can't send her off on her next big adventure without knowing I'm on track to that happily ever after she's always wanted for me.

Which means I need a stand-in.

A temporary forever.

A fake date, if you will, *a la* those made-for-TV romances my mom loves so much. I need a guy who's cool enough to make my gram happy, but not so cool my parents or sister will be upset when they eventually learn Mr. X and I aren't going to make it for the long haul.

But I don't know anyone like that, Diary.

I don't!

Don't you dare say his name.

He Who Shall Not Be Named isn't fit to lick the bottom of my shoe, let alone charm the slippers off my gram. I hate He Who Shall Not Be Named. I hate him so much I've completely forgotten about how hot that kiss was last September, and I hardly tingle at all when he drops by the apartment to boss Evie around in his capacity as the most irritating big brother in history.

And even if I didn't hate He Who Shall Not Be Named, I'm not going to *date*, not even *fake date*, my best friend's older brother. Evie is one of the most important people in my life. I don't know what I'd do without her, and I'm not about to put our relationship at risk over stupid old Derrick.

Okay, fine! I said his name.

You win this battle, Diary, but I'm going to win the war.

The next time Derrick shows his face at the apartment, I'll lock myself in my room and stay there until he's gone. I'll pee in an empty water bottle and survive on the stale granola bar chunks at the bottom of my purse if I have to.

I'm done with that man. *Done.* He's dead to me. Dead, I tell you!

At least while I'm awake. I can't help it if I

have the occasional steamy dream featuring Derrick's lips kissing his way up my thighs...

Ugh. Yep. I'm definitely staying in my room next time he shows up.

Definitely.

SCREWED is available now!

ABOUT THE AUTHOR

Author of over forty novels, *USA Today* Bestseller **Lili Valente** writes everything from steamy suspense to laugh-out-loud romantic comedies. A die-hard romantic, she can't resist a story where love wins big. Because love should always win. She lives in Vermont with her two big-hearted boy children and a dog named Pippa Jane.

Find Lili at...
www.lilivalente.com

ALSO BY LILI VALENTE

The Virgin Playbook Series

Scored

Screwed

Seduced

Sparked

Scooped

Learn more at Lili's site

Hot Royal Romance

The Playboy Prince

The Grumpy Prince

The Bossy Prince

Learn more at Lili's site

Laugh-out-Loud Rocker Rom Coms

The Bangover

Bang Theory

Banging The Enemy

The Rock Star's Baby Bargain

Learn more at Lili's site

The Bliss River Small Town Series

Falling for the Fling

Falling for the Ex

Falling for the Bad Boy

Learn more at Lili's site

The Hunter Brothers

The Baby Maker

The Troublemaker

The Heartbreaker

The Panty Melter

Learn more at Lili's site

Bad Motherpuckers Series

Hot as Puck

Sexy Motherpucker

Puck-Aholic

Puck me Baby

Pucked Up Love

Puck Buddies

Learn more at Lili's site

Big O Dating Specialists
Romantic Comedies

Hot Revenge for Hire

Hot Knight for Hire

Hot Mess for Hire

Hot Ghosthunter for Hire

Learn more at Lili's site

The Lonesome Point Series

(Sexy Cowboys)

Leather and Lace

Saddles and Sin

Diamonds and Dust

12 Dates of Christmas

Glitter and Grit

Sunny with a Chance of True Love

Chaps and Chance

Ropes and Revenge

8 Second Angel

The Good Love Series

(co-written with Lauren Blakely)

The V Card

Good with His Hands

Good to be Bad

Click here to learn more

Learn more at Lili's site

The Happy Cat Series

(co-written with Pippa Grant)

Hosed

Hammered

Hitched

Humbugged

Learn more at Lili's site

Printed in Great Britain
by Amazon

20709927R00180